Praise for

A SKELETON IN THE FAMILY

"Dr. Georgia Thackery is smart, resourceful, and determined to be a great single mom to her teenager. Georgia is normal in every respect—except that her best friend happens to be a skeleton named Sid. You'll love the adventures of this unexpected mystery-solving duo."
—Charlaine Harris, #1 *New York Times* bestselling author

"Adjunct English professor Georgia Thackery makes a charming debut in *A Skeleton in the Family*. Georgia is fiercely loyal to her best friend, Sid, an actual skeleton who is somehow still 'alive.' When Sid sees someone he remembers from his past life—who later turns up dead—Georgia finds herself trying to put together the pieces of Sid's past as she works to hunt down a killer. Amateur sleuth Georgia and her sidekick, Sid, are just plain fun!"
—Sofie Kelly, *New York Times* bestselling author of *Final Catcall*

"No bones about it, Leigh Perry hooked me right from the beginning. An unusual premise, quirky characters, and smart, dry humor season this well-told mystery that kept me guessing until the very end. It's too bad Perry's sleuth is fictional—I'd invite Georgia over for dinner in a heartbeat."
—Bailey Cates, national bestselling author of *Charms and Chocolate Chips*

"A delightful cozy with a skeleton who will tickle your funny bone."
—Paige Shelton, national bestselling author of *Merry Market Murder*

continued . . .

THE
SKELETON
TAKES A
BOW

Leigh Perry

BERKLEY PRIME CRIME, NEW YORK

THE BERKLEY PUBLISHING GROUP
Published by the Penguin Group
Penguin Group (USA) LLC
375 Hudson Street, New York, New York 10014

USA • Canada • UK • Ireland • Australia • New Zealand • India • South Africa • China

penguin.com

A Penguin Random House Company

THE SKELETON TAKES A BOW

A Berkley Prime Crime Book / published by arrangement with the author

Berkley Prime Crime Books are published by The Berkley Publishing Group.
BERKLEY® PRIME CRIME and the PRIME CRIME logo are trademarks of Penguin
Group (USA) LLC.

For information, address: The Berkley Publishing Group,
a division of Penguin Group (USA) LLC,
375 Hudson Street, New York, New York 10014.

ISBN: 978-0-425-25583-4

PUBLISHING HISTORY
Berkley Prime Crime mass-market edition / September 2014

PRINTED IN THE UNITED STATES OF AMERICA

10   9   8   7   6   5   4   3   2   1

Cover photos by Shutterstock.
Cover photo composition by Ben Perini.
Interior text design by Kelly Lipovich.

To Ginjer Buchanan,
who believed in Sid from the beginning

Acknowledgments

A skeleton is all about the connections, and I have many connections to thank for their help.

My husband, Stephen P. Kelner, Jr., for a ludicrous amount of support.

Charlaine Harris and Dana Cameron, who dropped everything to beta read. Again.

My daughters, Maggie and Valerie, for letting Sid join the family.

My agent, Joshua Bilmes, who always has my back.

Art Taylor, for last-minute homework assistance.

Bill Aronoff, for providing the perfect joke for Sid.

Dina Willner, for keeping me from making a real boner.

I

I should have known better than to let Madison talk me into letting Sid appear in *Hamlet*. Of course, he was made to play the part she had in mind for him. Like Yorick, Sid was a fellow of infinite jest and most excellent fancy, had borne me on his back a thousand times, and his flashes of merriment were indeed wont to set the table on a roar. More to the point, Sid and Yorick were both dead. But while Yorick is usually depicted as an inanimate skull, the Thackery family skeleton is a full set of bones and he is quite thoroughly animated.

It started on a Friday in late March, a few days after the Pennycross High School Drama Club held auditions for its production of *Hamlet*. My teenaged daughter Madison had spent most of the afternoon conferring with Sid in his attic room, and when they finally emerged, they cleaned up the kitchen, washed and folded two loads of laundry, and gathered the garbage and recycling to take out to the street—all without being nagged. So of course I'd known they were up to something.

Over our spaghetti dinner Madison said, "They announced the cast for the play today. Becca Regan is going to direct, and she's great."

"Excellent!" Madison had joined the drama club as soon as she started attending classes at PHS, but it had been too late for her to be in the fall show. This time she was ready. "What part did you get?"

"Guildenstern."

"Guildenstern?"

"He's one of Hamlet's friends. Claudius brings him and Rosencrantz in to try to cheer up Hamlet and then uses them to—"

"Sweetie, I know who Guildenstern is. English degree, remember? It's just that I thought you were going for Gertrude or Ophelia."

"I was, but so were all the other girls in the club. There are only two good female roles in the play, after all. Guildenstern will be interesting."

"Are you going to be the mature one this time? I want to know before I start complaining about club politics, playing favorites, and so on."

"Tonight I will be playing the role of maturity incarnate."

"Okay, then. They gave you such a small part because you're a freshman, right? And a new kid?" Even though we'd moved so often that Madison was remarkably adept at fitting herself into a school's society, some schools were more insular than others.

"Maybe, but to be fair, Becca doesn't know me well enough to know if she can rely on me to carry a big part.

This is her first time directing a show, and you can't blame her for wanting to go with a known quantity."

"Yes, I can. Especially if you gave a better audition."

"Oh, I nailed that audition!" Then she remembered that she was being mature. "Of course, we both know that plenty of people audition and get a role, then don't even bother to show up for rehearsals."

"Please. She could have checked your resume and realized that you were dependable enough for more than a small part."

"There are no small parts, only small actors."

"Which you are not, so you are going to rock that part!"

"Agreed. Besides, there are a lot of even smaller parts. And Tristan, the guy playing Rosencrantz, is really cool and we get to hang out together at rehearsal. He's a really good actor and would have been a great Hamlet, but the guy who got it is good, too, and he really looks the part. He's got that whole dark-haired emo thing going on—Tristan is blond."

I resisted asking the questions that sprang immediately to mind: Is Tristan cute? Is he cool for a boyfriend or just as a friend? Does he have a girlfriend? When can I meet him? In other words, all the questions that were guaranteed to make Madison's hackles rise. If she was going to be mature, I should take a stab at it, too. "So are you going to be a female version of Guildenstern, or dress in male drag?"

"Drag!" she said happily. "We talked about setting the show during the twenties or something, but decided to go full-out Elizabethan. Tights, swords, doublets. Jo Sinta is doing costumes again, and she's so excited!"

"Sounds great. I look forward to it. Just let me know the rehearsal schedule so I can put it in my book." As an adjunct

English professor, my classes tend to be at those odd times that full-time profs don't want, and I also have to keep office hours. Keeping up with that while monitoring the activities of a busy teenager was a constant challenge.

"There is one thing I wanted to ask about, schedulewise." Madison looked at Sid, and I knew the moment had come for them to ask whatever it was they'd cooked up earlier. "You know high schools have to work with tight budgets."

Sid spoke for the first time since we'd sat down to dinner. He doesn't eat, of course, or even drink, but he likes keeping us company during our meals. He also likes sneaking tidbits to Madison's Akita, Byron, under the table, not because he likes the dog but because he was hoping to convince him that there were much better treats available than Sid's own bare bones. He said, "I think it's shameful that the arts are so poorly supported in public schools. I'd like to do more to help."

There was a thump under the table that I interpreted as Madison kicking Sid in the shinbone. Had she known him as long as I had, she'd have known that, unlike her, he never could stick to a script. But I'd known him most of my life, while she'd only been formally introduced to him a few months before.

Madison said, "Becca said we're going to spend most of our budget on the costumes. That's the way they did it back in Shakespeare's time."

"I know. English professor, remember? Even adjunct faculty members are familiar with the way Shakespeare's work was originally produced."

"Right. So we'll have some props and scenery, but they'll be minimal, whatever we can scrounge up. And today Becca pulled out this really awful papier-mâché skull and said we'd be using it for the grave-digging scene."

Sid assumed a dramatic pose. " 'Alas, poor Yorick! I knew him, Horatio: a fellow of infinite jest, of most excellent fancy—' "

There was another thump under the table.

"Anyway," Madison said emphatically, "I thought that the scene would play so much better with a more convincing skull."

"Like Sid's?" I asked.

"What a great idea, Georgia!" Sid said, and I think he was trying for enthused surprise. He'd have never made it through an audition if that was the best he could do.

"Nice try," I said, "but we all know it wasn't my idea—it was yours and Madison's."

"Was doing the laundry too much of a giveaway?" she asked.

"Just a bit." Not that I was complaining—it meant fewer shirts for me to fold. I took a healthy bite of spaghetti so I could chew on it and the idea simultaneously. "Do you have any idea how you would work this out?"

"It'll be easy," Madison said. "I'll take Sid to school with me and keep him in my locker until rehearsal."

"You're going to take all of Sid?"

"No, just the skull."

"I'm fine with that," Sid added.

He really was eager. Usually he hated to be separated from the rest of his bones because it made him feel so helpless. The essential part of Sid—I never know if I should call it his soul, his consciousness, his ghost, or his memory chip—travels with the skull, which means that when the skull is elsewhere, the rest of his bones are just that, a pile of bones. He could move the rest of his skeleton from a few feet away, but not from as far away as the high school.

"Won't you get bored cooped up in a locker all day?" I asked.

"I'll put him on the shelf in front of the vents," Madison said, "so he'll be able to watch people."

Since Sid was an enthusiastic eavesdropper and peeper, I could see how that would appeal to him.

She went on. "I'll take him with me to rehearsals, then bring him home every night. All we need is some sort of padded bag to carry him in, and Aunt Deborah has an old bowling bag she's not using anymore that would be perfect."

"You told Deborah your plan?"

"No, no. I just noticed the bag the last time I was over at her place."

That was a relief. My older sister had grudgingly accepted that Sid was a part of the family, but I was pretty sure what her reaction to this plan would be. My initial feeling was the same, but after all the cleaning they'd done, I owed Sid and Madison a chance to convince me.

So I listened to the rest of their pitch as I finished my plate of pasta. Madison's argument that it would add a vital element to the play's success didn't sway me much. Yorick's skull appears onstage for exactly one scene—as long as the skull they used onstage was approximately the right shape and color, it would be fine. It was Sid's plea that really got me. Once he abandoned his "support the arts" platform, I could see how much he really wanted the chance to leave the house and spend more time with Madison.

Sid had moved in with us when I was six, but for obvious reasons, he only rarely left the house. As long as I'd been living at home, he'd had me for company, but once I moved out, he'd spent most of his time alone in the attic. Since I'd come back to Pennycross for a job at Joshua Tay University, and was house-sitting for my parents while they were on sabbatical, his life had been far more interesting. He had me and Madison to hang with, Byron the dog to fuss about, and when he discovered the Internet, a whole new world to play in.

But still, he hadn't had an opportunity to actually leave the house for months, and this sounded like it might be a safe way to allow him a little more freedom. After obtaining pinkie swears from them both—Sid's that he wouldn't play any tricks and Madison's that she'd be exceedingly careful with him—I agreed.

But late that night, after I went to bed, I started counting up the ways it could go wrong. The problem was, I couldn't go back on my word to my daughter and my best friend, no matter how much I wished I'd never let them talk me into it.

2

My misgivings were proven all too correct just three weeks later. Madison had just started down the street to take Byron for a walk when I got home from work, even though it was after five. Knowing that she usually takes him out first thing after she gets back from school, I deduced that she'd had a long day. So while she tended to his needs, I went inside to tend to hers. In other words, I thawed out some of the chili we'd made and frozen the weekend before and baked a can of crescent rolls. Since it was Thursday, we'd just about run out of fresh supplies from the previous weekend's shopping trip, but there was enough produce left to toss together a salad.

I had everything ready by the time Byron dragged Madison back in, and while she washed up, I made sure all the curtains were closed tightly for privacy before I went to the bottom of the stairs and yelled, "Sid! Dinnertime!"

This time, there was no answering clatter of bony feet.

"Sid? Are you coming down?"

Madison came out of the bathroom with an expression of guilt it didn't take a mother to interpret.

"What?" I asked.

"I left him at school."

"You did what?"

"I left Sid at school!"

"Madison! How could you—?"

"It's not my fault. I had to take that makeup Spanish test after school, and Senora Harper made me wait until after she finished tutoring some kids, and then the test took forever so I barely made it to choral ensemble. Then Samantha's wheelchair was acting wonky so she needed help pushing it outside, and I couldn't just leave her outside alone with her chair messing up, especially since her mother was late. Then when she finally showed up, they offered me a ride home, and it was so late and I was so tired—"

I held up my hand to stop the flood of excuses and asked, "Where is Sid?"

"Well, I didn't remember the test until after I'd gone to rehearsal, and we weren't working on any of my scenes today anyway. Only Becca wanted to keep Sid because she wanted to work on the graveyard scene, which I said was fine, so she said I could come pick him up later. But I had that Spanish test and—"

"Madison! Where is he?"

"He must still be backstage in the auditorium."

"Fine. We're going to go get him." I grabbed my purse and car keys, and she followed me out to our somewhat battered green minivan.

Rush hour was in full swing, something I usually manage to avoid by virtue of working in university settings that don't

9

keep standard business hours, and even in a town as small as Pennycross, the delays were annoying. Madison, realizing that I hadn't bought her explanations for why it wasn't her fault, was sunk in silence and I was too mad to say anything to make her feel better.

Had I been totally honest with her, I might have admitted that I was blaming myself nearly as much as I was her. I should have noticed sooner that Sid wasn't clattering around in the attic. When a person has no skin to mask the sound, and no reason to keep himself hidden, it can get pretty noisy. I'd figured he was on the computer, catching up with his myriad Facebook friends and Twitter followers.

Though the parking lot was nearly deserted when we got to Pennycross High, the two cars parked near the front door gave me hope that somebody would be available to let us in. No such luck. I pounded on the door repeatedly and Madison trotted all the way around the building to see if she could find a door that had been left unlocked, but there was no sound from inside the building. After fifteen minutes of raising as much of a ruckus as we dared, we admitted defeat and got back into the car.

We were halfway back home when Madison said, "I'm sorry, Mom. It was my fault."

"No, it was mine. I should never have let you talk me into letting Sid be in the play."

"But he's been having so much fun!"

"And now he's stuck at the school all night. Alone."

"At least it's not Friday—one night is a lot better than the whole weekend."

She wasn't even convincing herself, and I was not appeased.

I warmed up the chili and rolls in the microwave when

we got back to the house, but neither of us had much appetite. Afterward, Madison dove into her homework while I graded student papers. I'm afraid my students paid the price for my bad mood—I wasn't as patient as I usually was with grammar mistakes and confusion over syntax.

The night seemed long and empty without Sid, and once Madison went to bed, I snuck up to his attic room. With his skull gone, inhabited by whatever it was that kept Sid moving and talking, the rest of his bones were abandoned on the couch. Normal skeletons, meaning the kinds of specimens I see fairly often in the halls of academe, are held together with wires and bolts. Sid holds himself together, so the pieces he'd left had no reason to stick together. It was vaguely creepy seeing him like that, but I suppose it would have been creepier still if his body had been wandering around blindly, searching for his skull.

Byron was standing at attention outside the attic door when I got back downstairs, so I carefully closed it behind me. It was bad enough that we'd left Sid at school. I didn't want to think about what his reaction would be if we let the dog gnaw on his bones while he was gone.

3

Usually Madison rode her bicycle to and from school, but the next day I drove her and her bike, hoping she'd be able to get to the auditorium and grab Sid so I could take him home right away. Unfortunately the cheerleaders picked that morning to rehearse for a pep rally, so we had to postpone our apologies until later.

I blew off my office hours that afternoon and was back at PHS when the bell rang. Madison ran out to where I was waiting, gave me the battered black and purple bowling bag Sid had been riding to and from school in, and jumped on her bicycle to take care of an urgent errand.

"Sid, I am so sorry," I said as soon as I started driving. I'd unzipped the bag so he could hear me better, knowing that if anybody saw me talking, they'd assume I was on a cell phone.

"Georgia, we need to talk," Sid said, his voice a little muffled from still being in the bag.

"I know, I know, this was unforgivable. We went to the

school as soon as we realized you'd been left behind yesterday, but the doors were locked and nobody would let us in. Madison beat herself up over it all night long, and she really wants to make it up to you, so she's at Wray's Comics right now looking for something special to get you as an apology present."

"Forget the manga," he said. "This is important."

"Of course it is, but you know we'd never have left you there all night on purpose. It's just that Madison had to make up that Spanish test she missed when she was out sick last week, and it took longer than she expected, and she had choral ensemble practice after that, then went to help Samantha, and she just forgot to come back by the auditorium to get you."

"It's okay, but—"

"It's not okay!" By then I'd arrived at the house. "Hang on until we get inside." Normally I'd have zipped up the bag, even for the short walk from the driveway into the house, but under the circumstances, I just couldn't do it.

As soon as I was in the front hall with the door firmly shut, I pulled Sid out of the bag to continue apologizing face-to-face. Or at least face-to-skull.

"Okay," he said, "it's not okay and I will be happy to let you and Madison grovel for the next month. Maybe two. But right now I have to tell you something."

"Okay, what is it?"

"I witnessed a murder."

"Excuse me?"

"Last night, somebody killed a man in the high school auditorium."

4

"Say that again," I said, really hoping I hadn't heard him say that he'd witnessed a murder.

With an air of extreme patience, Sid said, "Last night, somebody killed a man in the auditorium."

"Are you serious? What happened? At school? Because I didn't hear anything about a body being found there." I couldn't imagine that a murder at the high school wouldn't have made an enormous splash in a town the size of Pennycross.

"I'll explain, but can we go upstairs so I can pull myself together first?"

"Yeah, sure." I stopped just long enough to drop my briefcase in the living room and give a quick pat to Bryon the dog, who seemed to be nonplussed that I wasn't giving him the attention he felt he deserved. He looked up at Sid's skull hopefully, and Sid snarled, "In your dreams, pooch!"

I carried Sid up the two flights of stairs to the attic, where he lived. Well, technically, Sid didn't live anywhere because he wasn't really alive, but I'd long ago learned that normal vocabulary and usage only go so far when dealing with the walking, talking skeleton who'd been my best friend since childhood.

As we were in the room, the bones snapped together into traditional skeletal form and he sat up and reached for the skull. It would have been unnerving if I hadn't seen it a zillion times before.

"Do you mind?"

"Right. Sorry." I handed the skull over to the beckoning hands, and Sid plopped it back where it belonged.

"That's better," he said, rolling his shoulders and twisting his neck to make sure everything was situated correctly.

While he was adjusting himself, I took a seat on the couch next to him and prompted, "You saw a murder?"

"Not exactly."

"Then what did you see?"

"I didn't see anything—I said I witnessed it."

"You lost me."

"I heard a murder. I couldn't see what was happening from where I was."

"Which was where?"

"Waiting in the wings. Which is the story of my life. Well, not life but—"

"Focus, Sid!"

"I was on a shelf filled with props in the wings. Stage right."

I'd helped out at enough of Madison's plays to know that he meant the wings that were to the side of the stage, not visible from the audience, and stage right was the left side from the audience's perspective.

He went on. "About all I could see from there was a side

view of the stage, and whoever it was was in the auditorium and not onstage. Needless to say, I couldn't exactly roll out to see what was happening."

I nodded. He could kind of hop around with his skull, but it wasn't silent or subtle. And it looked really freaky.

"I don't know for sure when it was because I couldn't see the clock in the auditorium, either, but rehearsal had ended hours before. It started when I heard some banging noises. Then I heard somebody come into the auditorium. I was hoping it was Madison coming to get me."

"We're so sorry about that, Sid."

He waved it away—I could tell how upset he was about what he'd heard because he didn't even pause to give me mournful puppy dog eyes. I knew darned well it should be impossible for a bare skull to make that expression, but somehow he managed when the occasion arose.

Sid said, "Anyway, since I wasn't absolutely sure it was Madison, I didn't say anything. Then the argument started and I knew it wasn't her."

"Who was it?"

"I don't know. I only heard two voices, so I think it was just two people, but I didn't recognize either voice."

"Were they students?"

"I don't think so. They sounded too old, but then again, some of the kids Madison knows have really deep voices. I do know they were both male."

"That's something. What were they arguing about?"

"I'm not sure. All I could get was tone and some random words. But they were going at it hot and heavy. Then one of them yelled, and there was a thump and a grunt and the sound of something falling. Like a body. The one left standing cussed and cussed—that I could hear. He stepped closer to the stage, too."

I could picture that, the killer not wanting to stand right next to a dead body.

Sid went on. "I think he got out a phone because he started talking to somebody, and I couldn't hear anybody else responding. After he stopped talking, he sounded as if he was pacing. Maybe twenty minutes later, I heard the auditorium door open and his footsteps going away from me. When the door opened again, there were two sets of footsteps. More conversation, but much quieter. They left for a few minutes, then came back again. And started washing up."

"How could you tell?"

"The janitor has this wheeled mop bucket, and it squeaks. I've heard it a lot while I've been in Madison's locker. Plus I could hear liquid sloshing and smell soap, so what else could it be but mopping the floor? They had to be cleaning up the evidence."

It did sound like something awful had happened, but I had to ask, "Are you certain it was a murder?"

"Oh yeah. When that first guy was on the phone, he said, 'Of course I'm sure—he's dead. Just get over here!' And when the other guy showed up, that one said, 'Damn, you really nailed him.'"

"So some man killed somebody and then called a third person to help take the body away."

"I think so."

I ran my hands through my hair, trying to make sense of it. "Jeez, I just had an awful thought. I know why the killer and the victim went into the auditorium."

"Why?"

"Because of me and Madison. That banging you heard? That was us beating on the main door trying to get somebody to let us in. There were two cars in the parking lot, so I know somebody was there. I bet those men you heard saw us, and didn't want to be seen, so they ducked in there. We could have been there when it happened."

Sid shuddered, which was a noisy operation. "That gives *me* goose bumps and I don't even have any skin."

"The worst part? Maybe it wouldn't have happened if we hadn't panicked the guy."

"Hey, hey, hey," Sid said. "The killer met with the guy in a building that is usually empty at that time of day. Do you really think he had good intentions?"

"Good point."

"No, the worst thing was that there was nothing I could do! I couldn't stop them, and I couldn't get to a phone to call the police, and I couldn't even move somewhere where I could see who it was. You can't imagine how awful it was to hear all that and not know what to do."

I put my arm around his shoulder blades. "It's not your fault, Sid."

"I should have yelled. I should have said that the cops were on the way or tried to bite him or . . . I don't know, Georgia. Something. But I was scared."

"Coccyx, Sid, you heard a murder. Of course you were scared."

"Yeah, but what was I afraid of? Them killing me? I'm already dead!"

I winced, but he was right. "Sort of, yeah, but you could still be . . . destroyed." Though Sid had lost a couple of small bones without harming him, and we'd repaired one he'd broken, we didn't really know how Sid would be affected if more of his bones were damaged. It wasn't an experiment we cared to make.

"Anyway, I didn't hear anything else, not until it was morning and the cheerleaders came in and started practicing."

"And there was nothing said at school about a body being found in the auditorium?"

"I told you, they carted the body away and cleaned up after themselves. They must have dumped it somewhere."

"I didn't hear anything about a body being found around town, but I haven't looked at the news. Can I borrow your computer?"

"Let me. I'm faster."

I'd been using a computer for a lot longer than Sid had, but since I was still in groveling mode, I didn't argue as he booted up his Mac. When he'd first discovered the wonders of the Internet, he'd had to make do with using my parents' old and slow desktop computer or borrowing mine, but I'd used my educator's discount to get him his own system for Christmas. Given the hours he spent on it while Madison and I slept, he probably was faster on the keyboard than I was.

The first site he pulled up was the one for the *Pennycross Gazette*, but the lead story was about the city council meeting. I noticed that the author of said piece was an ex-boyfriend of mine, but I didn't feel even a twinge. Well, not a big one. The guy was pretty cute.

"Nothing there," I said.

Sid moved on to the site for the local TV station, but its lead was a landmark restaurant closing its doors. Then he tried Googling for dead bodies being found.

"There's one," I said, tapping the screen.

He clicked on it, and I read. "Hunters found a male body

out near Springfield. No, wait. The remains were skeletal. I don't think that would happen so quickly."

"It could, but it would require special expertise," Sid pointed out, reminding me of one of the more unsavory aspects of his existence before joining my family.

"Um, right. But this can't have anything to do with what you heard. The cops think that body has been there for months."

"I'll keep looking."

But while he gave it his best, spending half an hour running down links, he couldn't find anything. Finally I said, "Sid, there's nothing here. The body hasn't been found yet."

"Yet? Then you believe me," he said hesitantly.

"Of course I believe you. One, you don't make things up. Two, your hearing is solid even if you don't technically have ears, and I just don't see what else could have made the sounds you heard."

"So what do we do now?"

"I don't know. We could call the cops, but what would we tell them? There was a murder, but we don't know who the killer was or the victim, and there's no body anyway. I don't think they'd take something like that very seriously."

"But we can't ignore it," Sid protested.

"I know, I know, but—"

Before we could discuss it further, I heard the pounding of sneakers on the attic steps and Madison burst in.

"Sid, I am so sorry! I have no excuse, none at all, but please, please, please let me make it up to you." She shoved a shopping bag onto his lap. "Look, I got you the latest issues of *One Piece* and *Black Butler*—"

"You didn't have to do that," Sid said, but he was reaching inside the bag. "Two books of *Fairy Tale*?"

"And Samantha let me borrow her DVDs of *Doctor Who*

season six so we can have a movie night. Just please say you forgive me."

"Of course I forgive you!" he said magnanimously, and she threw her arms around him for a big hug.

In the midst of that, Sid looked at me and mouthed, "Do we tell her?"

I shook my head.

He nodded his agreement and, out loud, said, "Which first? Manga or the Doctor?"

"You two discuss options while I figure out what we can have for dinner," I said, but I wasn't completely sure they heard me.

Poor Byron was waiting at the bottom of the stairs, looking neglected. He wasn't—his water dish was full and he had a doggie flap so he could get into the yard to take care of business—but he was used to getting more attention from Madison when she came home.

I called up the stairs. "Madison, Byron wants his walk."

If Madison had tried to beg off, I'd have reminded her that Byron was her dog and therefore her responsibility, but instead it was Sid who came down and said, "Do you think you can take him this once? Madison and I are in the middle of something." This time he did pull the puppy-dog-eye trick.

"All right," I said, "but keep in mind that this will fulfill my groveling obligations."

"Fair enough!" He zipped back to the attic, and I found Byron's leash to do the honors.

Though I wasn't going to admit it to either Sid or Madison, I didn't really mind. Byron was well behaved, thanks to the training classes Madison had taken with him, and it was a lovely spring evening. Fall in New England gets all the good press, but spring has a special magic, probably because it's so short. Some years, Massachusetts goes straight from winter to summer with no spring at all, but this year we'd had several weeks of warm weather and the trees were lightly painted in bright green.

Byron seemed to be enjoying our jaunt as much as I was, so I went farther than I'd intended, passing through our residential neighborhood and into the nearby business district and its handful of shops and restaurants. The fact that I went by Town House Pizza and Subs was entirely accidental. Of course, once I was there, I smelled cheesesteak subs cooking, and there was no resisting their allure. Though I couldn't take the dog inside, I could use my cell phone to call in an order while standing on the sidewalk.

The middle-aged woman behind the counter laughed when I explained the situation, and she obligingly brought the two subs and the Greek salad I'd asked for out to me, and even had a bone for Byron.

I was about to leave when she said, "You be careful walking home. This town is getting scary."

"Pennycross? Since when?"

"First that murder back in the fall, and just now I heard they found another body."

"Another body? Was it murder?"

"All I know is that a cop was getting a sub and got a call that made him run out of here without it. My son looked up the code they called out on the radio, and it means there was a body found. I don't think a cop would leave his sub behind if it was somebody who'd had a heart attack, so you might want to go straight home."

"I'll be careful," I promised, but I didn't say anything about going home. I had a phone call to make first.

5

Pennycross had recently implemented an anonymous tip line, so theoretically it should have been safe for me to call from my cell phone or the house's landline, but the idea of the police tracking a call back to me and then somehow getting to Sid was enough to give me nightmares. So that meant I needed a public phone. The last time I'd needed to call the police with an anonymous tip—and it was a symptom of the oddity of my life that I'd had to do so more than once— it had taken me a while to find one, but this time I hit it lucky. There was one next to the convenience store two doors down from the sub shop. I only had to wait a couple of minutes for a pair of smokers to finish their break to make my call.

"Pennycross Police Department Tip Line," a bored-sounding voice said.

"Hi, I need to report something about the body that was just found."

"Yes?" was all the woman said, but she no longer sounded bored.

I launched into the story of how a friend had been back-stage at the high school auditorium and overheard the murder and the cleanup. I'm pretty sure she was assuming that I myself was the friend, but she politely maintained the pretext. Of course she wanted to know why my friend hadn't tried to do something, but I explained he wasn't supposed to be in the building and that he'd been afraid to do anything. That was true enough, though not for any reason she was likely to come up with. Then she wanted to know why he hadn't called them sooner, and all I could say was that he didn't want to get involved. The longer we talked and the more details she asked for, the more bizarre it sounded to me, and I could only imagine how crazy it sounded to her. Finally I said, "I'm sorry, but that's all I know," and hung up.

I walked home considerably faster than I should have, but I told myself it was because the subs were getting cold, not because I was worried that a squad car was going to come squealing around the corner and chase me down.

Madison and Sid were already in the middle of an episode of *Doctor Who* when I got home, and since it was Friday night, I figured it wouldn't hurt for us to eat in front of the TV. I wanted to tell Sid about the police finding his murder victim, but I didn't want to bring it up in front of Madison. We'd have to tell her something sooner or later—she was bound to hear about a murder taking place in her high school auditorium—but I'd rather be able to assure her that the police were well on their way to finding the killer. Sid's infor-mation, as incomplete as it was, would have to help.

We vegged out in front of the TV for the rest of the night, but I kept using my phone to go online every half hour or so to see if the news about the murder had hit the Web. It hadn't by bedtime, which was frustrating. Had my relationship with the *Pennycross Gazette* reporter ended better, I'd have called him with a tip.

It was after eleven when I finally called it quits. Madison and Sid were still going strong, so I told them good night, reminded them to tend to Byron and set the alarm system before going to bed, and turned in. If I'd had a camera handy and any skill whatsoever as a photographer, I'd have paused and taken a picture of the homey scene. Madison curled up on the couch, Sid with his hands behind his skull and his feet up on the ottoman, and Byron gnawing happily on his bone with only the occasional longing look at Sid's femur. Admittedly, it was more Charles Addams than Norman Rockwell, but it was home.

I love weekend mornings because I don't have to set the alarm clock or run around in a frenzy getting myself ready for work and Madison ready for school. Recently, I've also come to enjoy the sight of my daughter in her own frenzy. She worked with my sister, Deborah, at her locksmith business every Saturday to earn money to help pay for Byron's upkeep, and Deborah was not one to take excuses for tardiness, even from her only niece. Madison made it by the skin of her teeth that day, running out the door just as Deborah drove her truck into the driveway. Knowing that Deborah would dock her pay for being late, I forgave her for not kissing me good-bye.

With Madison safely out of earshot, I could go up to the attic to tell Sid what I'd heard and about my call to the police. He was reading—or more likely rereading—one of the manga Madison had brought him the day before. Sid didn't sleep, so he spent most of his nights reading or tapping away on the computer.

"That's a relief," he said when I was done. "Maybe I helped a little after all."

"Sid, you did everything you could do, and though I'm still sorry Madison left you overnight, I'm glad you were there. Otherwise the police would probably never have been able to figure out where the murder took place, and that's got to be a big part of the investigation."

"I guess," he said.

"Have you seen anything new on the Web?"

"I've been afraid to look," he admitted. "Let's see what the word is." After a few minutes, he said, "Here it is! 'Body found in Pennycross.'" But when we followed the link to the *Gazette* article, all it said was that a body had been found on the east side of town and that identification was being withheld until the family could be notified.

"Wow, the police are really keeping a lid on this," I said.

"Maybe there's more to this murder than we thought."

I shrugged. "I guess we'll hear soon enough."

After that, I figured I better get started on my usual Saturday joys: laundry, cleaning, paying bills, and going grocery shopping. Sid helped with the first two, and though he couldn't help pay bills or grocery shop, he did bring me coffee while I was writing checks and insisted on putting the groceries away once I got them home. Obviously he'd forgiven Madison and me. The day passed quickly, punctuated by fruitless online checks for more news about the murder.

Madison texted me at four and said that Deborah had volunteered to bring over Chinese takeaway for dinner. I debated the bad example of eating take-out food two nights in a row versus knowing that Deborah would almost certainly turn down my offer to help pay, and replied that that would be great. By the time I had the table set and drinks ready, the two of them had returned, laden with bags from which arose a heavenly odor. Byron showed immediate interest and if I'd had a tail, mine would have been wagging, too.

"How'd work go?" I asked, taking Madison's load and getting the kiss I'd missed that morning.

"Would you believe we had to help the police with a murder investigation? At PHS!" Madison said.

I froze and was trying to think of what to say when she and Deborah burst out laughing.

6

Though Deborah and I haven't always gotten along, I wouldn't have accused her of being so callous as to laugh at a murder—let alone to get Madison to demonstrate such insensitivity—so clearly I was missing something.

"A murder? At the high school?" Sid said in a tone of surprise that sounded patently false to me, but apparently neither Deborah nor Madison noticed.

"There was no murder at PHS," Deborah said, still snickering. "Let's get something to eat before it gets cold, and I'll tell you the story."

Once the sweet-and-sour pork, rice, and egg rolls had been distributed, Deborah said, "I got a call from the police department this morning. They needed to get into the school, and Principal Dahlgren is out of town and nobody could find whoever it is who's supposed to open up when he's gone, so Dahlgren had them contact me because I put in all the school's locks and have spare keys.

"Madison and I get to PHS, and Louis Raymond and his partner are there, looking disgusted."

"By the way," Madison put in, "I think I deserve extra points for not saying anything about Officer Raymond being your beau."

"He's not my beau," Deborah retorted. "And what normal kid says 'beau' anyway?"

"Who are you calling normal? But if you prefer, your BF, your boo, your fella, your hookup, your friend with benefits. Or you could go old school with 'boyfriend.' "

"How about my bowling buddy?"

"Is that what the kids are calling it these days?"

Deborah gave her a look, which I had to admit was a good one for a nonmother. "Anyway," my sister said emphatically, "I let them in but then we had to hang around to lock up after them, and in case they needed any other keys. Maybe half an hour later, they came out looking even more disgusted."

"What were they looking for?" I asked, hoping I sounded more natural than Sid had.

"Louis said they'd gotten some crazy anonymous tip last night. Some woman called and claimed 'a friend' had overheard a fight at the high school auditorium Thursday night, and she was afraid somebody was dead. She couldn't explain how the friend had overheard without seeing anything, or why it was she'd waited so long to call, and naturally she wouldn't give her name or the name of her friend. They knew it was a crank call, but they checked it out anyway. Louis said they have to check out all the tips that get called in, even the ones that are clearly from nut jobs."

"Didn't they find anything?" Sid, my favorite nut job, asked.

"Nothing, other than the fact that the school overpays the

janitor," Deborah said. "Louis figures the call came from a kid who was hoping they'd close down school for the day."

"Hey! Profiling much?" Madison said indignantly. "A kid would have called on Sunday night to get them to cancel school on Monday."

"Good point," Deborah said. "It must have been an adult nut job."

Madison nodded, took a bite of rice, then looked at Sid. I could see her starting to figure something out. "Wait, Thursday night?"

Wanting to stave my daughter off from realizing who the adult nut job was, I said, "But didn't I hear there was a dead body found in town on Friday? How do they know there wasn't a link?"

"Because that woman wasn't murdered," Deborah said. "It was an overdose. Louis says the guys in the department are still taking sides on whether it was suicide or accidental, but nobody is thinking murder."

"A woman? And it was an overdose?" Sid said. "They're sure?"

"They're still waiting on the lab guys to test whatever it is they test, but Louis says that's what it looks like."

I tried to subtly signal Sid to stop looking so shocked. Of course, it was irrational for a skull to have any expression, but either Sid managed or I was really good at interpreting body language. Bone language?

Unfortunately, Sid wasn't paying attention to me, and since Deborah also had a lot of experience with Sid's non-verbal cues, she caught on.

She said, "What's bugging you, Sid? Hoping to have another chance to play Sherlock Bones?"

"An overdose?" Sid said again. "Not a blow to the head?"

She rolled her eyes as she helped herself to another egg roll. "I think the police can tell the difference between a blow to the head and an overdose. They're sticklers about that kind of thing, you know."

"Why were you so sure it was a blow to the head?" Madison asked.

"What?" Sid said, trying to act innocent far too late in the conversation.

"Sid, were you the 'friend' who overheard something in the auditorium Thursday night?" she asked.

Deborah said, "What are you talking about?"

"Sid spent the night at school Thursday night," Madison explained.

"Well, it wasn't on purpose. If you hadn't left me there—"

"I know, I know, it was my fault for forgetting you, but—"

"Why was Sid at the school in the first place?" Deborah wanted to know.

Madison turned to me. "That's why you were gone so long when you took Byron for a walk last night. You were the woman who called the cops!"

"Georgia made the crank call?" Deborah was still trying to catch up.

"Well, I couldn't very well be the one to go out to a pay phone," Sid said, "and somebody had to report the murder."

"There was no murder!" Deborah said, then took a deep breath. "One of you, just tell me what happened."

Sid went through the circumstances of why he'd been at school and the story of what happened Thursday night, ending with, "So I talked Georgia into calling the cops."

"You did not," I said. "I called because I had no intention of letting my daughter spend all day where a murder had taken place without telling the police."

"But there wasn't a murder, was there?" Deborah said.

Sid said, "Yes, there was!"

"So where's the body?"

"How should I know? If the cops are right about that woman they found being an overdose, I guess the real victim hasn't been found."

"This mess is all my fault," Madison said. "If I hadn't forgotten him, it wouldn't have happened."

"It still would have happened. We just wouldn't know about it. Right?" He looked at Madison. "You don't think I imagined it, do you?"

"Well, no, not exactly," Madison said, "but I know how spooky it can be being at school at night. One time I had to go to my locker after rehearsal, and it was all dark and echoey, and I got really freaked out."

"You do think I imagined it."

"I'm sure you heard *something*. Maybe some of the kids in the play were running lines."

"I know the difference between *Hamlet* and a murder," he said, but he wasn't exactly emphatic.

"Don't worry about it, Madison," Deborah said, and I'm pretty sure she meant to be reassuring. "The call can't be tied back to you guys, so there's no harm done other than a couple of cops missing a Dunkin' Donuts run. Though if you'd asked me, I could have told you that taking Sid to school wasn't a good idea."

Madison didn't even bother to argue with her aunt, which I didn't appreciate. I was the one she was supposed to ask for advice, not Deborah.

Sid didn't say anything, either, but I could see the connections between his bones loosen, as they did when he was feeling unhappy.

"I believe him," I said firmly.

"You do?" Sid and Deborah said simultaneously, albeit with very different intonations.

"Of course I do. Sid didn't hear every word spoken, but he heard enough to know that it wasn't *Hamlet*."

"You do remember that the dead woman died of an overdose, right?" Deborah said.

"All that means is that that woman's death didn't have anything to do with what Sid heard. Pennycross is a small town, but it's not out of the realm of possibility to have more than one person die in the same week. I don't blame the cops for thinking my call was a crank—I just assumed the body found was the one Sid heard being murdered. Now we know differently. As soon as the second body is found, the police will realize that my call had useful information, even if there wasn't any physical evidence in the auditorium."

Deborah looked aggravated, but she does that a lot around me anyway. Madison's reaction troubled me more. She wouldn't meet my eyes or Sid's, so she was clearly having doubts. I was disappointed but I understood. She hadn't known Sid as long as I had. She'd come around.

As for Sid, his bones were right back where they were supposed to be.

7

There was no more discussion of the murder that night. Instead we watched DVDs until Deborah started snoring in the middle of an episode of *Leverage* and I sent her home. Then I did a cursory kitchen cleaning and booted up my laptop to jot down some lecture notes for the next week's classes while Sid and Madison watched more of *Doctor Who*. In other words, it was a typically festive Saturday night at the Thackery house.

Eventually Sid headed upstairs to catch up with his ever-increasing number of Facebook friends, and Madison and I started getting ready for bed.

When I went into her room for a good night kiss, I saw from the look on my daughter's face that she had something on her mind.

She said, "Mom, why didn't you tell me about what Sid said he heard at school?"

"Ah. Mind if I have a seat so we can talk about it?"

She pulled Byron onto her lap so there would be room for me to sit down.

I said, "That's a fair question, but I'm afraid I don't have a very good answer. Sid and I were still discussing the murder when you came home from Wray's, and my knee-jerk reaction was not to tell you. At least, not yet."

"When were you going to tell me?"

"As soon as the story had an ending. I really thought that calling the police last night would give them what they needed to find the killer and arrest him, and then I could explain it to you once it was a fait accompli, and you wouldn't be scared about going to school."

"I'm not scared of going to school."

"It doesn't bother you that there was a murder committed in the auditorium?"

She hesitated and picked up the stuffed pig that she still keeps on her bed. "Do you really believe Sid heard what he says he heard?"

"Yes, I do. But you don't, do you?"

She shook her head.

"Do you think he's lying?"

"Not exactly lying. But could he have misinterpreted? Made it sound worse than it really was?"

"Sid's not the kind of person to make something up just to get attention."

"I guess not, but—"

"But you still don't believe him. Okay, I accept that. But you have to accept that I do believe him. I've known him most of my life—I trust him completely."

"But Aunt Deborah said—"

"Aunt Deborah has her own issues with Sid. Don't forget that she spent years not even speaking to him." Around the time Deborah graduated from high school, she'd decided that Sid was too ridiculous to exist and therefore she wouldn't acknowledge him directly in any way. I suspect that she still thought he was too ridiculous to exist, but some events the previous fall had convinced her to revisit her interactions with him.

"That was uncool," Madison said, "but it must have been kind of weird for her. Having Sid around, having to keep him hidden, and never being asked about having him in the family or anything."

Okay, I thought I knew what was going on. It wasn't an issue that had ever shown up in any parenting article I'd ever read, so I was going to have to play it by ear.

"You're right, nobody asked Deborah if she was okay with Sid joining the family, but you have to remember that Deborah was only ten years old when Sid showed up at our door, and it was a very different time. Though our parents were pretty open-minded, they didn't always consult us kids before making big decisions. You, on the other hand, are significantly older than ten and you and I do discuss decisions. Usually. But maybe I blew it with Sid. I mean, I'd never get married or adopt another kid or even let a room-mate into the house without talking to you, but I did spring Sid on you." It hadn't been planned that way. I'd wanted to introduce Sid to Madison for years, but when the time finally came, it had been a spur-of-the-moment decision.

"No, you didn't. I mean, you did kind of surprise me with Sid's . . . Sidness, but once I knew him I wanted him to stay with us. And this is his house anyway. I just hadn't known he was living in the attic until then."

"True, but now that you do know, Sid has really inserted himself into our lives. Does it bother you that we're a three-some now and not a duo?"

"No, of course not."

"No, not 'of course.' I want a real answer."

This time she took a moment to think. "Okay, it is different. I mean, you and he have a lot of history, and you and I have history, but he and I really don't have much. Except that he knows so much about me from talking to you."

"He always loved hearing about you, if that makes you feel any better. Did you know he has a photo album of pictures of you?"

"He does? That's kind of sweet."

"He's a sweet guy, which you wouldn't expect from somebody without a heart."

She halfway smiled. "That whole skeleton thing is taking some getting used to, I guess. I feel awkward inviting people over to the house."

"Don't!" I said. "Sid won't mind spending an evening or a whole weekend up in the attic. I can sneak up there if he wants company, but now that he's got his computer—plus books and movies—he's fine with it. Your aunt and I had company when we were growing up, and it didn't bother him. It gave him new people to spy on, which he loved. But even if he did mind, he'd be willing to stay out of the way so you could have friends over. He doesn't want you to miss out on anything. Okay?"

"Okay. I guess it has been kind of weird, but mostly it's good. I love Sid, I really do."

"I'm glad you feel that way. And I'm even more glad that you're willing to talk to me about the situation. Because it would be really hard for you to go to the guidance counselor at school with this particular problem."

She snickered. "Yeah, Mr. Carabello is great, but I don't think he'd be prepared for helping set up a family meeting with Sid."

"Exactly. And while we're at it, there's something I want you to know. My first priority is and always will be you. I love Sid, I love my parents, I'm pretty fond of Deborah—"

"Mom!"

"Okay, I love Deborah. But I love you most-est of all!"

"Most-est? They are so going to kick you out of the English professor club."

"All English professors have a creative license, with special dispensation for amphigory."

"Uh-huh."

"Anyway, as I was trying to say, you are the most important thing in my life. If you're not happy with our living arrangements, then we will rearrange them until you are. Okay?"

"Okay."

"Okay. Now it is past bedtime."

Hugs and kisses were exchanged, and I headed for my room. A couple of seconds later, I heard tiny sounds from the attic stairs.

I was really going to have to talk to Sid about eavesdropping, but maybe it was just as well that he'd overheard that particular discussion.

8

After she swore that she'd finished her homework for the weekend, I took Madison and her dog to spend Sunday afternoon at her friend Samantha's house. Once I got home, I took my laptop up to Sid's attic room to keep him company.

The place was looking much brighter than it had when I'd first moved back into the house. His furniture was still used, but I'd replaced some of the more obvious castoffs. Sid might be completely secure in his masculinity, but no grown man—not even a skeletal one—wanted to have to rely on Deborah's old Hello Kitty flashlight.

Sid was typing away enthusiastically when I came into the room and got settled on the couch. Finger-bone typing is considerably louder than any other kind of typing, but I can filter it out well enough to do my own work. In fact, I filtered it so thoroughly that I didn't notice at first that Sid had stopped, and when I did, I looked up and saw him looking at me with an air of expectation.

"So what's our plan?" he asked.

"Um . . . I'm going to grade papers, and you're going to play on Neopets?"

"No! Well, yes, but I mean what's our plan for solving the murder."

I blinked. "Excuse me?"

"We're not going to just let a killer get away with it, are we?"

"I didn't realize we had a choice in the matter, Sid. We told the police what we could, which should help as soon as they find the real body—I mean, the second body— Or have they found it?"

"Nope. I've scoured the Web, and the only body found was that woman Deborah was talking about. The overdose."

"Well, when the other body is found the police can take it from there."

"But what if they don't find it? Or what if the physical evidence has deteriorated by the time they do? The first few days after a murder are key to solving the crime, Georgia. Key!"

"And that's very important for the police to keep in mind, but considerably less so for us. I've got plenty on my plate already."

"But you said you believed me."

"I do believe you. That doesn't mean I'm going to get myself into a mess like I did last time. You do remember what nearly happened, don't you?" Being knocked out and tied up wasn't nearly so much fun as it looked in the movies, and though I wasn't a hundred percent sure my death would have been next on the list, I didn't want to chance it a second time.

"We're more experienced investigators now. We've learned from our mistakes."

"Exactly. I learned not to make the mistake of getting mixed up in a murder investigation again."

He just looked at me.

"Sid, stop making Bambi eyes! You know it's completely impossible for you to make Bambi eyes, so stop it!" I pointedly looked at my computer screen, but I could feel his Bambi eyes boring into my brain. After an eternity—which translated to about ten minutes of my reading the same paragraph over and over again—I said, "Besides, I have no idea how to start."

"Me, neither," he said cheerfully. "That's why I thought we should brainstorm."

"Don't you need a brain for that? Because your skull is noticeably empty."

He ignored that. "I'm thinking that we can assume the murder was unplanned."

"Since you seem to be assuming we're doing this," I muttered, "what's one more assumption?"

He ignored that, too. "If the killer had planned the killing, he'd have had a way to get rid of the body without making an emergency call for help with the cleanup. Right?"

"I guess, but where does that get us? We don't even know who the victim is, let alone the killer. There was no evidence the cops could spot, so we're not going to be able to find anything, either. All we've got is what you heard, which was just enough to convince us that it was murder. What can we do with that?"

"I don't know," Sid said, "but we've got to do something."

"Why?"

"Because if we don't . . ." He paused dramatically. "Madison could be in danger."

"That's not funny!"

"I don't mean it to be funny. What if the killer is the

principal or one of Madison's teachers or one of the cafeteria workers? What if he's at the school every single day with Madison?"

"Come on, you said yourself that it sounded like a spur-of-the-moment thing. Even if it is somebody at PHS, he's not going to start attacking people at random."

"We don't know that."

"What do you expect me to do, Sid? Take Madison out of school? Homeschool her? She'd never go for that, not even if she did believe—"

"Not even if she believed me?"

"You were eavesdropping last night, weren't you?"

"Sorry. I didn't mean to—I just wanted to get a book I left downstairs. But I heard my name, and, well, old habits die hard."

"I get that." Before Madison had learned about Sid, eavesdropping had been his way of being part of the family. "I'm sorry Madison doesn't believe you. Just give her time."

"I can do that; I will do that. But for now, her not believing me means she won't be careful the way she should be with a killer on the loose."

"I just don't see why she would be a target. And I have no idea what we can do to find the killer anyway." He started to speak, but I interrupted him. "So this is what I think we should do. I want you to keep going to school with Madison, and I want you to eavesdrop like you've never eavesdropped before. If you hear anything that will give us a starting point, we'll go from there. Okay?"

Sid wouldn't have been the skeleton I know and love if he hadn't argued, but he finally had to agree because he couldn't think of anything more proactive to do, either. If he did hear something, he would be able to let me know right away because instead of just sending his skull to school, we were going to put one hand and an old cell phone in his bag so he'd be able to text me if he heard anything important. During classes, he'd eavesdrop from Madison's locker, and during rehearsals, he'd be listening from backstage.

Despite having recently fussed because I hadn't told her everything, Madison did not seem enthused by being let in on the plans that evening. In fact, she rolled her eyes when we explained the idea to her. The expression reminded me far too much of Deborah, which was probably why I played dirty and pointed out that if Sid had had a hand and phone the Thursday before, he would have been able to remind her to come get him. She wasn't happy with me, but she agreed to carry out her part of the scheme.

None of us brought up the fact that Madison didn't believe Sid's story.

Even though I still did believe, I didn't really think Madison was in any danger at school, even if Sid hadn't been there to keep an eye out. Or at least an eye socket. But apparently my subconscious had other ideas—that night I had one bad dream after another.

9

For once, I was glad to see Monday morning. Normally I greeted it with dread. That semester I was teaching five sections of freshman composition at McQuaid University, and since there's an unwritten rule that adjuncts get the most inconvenient schedules imaginable, I had classes on Mondays, Wednesdays, and Fridays at eight AM, nine AM, ten AM, and eleven AM. Naturally I had to change classrooms for each of those—adjuncts don't get permanent classrooms. If I survived that, I had enough time to run by the adjunct office to check messages and go grab lunch before keeping office hours from one thirty to three thirty, which was always a mob scene on Monday because that was the day I handed back the previous week's assignment—usually either reading response papers or essays—and announced that week's assignment. That meant I usually didn't shake loose from anxious freshmen until after four, which gave me an hour or two to catch up on accumulated paperwork and get home. By that point Madison was usually starving, so I'd throw together dinner, eat, clean up, and collapse. I sometimes skipped the cleaning part.

I only had one McQuaid class on Tuesdays and Thursdays. I was stuck with the eight AM slot again, but at least it left me time for grading and doing paperwork.

The routine was complicated enough that I lived in fear that I'd forget which day it was. The only good thing to be said for my schedule was that it would only last another month and a half until the semester ended. Of course, I had the added pleasure of not knowing whether or not I'd be hired for another semester. I could make out fairly well if I didn't get anything in the summer, but if my "vacation" lasted into the fall, I'd be sunk, financially speaking.

At least my life wasn't boring.

I made it through my Monday morning classes and headed for the adjunct office. My mailbox, one of a rack outside the office, was halfway filled with McQuaid internal memos, notes from students, and a few pieces of actual mail. First up was a reminder that parking passes were not to be given or sold to students. "If you paid adjuncts enough, we wouldn't be selling them to the highest bidder," I muttered as I tossed it into the conveniently located recycling bin.

Next was a postcard announcing the date of the next Northeast Popular/American Culture Association conference. It was being held in Providence in October, and I would have given my left arm to attend. Well, Deborah's at least. True, I had no paper to submit, but I knew of a dozen New England schools that would be screening prospective hires there.

Most colleges began their hiring process for tenure-track positions at conferences, and some even provided grants for graduate students to attend and get a shot at those carrots of employment. Adjuncts like myself, on the other hand, only got grants when we had papers to present, which we rarely did because we didn't have time to write papers. And of course we didn't make enough money to pay our own way.

I'd been hoping to take advantage of living at my parents' house to scrape up enough money to attend a conference or two, but now that Sid had joined my household permanently, I had to plan for the future expense of a third bedroom once my parents returned and wanted their house back. That didn't leave enough in my budget for conferences.

Reluctantly, I put the postcard into the recycling bin and turned my attention to the messages from students. They were the usual excuses for late homework along with the late homework papers themselves. I added them to my satchel with a sigh—I really preferred that work come in electronically to cut down on the paper I was forced to carry and keep track of. But, no matter what I said, some students were convinced that actual paper, placed in a snazzy report folder, would give them extra points.

As I continued to sort, somebody came up behind me and said, "Dr. Thackery, you're looking well today."

I turned to see who it was. "Thank you, Dr. Peyton. You're looking pretty natty yourself."

History adjunct Charles Peyton was in fact one of the more nattily dressed men of my acquaintance. Though he made no more money than the rest of us adjuncts, he once told me that buying classic clothes of quality is actually more frugal than buying cheap and trendy. What he didn't tell me, but which I discovered for myself, was that squatting in unoccupied offices was a swell way to save money, too. He went to great lengths to conceal that fact, both because he was embarrassed by it and because he could lose his job if it were found out.

I noticed an accessory Charles didn't usually sport. "Why the black armband?"

"Haven't you heard? We lost one of our own over the weekend. Patty Craft succumbed to her illness."

Sara Weiss, an adjunct in biology who'd never heard a piece of gossip she didn't like, had walked up as we were speaking and piped up with, "Yeah, mental illness. She killed herself."

Charles looked vexed. "It is my understanding that the authorities have yet to determine the precise cause of death. For all they know, it was the cancer from which she'd been suffering. Or perhaps she accidentally ingested too much of her medication."

Sara snorted and went inside the office.

"An overdose?" I said. "I think I heard something about that." Craft's death had to be the one that Deborah had been talking about Saturday night. "I didn't know she taught at McQuaid."

"Actually, she wasn't currently employed here. She was an adjunct in the Mathematics Department for several years, but was diagnosed with pancreatic cancer perhaps a year and a half ago. She managed to keep teaching for a while, but I suspect her work wasn't up to its previous standards. So she hadn't been offered any classes since the last summer semester."

That meant she and I hadn't intersected—I'd started at McQuaid partway through the fall.

"She had insurance, but it was minimal, and between her expenses and not being able to work, she'd been having a very difficult time these past few months. Frankly, I'm not sure how she managed to keep her bills paid." He hesitated. "I'm not saying that she did take an excess of medication intentionally, but if she had, I would find it difficult to censure her."

I nodded. I carried insurance, both for myself and for Madison, but keeping up the premiums was sometimes a strain.

"I've been letting people know about the arrangements, but I don't suppose you would care to attend the funeral, since you didn't know her."

"When is it?" I asked.

"Thursday morning. Patty's sister Phoebe is her only living relative, and she can't get here any sooner."

"Sure, I'll go. Police and firefighters will travel halfway across the country to honor one of their fallen brethren. I think I can manage a drive across town."

We made plans to meet beforehand, then went into the office.

The room we adjuncts called home was large, but not nearly large enough for privacy. It was filled to the bursting point with rows of mismatched desks, squeaky chairs, and other hand-me-downs from when the offices of tenured faculty and loftier administrative personnel were redecorated and upgraded.

My own spot was against a wall near the door, which would have been a prime location if Sara's desk weren't right in front of mine. Her constant presence scared most people off, but I hadn't had many choices when I picked my spot, and that one was the best available. I didn't like the woman—she was nosy and vindictive—but with practice, I'd learned to ignore her most of the time. Sadly, I'd had worse office neighbors.

I started grading the late homework assignments—one-page responses to a reading about Freud's influence—while Charles made his way through the office, telling people about his friend's death and when the funeral would be.

Sara sniffed loudly and said, "I hope Charles doesn't expect me to go to his girlfriend's funeral."

Had it been anybody else speaking, I'd have asked what she meant by "girlfriend," but not with Sara. For one, I didn't want to encourage her, and for another, I knew that she'd spill any dirt she had anyway.

Sure enough, a minute later she said, "Of course he claims they were just colleagues, but I used to see them coming to work together in the morning." She raised her brows. "Early in the morning, if you know what I mean."

Our dog Byron would have known what she meant. "Was she married?"

"Not that I know of."

"Neither is Charles, and both were adults. You're a biologist—why would you think this was odd?"

"Well, if it wasn't odd, why won't he admit it?"

"You could ask him."

That was far too direct for Sara. "I wonder if it was because she was so much younger than he was. I don't really know how old she was, but she sure dressed like a kid—if I hadn't known she was an adjunct, I'd have thought she was a freshman. I always think that it should be possible to tell a professor from a student at first glance."

She certainly lived by that credo. No student on campus would have been caught dead in the long skirts she wore with black oxfords. I had no idea where she got those blouses with the bow collars—she must be hunting them down at vintage stores.

"The only thing worse than the way some professors dress," she said, "is the way some students dress."

I looked up to see what had provoked such an emphatic sneer.

Standing just outside the doorway and peering in was a young woman in a black miniskirt with chain trim, a black jean jacket, and Doc Martens. Her hair was precisely the shade of the red in her red-and-black-checked stockings—in other words, a color never found on human heads without chemical assistance.

"Yo?" I said. It wasn't a vain attempt at street cred—Yo was her name, short for Yolanda. She was a graduate student in anthropology I'd met during the fall semester when I'd needed somebody to examine Sid's bones.

She was looking considerably less frazzled than the last time I'd seen her, which I calculated to mean that she'd nearly finished her dissertation but was still in rewrites. I'd been around enough grad students to be able to make fairly fine distinctions with a high degree of accuracy.

"Hey, Georgia." She came in and looked around the room with a disdainful expression surprisingly similar to Sara's. "So this is your office."

"Mine and many others'. Welcome to the adjunct corral—our home away from home."

"Yeah, right. Look, can I pick your brain about something?"

"Sure."

She looked around the office. "Maybe somewhere more private?"

"I was going to get lunch anyway. Hamburger Haven?"

"Suits me."

I probably shouldn't have enjoyed the look of disappointment on Sara's face when I gathered up my belongings without saying anything else to Yo, but I really did.

After we got our burgers, fries, and sodas from the counter, we found a table in the corner where we could talk without being overheard.

Once my burger had been enhanced appropriately with mustard, I said, "So what can I do for you?"

"What do you know about grants for attending conferences?"

"I know that most of us would give our eyeteeth for one, but they're getting harder and harder to land. I hope this means you're one of the lucky ones."

"You tell me." She reached into her backpack and handed me a piece of paper to read.

Dear Ms. Jacobs,

The Sandra Sechrest Foundation has funding available for graduate students to attend academic conferences as part of their academic growth and to facilitate their search for employment. If you would like to meet and discuss this opportunity, and whether or not you are eligible, please call this phone number.

Best regards,
Ethan Frisenda

"Have you ever heard of the Sechrest Foundation?" Yo asked.

"No, but if it's for forensic anthropology grad students, I wouldn't have."

"It's not. Some buds of mine got the same letter. One was in history, one in women's studies, and another in English."

"Did you Google them?"

She gave me a look that plainly said, *If I could have found out what I need by Googling, I wouldn't be wasting my time with you.* "They have a site, but there's nothing there but the same kind of spiel as in this letter."

"Sorry, Yo. I've never heard anything about this. It sounds kind of hinky to me."

"Yeah, my spider sense went off, too, but I was hoping I was wrong. There's a couple of conferences coming up where I could do some serious networking, maybe get a job nailed down right away so I don't end up in that corral where you have to hang out. No offense."

"None taken. If I could swing a tenure job, I'd be on it like white on rice."

"But you don't think this is legit?"

"I think it's a case of the old saying 'If it sounds too good to be true, it probably is.' Though it probably wouldn't hurt to make the call, see what they say."

She shrugged and shoved the letter back into her backpack. "Maybe. I'll think about it."

"Sorry I couldn't help. I'll ask around back at the corral, see if anybody else has heard of it."

"Cool. Thanks."

We went on to chat about other things, which was a little awkward because we really didn't know each other that well, but finding common ground in our admiration of the works of Joss Whedon carried us through lunch. Then Yo headed her way, and I headed off to attend my office hours.

Given the overly open nature of the adjunct office, and the fact that my parents were on sabbatical, I'd taken to using my mother's office for anything that was better done in private. I could have used that office for all my personal chores, but if one is living the adjunct lifestyle, it behooves one to maintain relationships with as many other adjuncts as possible because one never knows where a job tip will come from. Besides, I didn't want to get overly accustomed to the accoutrements of a tenured professor—it would make going back to my adjunct corral all the more difficult.

Thanks to their long tenure at McQuaid, my parents had adjoining offices, with a door between them. When I'd first arrived on campus, I'd used both offices, but a few months back I'd handed over my father's to Charles to squat in. He'd had to vacate his previous place after the rightful owner returned from maternity leave, and I'd known him long enough to know that he wouldn't snoop, and when he moves out of an office, he leaves it cleaner than when he found it.

I still had a few minutes before students started showing up, so when I heard movement from next door, I knocked on the adjoining door. Charles answered as promptly as if he'd been waiting for me.

"Dr. Thackery, to what do I owe the pleasure?"

"I'd like to consult you about something, if you've got a minute."

"Of course."

"A grad student I know got a letter from a group called the Sechrest Foundation. They're inviting people to apply for grants for conferences. Have you ever heard of them?"

"Had you asked me just a few hours ago, I would have answered in the negative, but just today Dr. Goodwin mentioned that she'd received a similar letter."

"She's in your department, isn't she?"

Charles nodded. "Her period is Colonial America."

"Interesting. My friend is in anthro, and she says grad students in other departments got letters, too. You didn't get one, did you?"

"Not as of today. And you?"

I shook my head. "Maybe it's a new foundation. Is Dr. Goodwin going to call them?"

"She wasn't sure—like your friend, she was hoping to learn more about the organization first."

"We're a cautious bunch, aren't we? Let me know if you hear anything else about them, okay?"

"With pleasure."

There was a knock on the other door to my office, the one leading to the hallway. "Students await," I said. "Any bets on how many will be asking for extra credit?" There were always students who spent more time begging extra credit than they would have spent doing a decent job on the original assignments.

"This late in the semester . . ." He rubbed his chin speculatively. "I would venture forty percent, plus or minus five percent."

"I'm betting it'll be more like sixty, but that's only because I saw the last batch of grades. Whoever is furthest away brings doughnuts tomorrow?"

"It's a wager."

We shook hands, and I went on to my meetings. When the last student left, I told Charles that I wanted mine chocolate iced, with sprinkles.

10

Madison must have been hungry that night. By the time I got home, she had thawed out some stew we'd frozen a couple of weeks back and had rice ready to serve. She hadn't done anything with the salad fixings that had also been intended for the night's meal, but I wasn't about to criticize her. It might discourage her from doing it again.

I was glad when Sid joined us at the table, even though I knew he'd be slipping illicit scraps to Byron again, because it was the first chance I'd had to talk to him about what he'd overheard at PHS. I had checked my phone several times during the day, and there had been no messages, but since he'd promised to text only in case of emergency, I still had high hopes. "So what was the scoop at school today? Did you hear anything?"

"I heard so much I was afraid I'd forget stuff," he said. "Tomorrow I'm taking a pad and pencil with me."

"Well?"

"First off, Dante and Mina broke up."

"You're kidding!" Madison said. "They were such a cute couple."

"I know, right? But she said he wasn't paying enough attention to her. She texted him Friday night, and he didn't reply until Saturday morning, so she knows he was out with somebody else."

"Maybe he went over his texting limit."

"The perennial problem of the age," I put in.

Sid went on. "No, because he texted Nikko Saturday afternoon to check on a homework assignment, which proves he still had minutes. So she texted him that night and broke up."

"That's harsh!" Madison said. "The least she could do was to break up in person."

"It gets worse," he said. "They were both invited to a party Saturday night, and she took another guy."

"You're kidding! Did Dante freak?"

"He would have, but he was with Rhonda. So apparently he was seeing her all along."

"Wow," Madison said. "What else?"

"Tristan wants to quit the softball team because he really doesn't like it and he feels tired all the time trying to keep up the schedule, but his father says he needs a sport on his high school resume to get into college."

"Mom! Do I need a sport?"

"You have drama and choral ensemble, plus a part-time job with your aunt and good grades. You're fine."

"That's what I wanted to tell Tristan," Sid said, "but under the circumstances . . ."

"Anything else?" I said impatiently.

"One of the teachers is sneaking out every chance she

gets to smoke. I couldn't see which one it was, but I could smell the smoke on her when she came back. Just tobacco, though."

"That's Ms. Gilstrap," Madison said. "We all can smell it on her, so it's no secret, and everybody knows she's trying to quit."

"Good for her. Anyway, that's all I got while in the locker. When I was backstage I heard Becca on the phone telling somebody that she's having second thoughts about casting Holly as Ophelia because she isn't sure she's up to it."

"I could have told her that," Madison muttered.

"And I didn't see who it was, but somebody was doing some serious kissing in the dressing room while you guys were doing act four."

"Really? Now I've got to think about who's not in that act."

"Excuse me," I said, "though this is undoubtedly valuable information, can we focus on whether or not you heard anything that might apply to the murder?"

"Well, we don't really know what could be important, do we?" Sid said defensively.

"Did any of the voices you heard sound like the murderer? Or the person who came to help the murderer get rid of the body?"

"No, not really."

"Was there any mention of anybody being missing? Like a teacher or any other adult who didn't come in to work?"

"No."

"Then how likely is it that any of this gossip is meaningful?"

"It's a lot more likely than a walking, talking skeleton."

I couldn't argue with that. "Tell you what. Write it all up tonight so we can keep track of everything."

"Can I create a spreadsheet? Or would a database be better? Maybe a word processing file with tags, or—"

"However you like."

"Oh boy," he said, rubbing his bony hands together in anticipation. Then he gave me a look. "You're not just assigning this as busywork, are you?"

"Maybe a little, but the fact is we know so little now that we can't afford to ignore anything. If you get it all down, we might find a pattern later." I didn't know if that made sense from an investigative perspective, but the technique had worked pretty well in the past when I was working on research papers.

"If nothing else," Madison said, "it would be a great column for the school paper."

From there, the conversation evolved into a discussion of the ethics of spreading gossip, even gossip confirmed by an impeccable source. By the time that was done, dinner was over, so after cleaning up, we headed for our respective computers: Madison to do homework, Sid to write up notes, and me to grade another couple of late homework papers and answer e-mail about the current week's assignment. On the whole, I thought Sid had more fun than either Madison or I did.

II

Monday set the pattern for the next couple of days. Each night at dinner Sid would regale us with the latest goings-on at PHS: shy flirtations, torrid romances, and dramatic breakups; tests failed, papers aced, and memes shared; teachers who blamed all their problems on the administration, administrators who blamed the students' parents, parents who blamed teachers, and students who either blamed everybody else for everything or were sure everything was their own fault. It was entertaining, to be sure, but wasn't really moving our investigation along.

Thursday morning I was considerably better dressed than my usual combo of slacks and a decent top or sweater because as soon as my class was over, Charles and I were going to head to the funeral of that adjunct who'd died. I'd tried to rise to the occasion by wearing a navy dress with a charcoal blazer and a pair of heels. Charles met me outside my classroom, and he took me up on my offer to drive.

Though he was perfectly polite on the way, and of course impeccably dressed for the funeral, Charles was not his usual buoyant self. I even wondered if Sara had gotten something right for a change. Maybe Charles and Patty Craft had been an item. Of course it wasn't really my business, any more than it was Sara's, but sadly I was just as curious as my office neighbor. I managed to restrain my curiosity until I'd had to ask Charles three times how many were expected at the services.

"Please forgive me, dear lady," he said. "I'm afraid I'm preoccupied."

"Don't apologize. I know this is hard for you." I hesitated, but then asked, "Were you and Patty very close?"

"In all honesty, not close at all until she became ill. We'd worked together, and were collegial, but I never spent that much time with her until her distressing diagnosis. It was then that I saw that many of her friends were drifting away, as happens when times are difficult. So I offered as much support as I could."

"Charles, you are such a sweetie."

"No, Georgia, it was not from sweetness or anything so noble. It was guilt. I'd known that Patty was starting to . . . Let us say that I saw that she was heading down the wrong path in her life, and I did nothing to stop her. Though her poor choices had nothing to do with her illness, I know she had regrets later, and she carried those regrets to her grave. My own regret is knowing that I failed to act."

"Poor choices?" I prompted.

But he shook his head. "These are not my secrets to share. All I can tell you is that I hope that the next time I have an opportunity to intervene and prevent a friend or colleague from making a mistake, I shall do so immediately."

I patted his hand in a way which I knew Sara would misinterpret, but which I knew Charles would understand. With most of my friends, I'd have followed up with a hug once we arrived at the funeral home, but Charles just wasn't the hugging kind.

Given what he'd said about Craft's family and circle of friends, I wasn't surprised that the services were being held at the smallest chapel of the Spadina Funeral Home. Charles excused himself to go find his friend's sister Phoebe as soon as we came in, but after I signed the guest book, I spotted several other adjuncts from McQuaid and we found an empty pew to sit in together.

None of us talked much—I gathered none of the others had known Patty Craft that well, and of course I'd never even met her. Soon enough the music started playing and the funeral director asked us to stand.

Charles was one of the pallbearers, and the coffin was followed by the saddest funeral party I'd ever seen: one lone woman, looking frazzled and confused in a dress that I guessed had been bought specifically for the funeral. She had to be the dead woman's sister Phoebe, though as far as I could tell, she looked nothing like her sister. There was a blown-up photo of Patty Craft on a stand by the coffin, and the late adjunct's features had been so delicate that, especially with her short, asymmetric haircut, she looked almost elfin.

The service was given by a pastor who clearly hadn't known the deceased and who either hadn't bothered or been able to find out enough about her. His words sounded as if they'd been cribbed from a rack of sympathy cards.

At least Charles was able to do his friend proud with his eulogy, speaking about her devotion to academia, her gifts as a teacher, and the courage with which she faced death.

Probably everybody in that room knew that there was a good chance that the woman had killed herself, but she still sounded heroic when Charles pointed out how hard she'd worked to keep her job and to stay current with research in her field. Since I hadn't really known her, I hadn't expected to need the package of tissues in my purse, but I ended up using several and sharing the rest with my colleagues.

At the end of the services, the funeral director announced that there would be no graveside service, because the remains were being cremated according to the wishes of the deceased, and invited us to join the family for refreshments in the room next door.

The receiving line was just the sister Phoebe with Charles staying by her side to introduce those people he knew. I offered my condolences without explaining that I hadn't even met the deceased. I'd have left after that, but I was Charles's ride and he didn't look as if he was going to be leaving anytime soon.

So I made a beeline for the refreshment table. There's something about awkward social situations that makes me crave salty snacks and sweets. At least eating chips and dip and fudge brownies gave me something to do with my hands.

I joined a couple of McQuaid adjuncts, who introduced me to a trio of adjuncts from other New England colleges. We all nodded cordially. There was no secret handshake for adjuncts, but we generally tried to play nice because chances were that sometime over the course of our careers, we'd be sharing the adjunct lifestyle at the same college.

We talked a little shop, and eventually Charles finished with his self-appointed duties and joined us. He knew all the adjuncts present—he'd been making the rounds even longer than I had and was better at maintaining networks.

After he made sure everybody had been introduced, a sharp-nosed brunette named Dolores said, "Did Bert not even show up? I know he and Patty broke up, but they lived together for, what, three years? The least he could do was show up at her funeral. Or did he not know she'd died?"

"I can't say for sure," Charles said, "but I did my best to inform him. I left a voice-mail message for him and sent an e-mail, but he never responded. I understand he's been job hunting, and he may have relocated, so perhaps my contact information is out of date. I haven't attempted to stay in touch with him."

I was surprised by that last comment. Charles stayed in touch with everybody—he'd probably keep in touch with Sara if they ever worked for different universities. For him to drop a colleague told me that the guy must be a real loser. Or maybe he was one of the fair-weather friends who'd deserted Patty Craft when she became ill.

"That's right—I forgot that his career had nose-dived," the brunette said with a smirk. "He's teaching high school. Can you imagine? Reading 'How I Spent My Summer Vacation' and 'My Favorite Character in *Romeo and Juliet*' essays?" She actually tittered.

I shouldn't have, but I've met a lot of Madison's teachers over the years, and I had a lot of respect for the vast majority of them. So I said, "I know, right? I mean, why would anybody give up the halls of academe to take a job with sick days and health insurance? Where you get your own permanent classroom instead of a shared office? And you know his brain will just rot without having to write all those research grant proposals and rushing articles out the door so he can make quota. Who wants all summer off anyway?"

The brunette blinked, and I saw a couple of the others hide grins.

After that, the conversation wandered a bit, mostly stories about how annoying college administrators could be, which was always a good topic for adjuncts. The room started to clear out, and finally Charles said, "I think it is time for us to take our leave. If you don't mind, Georgia, I'd like to have another word with Patty's sister."

The woman was standing by herself with a cup of coffee in one hand, looking more awkward than mournful.

"We must be going," Charles said. "Please do let me know if there's any assistance I can offer in your time of need."

"Thank you, Charles," she said, "but I couldn't ask you for anything else."

"Then there is something else?"

She looked embarrassed. "I was going to go to Patty's place today to pack up her things, but I won't be able to take much back with me on the plane, and I'm not sure what to do with the rest. I'd like to ship things to my house, but my flight leaves tomorrow before the post office opens."

"I would be honored to help with both packing and any necessary shipping."

She made a token attempt to refuse, but I could see how relieved she was—apparently there was nobody else she could ask. They made arrangements to meet at the dead woman's apartment that afternoon.

She did make one last protest, saying, "Are you sure you don't mind? You've done so much already! I mean, helping with the funeral and all. I couldn't have afforded to do things nice like this."

"Think nothing of it. We took up a collection at the

university to raise funds, so it's really all of Patty's friends and colleagues who have helped."

"Really?" she said. "That's so nice. I know adjuncts don't make much money and—"

The funeral director approached discreetly, and we said our good-byes and let them finish their business.

"Jeez, Charles," I said, "you didn't tell me you were passing the hat. Is it too late for me to add to the pool?"

"It's all covered," he said.

"What about the flowers and—"

"All covered."

I looked at him. "Charles, did you pay for this out of your own pocket?"

He held the door open for me. "It's turning out to be a lovely day, don't you think?"

That was all the answer I needed, and I resolved to have him over for dinner as often as I could manage for the foreseeable future. It wouldn't make up for paying for a funeral, but I figured it was as much repayment as he'd accept. I did offer to help him over at his friend's apartment, but was just as glad when he turned me down. Rifling through a dead stranger's belongings didn't sound like a good way to spend the day.

Instead I treated myself when I got back home and out of my good clothes. The house was empty except for me and Byron, so after I'd graded a couple of essays that had actually been turned in ahead of the next day's due date, he and I curled up together on the couch and took a nice, long nap. It was terribly self-indulgent, but I would have been happy to nap longer if Madison and Sid hadn't come bursting in.

Something had broken at last!

12

"Mom! We've got news!" Madison said. She dropped her backpack onto the floor with a loud thump and ran into the living room with Sid's bowling bag. As she unzipped it and put Sid's skull on the coffee table, he added, "Big news! There were police at school this afternoon!"

"They found the body?" I asked.

"We don't know—nobody told us anything," Madison said indignantly. "All we know is that a police car showed up right after lunch, and the cops were still there when school let out."

"I wanted Madison to leave me out somewhere," Sid groused. "Then when a student turned me in to lost-and-found, I'd have been in a prime location for listening."

"And I told him it was a terrible idea!" Madison said. "What if the kid who found you decided to keep you?"

"But—"

"Madison's right, Sid," I said. "It would have been too risky."

"Anyway," Madison said, "the cops were in Mr. Dahlgren's office, and lost-and-found is kept in the secretary's office, so you wouldn't have heard anything anyway."

"They were just in the principal's office? Didn't they seal off the auditorium to examine the crime scene?" I asked.

Madison shook her head. "I heard the jazz band rehearsing in the auditorium, so it definitely wasn't sealed off."

"So what were they doing?"

"We don't know. There was nothing about it in the afternoon announcements. But I did see a couple of teachers heading into the office as soon as the afternoon bell rang."

"Which ones?"

"Mr. Chedworth and Ms. Rad. And that's all we know. I guess we should have stayed at school to see what else we could find out."

"No, no, this is fine. The body must have been found and now that the police are on the job, it's not our problem. There's no reason to draw their attention to you. We can wait until the story goes public."

Sid looked aggravated. "Well, I can't—I'm dying of curiosity. Or I would be if I weren't, you know, already dead. Madison, can you take me upstairs so I can get onto my computer? Maybe the news has hit the Web!"

She hastily obliged and I was right behind them. We were most of the way up when Sid noticed that Byron was behind me.

"Don't let that dog into my attic!" he said.

"Sorry, fellow," I said, giving him a couple of good pats before closing the attic door with him on the other side.

Before long Sid had pulled himself together and was tapping enthusiastically away while Madison and I watched from either shoulder. I considered pointing out that Madison sure seemed to be sold on Sid's story of overheard murder, but I didn't want to spoil the moment.

"No body," Sid said.

"Just like you," I couldn't help saying.

"Mom!" Madison objected.

"What? It was funny, wasn't it, Sid?"

"Not your best effort, but not your worst." Tap, tap, tap. "I'm still not finding any mention of any bodies being found in the area."

"But the police were at the school!" Madison said.

I said, "Sid, search for recent mentions of Pennycross High School or the principal: Mr. Dahlgren."

"Good idea." Tap, tap, tap. "And I have a hit for PHS!"

He pulled up a news story, but it wasn't about a murder. It wasn't even a Pennycross listing—it was from the *Medford Transcript*, the paper in Medford, Massachusetts. " 'Medford man missing,' " I read over his shoulder.

"Gotta give 'em points for alliteration," Sid said.

I read the rest of the article. " 'Medford resident Robert Irwin, twenty-nine, has been missing since last week when he failed to pick up Melissa Laplante, his girlfriend, when she flew into Logan Airport Friday evening after a business trip. When Laplante was still unable to reach Irwin by phone the next day, she went to his High Street apartment. Not only was Irwin not there, but accumulated mail led her to believe that he had been gone for several days. She notified the police, and after investigation they found that the last confirmed sighting of Irwin was in Pennycross, Massachusetts, this past Thursday. He had driven to Pennycross to meet with officials at Pennycross High School about a job opportunity, but witnesses report that he dined at the River Inn in town several hours after the interview. Irwin was last seen wearing a dark gray pin-striped suit and was driving a dark blue Honda Accord with Massachusetts plates. The Pennycross Police Department has been assisting with inquiries, and anyone with information about the missing man is asked to contact either the Medford or Pennycross police.'"

Sid rummaged around the Web a little more, but the *Transcript* article seemed to include all the available details.

"Do you think this Robert Irwin was the man Sid heard being murdered?" Madison asked.

"Either he was, or he's somehow connected. What are the odds that a disappearance and a murder linked to the same location, on the same night, aren't connected?"

"I wish we knew what his voice sounded like," Sid said. "Wait, maybe we can find out." His metatarsals flew across his keyboard, and a minute later he said, "I've got his home phone number."

"He's missing, Sid. I don't think he's going to answer."

"But he probably has an answering machine, and he might have recorded his own answering machine message."

"That's brilliant," Madison said, and I couldn't argue with her.

Sid used his own cell phone to call the man's number, but put it on speakerphone so we could all hear. After only three rings we heard, "Hi, this is Robert Irwin. I'm not at home now, but if you'll leave your name, phone number, and a brief message after the beep, I'll get back to you."

Sid hung up without waiting for the beep and said, "What was he doing, reading from a script? No creativity, not even any personality."

"It sounds like most people's messages," I said, thinking of my own exceedingly bland one. "But artistic critique aside, do you think it was him?"

He hesitated. "Let me listen again." He repeated the process and sat thinking so hard I could almost see the wheels turning. If, of course, he'd had wheels in his skull. "One more time." He repeated the procedure.

Finally he said, "It was him."

"You're sure?" I said.

"One hundred percent certain."

"How can you be that sure?" Madison said. "I mean, you barely heard him at the school, and that message was, what, ten seconds?"

"It was him," Sid insisted.

"Madison, you have to realize something about Sid. Other than unusual events like Halloween and that anime convention back in the fall, the only contact Sid has ever had with people outside this family has been from listening to them from the attic or from the armoire in the living room or from wherever he hid when somebody else came into the house. He recognizes people from their voices as accurately as I can from their faces. Maybe more so—I knew a pair of twins, and I used to get them mixed up, and Sid never did. He may not have ears, technically speaking, but he is the best eavesdropper in the world."

Most people wouldn't take being called an eavesdropper as a compliment, but Sid looked inordinately pleased with himself.

I went on. "So if he says Robert Irwin was the man he heard being murdered, then I guarantee that Robert Irwin is dead."

"Okay, then," Madison said. "What next?"

"Well, I hate to sound like a broken record, but I still say it's a job for the police. I already told them what Sid heard, and now they'll be able to make the connection with the disappearance."

"Come on, Georgia," Sid said. "Deborah told us what they thought of your call. They've probably already forgotten about it."

"He may be right, Mom."

"Yeah, you've got a point. Perhaps it's time for another call." So while Madison took Byron for his much-delayed walk, I took a drive to find another pay phone. I knew I was being paranoid from watching too many episodes of *Leverage*, but I just wasn't comfortable making the call from our landline and didn't want to call from the same phone as last time, either. It took me long enough to find a pay phone that I was actually starting to wonder about how much a burner phone would cost and exactly where I could buy one.

I finally spotted a pay phone outside a drugstore, parked, and tried to walk casually over to the phone, which meant I tripped over the curb and nearly ran into a shopping cart. So much for being circumspect. Fortunately nobody paid any attention to me as I dialed the number.

"Pennycross Police Department Tips Line," that same voice said, sounding just as bored as she had the first time I called.

"I need to report something about that missing person, Robert Irwin."

"Yes?"

"I don't know if you're the person I talked to before, but a few days ago I called in a tip about a suspicious incident at Pennycross High School's auditorium. A friend of mine said he'd heard something that sounded like a man being bludgeoned to death."

"Yes, I remember your previous call quite well."

It was probably physically impossible to hear somebody's eyes roll, but as the mother of a teenager, I can sense when it's happening. I went on anyway. "At the time I thought it was something to do with the body that had just been found, but that was before I found out that that body was a woman and an overdose victim. So now I'm thinking that the murder my friend overheard has something to do with Irwin's disappearance. I'm pretty sure that he was the victim, and that the murderer hid the body somewhere."

"Do you—I mean, does your friend have a reason for suspecting that Mr. Irwin was the victim in this alleged event? I seem to recall that you—that nobody actually saw the event."

"No, he didn't see anything," I admitted, "but it stands to reason, don't you think? Since Irwin is missing? I know the police took a look at the auditorium when I called before."

"Oh?" she said.

I realized I shouldn't have been so certain about that—it implied more knowledge than I was supposed to have. "I mean, I'm sure they investigated because you guys are so thorough. But now that we know who the victim was, probably, it might be worth more investigation."

"I'll certainly pass on the information," she said. "Are you sure you—or your friend—don't want to come to the station so we can get all the details?"

"I'm sure," I said. "You know all I do—I'm confident that you guys can handle it from here." Then I hung up and walked back to my car, going as fast as I could without running. At least I didn't trip again.

"What did they say?" Sid wanted to know as soon as I got back home. He and Madison had been waiting for me in the living room.

"It's not really a conversation—I give information, I don't get any back. She did ask a few questions, but nothing I could answer."

"But she believed you, right?" Madison asked. "The police are going to investigate?"

"I hope so."

"They have to," Sid said, sounding as if he was trying to convince himself. "I just hope they wait until tomorrow to process the scene so I can be there to watch them go all *CSI*."

It seemed to me that if the police believed me, they'd investigate that night and not wait for the trail to get even colder, but then again, it seemed to me that the woman I'd spoken to still thought I was a nut job.

13

The rest of the evening was spent on normal stuff; at least, it was for me and Madison. We had dinner; she did homework; I cleaned the kitchen. Meanwhile Sid scoured the Web for more information about the missing man and kept checking local news outlets to see if anything investigative was happening at PHS. He was still at it when those of us in the family who require sleep retired for the night, though by the time I got up the next morning, I think he'd temporarily abandoned his efforts in favor of online gaming.

The second of the semester's three required essays was due on Friday, so I had an avalanche of work to look forward to for the weekend, but nothing of note happened otherwise. I did take Charles out to lunch after I noticed he seemed as if he'd been upset by the time spent packing up his dead friend's apartment, and I think it cheered him up some. I also found myself checking my cell phone over and over again, hoping there'd be a text from Sid, but there was nothing.

It was ridiculous to be so focused on murder on a day like that. Spring had arrived with a triumphant fanfare, bringing along a bright, clear blue sky. The temperature was perfect for opening windows sealed all winter long, and a breeze was blowing away every bit of academic interest for students and faculty alike.

When only one student showed up for the first half of my office hours that afternoon, I decided to play hooky for the rest of the day. If anybody showed up—which seemed incredibly unlikely on such a spectacular day—they'd find a note to send me an e-mail with any questions. Then I headed out into the glorious day myself.

I just barely beat the others home. As I was unlocking the front door, Madison pulled up on her bicycle with Sid's bowling bag in the basket.

"Well?" I asked when we were all inside and Byron had been appropriately greeted.

But before Madison could answer, there was a muffled complaint from Sid's bowling bag, so she unzipped it so he could join in.

"Jeez, a guy could suffocate in there!" he said.

"Sorry," Madison said.

"Ignore him," I advised. "He doesn't breathe. No lungs, and if he did have any, they'd be up in the attic with the rest of him."

"Technically true, but it still *feels* stuffy. Probably because I feel cranky."

"The police didn't show, did they?" I asked.

Madison shook her head.

"Coccyx!" I said.

"I know!" Sid said. "Somebody take me up to my body, will you? I want to hit something."

"You do it, Madison," I said. "You're younger than I am."

"I just rode home on a bike while you were seated in a luxurious minivan."

"One, I'm impressed you can call our minivan luxurious, even in jest. Two, all that bike riding means that you're in considerably better physical shape than I am and therefore better able to withstand the trip."

"Sid, can't the rest of you just come downstairs by itself?" she asked.

"Sorry, kiddo, I don't make the rules."

"Then who does?" she asked.

"Excuse me?"

"I mean, we all know your existence doesn't really make sense, right?"

"So you're not buying my story about having been bitten by a radioactive skeleton?" he said with a grin.

"That's a new one," I said. The most logical theory we'd ever come up with was the idea of a ghost haunting his own remains, but in that case, why had he lost all memories of his life before waking as a skeleton? Most ghosts were all about the memories, after all, or they wouldn't know who to haunt.

Apparently Madison wasn't buying the story. "Anyway, it seems to me that you're the only one who sets your limits."

"Like in *Roger Rabbit*," I said.

They both turned to look at me.

"Remember that scene when Eddie the detective and Roger are handcuffed together? Eddie tries to saw through the cuffs and gets mad when Roger slips out to make it easier for him. He says, 'Do you mean to tell me you could've taken your hand out of that cuff at any time?' And Roger says, 'No, not at any time. Only when it was funny.'"

They continued to stare at me.

"I just thought it was applicable."

They stared a moment longer. Then Sid said, "So, Madison, about the rest of my bones . . . ?"

"Fine!" She made an exasperated noise I would never be able to describe or repeat and stomped up the stairs carrying Sid's skull. A few minutes later they returned, and both of them were stomping a bit. Well, technically Sid was just making louder rattles, but it was the closest he could get to stomping.

I said, "Okay, starting Monday, Sid can leave his skeleton in the armoire in the morning and then nobody will have to lug him up the stairs. Will that make everybody happy?"

"Yeah, that'll work," Madison said.

"Good. Now you two can stop stomping. Madison, you're going to knock the pictures off the wall, and Sid, you're going to break a bone."

"Speaking of broken bones," Madison said, taking her seat on the couch again, "Mr. Chedworth fell down the stairs at school today."

"Jeez! Is he okay?"

"There's been no official word, but the rumor mill says they had to call an ambulance to take him to the emergency room."

"The rumor mill speaks truly," Sid said. "I heard the EMTs arriving and then taking him away. He was conscious, at least—I heard him talking. I don't think he sounded like the killer, but it wasn't the best opportunity to listen to his voice."

"Sid!" Madison said. "The man fell down the stairs."

"Did he fall, or was he pushed?" Sid speculated. "Did anybody see it?"

"Yes, Liam was there—and no, he did not push him," Madison said. "Anyway, I heard that he broke his leg or maybe his foot, which is bad at his age."

"Broken bones are bad at any age," Sid said with a noisy shudder.

I said, "Madison, remind me. Which one is Chedworth?"

"White hair, reddish face, chair of English Department, has been teaching since the founding of Massachusetts. I have him for SAT prep. Since he wasn't there for class, Samantha drew him a card and all of us in the class signed it. Ms. Rad said she was going to go visit him after school and that she'd take it to him."

Sid said, "Since the subject of people missing from school has been raised—"

"Smooth segue, Sid," I said.

He ignored me. "So what's the next step of the investigation? I mean, if the police aren't going to do anything, we're going to have to."

"Sid, I'm sorry, but I'm out of ideas," I said.

"Madison?" he asked. "You wanted in on this. Any out-of-the-box ideas?"

She shrugged her shoulders. "I've got nothing."

"But we've got to do something!" he said. "The police are completely ignoring this important link, and there's a murderer on the loose."

"We know, we know," Madison said with some irritation. "What do *you* think we should do?"

Sid's jawbone moved up and down a few times, but no words came out.

"That's what I thought," Madison said.

Sid's jaw moved again, and I was pretty sure words were going to come out this time and that I wasn't going to like them. "Look, we're all tired and we're all frustrated. It's been a long week, so why don't we let it alone for a while?" Before Sid could argue, I added, "Just for a while. Madison, why don't you take Byron for a walk? The weather is gorgeous."

"Good idea," she said, still glaring at Sid. "Mind if I go to Wray's, too?"

"Sure, no problem." I handed over her allowance just in case a comic or volume of manga needed to come home with her, and she and Byron went happily on their way.

Sid had moved onto the couch and was sitting with his arms crossed, looking rebellious. "Comic books? When there's a murderer on the loose?"

"Even cops take time off," I reminded him as I sat down beside him. "We're not giving up, Sid. We're just regrouping."

"Yeah, right."

"A few hours of doing other things, maybe even taking the whole evening off, is just what we need. We do have other things going on in our lives."

"No, Georgia. You and Madison have lives."

"Oh, Sid," I said helplessly. "Are you really that miserable?"

"No, no, not really. It's just that I feel so useless. You've got a job—you're teaching kids and you're making the money to support the house. Plus there's all you do to take care of Madison. Madison has school and choral ensemble and drama and friends, and she's taking care of Byron. What do I do for anybody?"

"You have lots of online friends."

"I don't think that sharing cat pictures and *Star Trek* jokes is adding that much to anybody's life."

"You're helping Madison in her play. You help us around the house."

"Being a prop and putting away groceries. There's a pair of achievements to be proud of."

"You do more than that," I said, but I didn't think that pointing out how many loads of laundry he'd done in the past week or the times he'd run the dishwasher would make him feel any better. "Do I have to remind you of how we met and what you did for me when I was pregnant with Madison? Not to mention more recent incidents?"

"And how long ago was that? What do I do for the family *now*? I can't get a job—even if I knew how to do anything, I couldn't get a job. Not like I am." He held up his bony hands and stared at them.

"It's not that bad." I was hoping to jolly him out of his black mood, but instead I said one of the most monumentally stupid things I'd said in a long time. "Look at Byron. He doesn't add to the family revenue stream, and it doesn't bother him a bit."

"I'm not a pet, Georgia," he snapped.

"Oh jeez, Sid, of course you aren't. I didn't mean it that way, I just meant—"

"I know what you meant, but— But sometimes I don't know *what* I am." His voice was tight, and if he'd been able to cry, I think he would have.

My eyes filled for him. I reached for his hand and held it between mine. "You're my friend, Sid. You are the best friend I've ever had, and I am so lucky to have you."

"Thank you, and I know you mean it—"

"You can bet your coccyx I mean it."

"Okay, you mean it, but Georgia, it just isn't enough for me. I know I'm being ungrateful—my world is so much bigger than it was before you came back to Pennycross—but some days it just reminds me of how much I can't do. I thought finding this killer was something I could do."

"Sid, I am not giving up on finding that killer. We'll come up with something, okay?"

"Pinkie swear?"

"Shouldn't that be phalange swear?"

"How about a phalange vow, then?"

"Deal!" I said, and we completed the ritual entwinement of fingers. "Tell you what. You can start earning your keep right now and help me make pizza for dinner."

"Can I flip the dough into the air?"

"As long as you clean it off the floor after you drop it."

When Madison brought Byron home, she found us laughing and covered in flour, which got the evening off to the right start. After a night of watching TV together, we all felt better.

Of course, I knew it was only a temporary reprieve. In fact, even if we did manage to get our amateur investigation back on track and find the missing body and the killer, it would still be a short-lived resolution to Sid's problem. Whether it was a job, a vocation, or a hobby—he needed something that was his own.

I kept thinking about how Sid had come into my life. I'd been in trouble, and I'd needed his help—that was the only possible explanation for why the skeleton of a murdered man had suddenly started to walk and talk. He continued to hold himself together because I still needed him. As far as I was concerned, I always would. But what if he ever stopped believing that? What if he decided he wasn't important to me? I was afraid that he'd just fall apart and fade away. For good.

14

We stayed up late that night finishing up the *Doctor Who* DVDs Madison had borrowed so she could take them back to Samantha, but since the next day was Saturday, I figured I'd sleep in and let Madison get off to work with Deborah without my presence. It didn't work out that way. Instead, I was woken by Deborah shaking my shoulder.

My sister knows that unless there's an emergency, she's supposed to warn me before coming inside the house. So naturally, I assumed the worst. "Deborah? What's wrong?"

"That's what I want to ask you."

"We're fine—I was asleep. Nothing's wrong."

"Well, something's wrong with you. Did you or did you not call the police again and give them that same cock-and-bull story that Sid dreamed up?"

"It's not a cock-and-bull story, and Sid didn't dream it up." Technically Sid can't dream anything up, since he doesn't sleep, but I didn't think it was a good time to remind her of that fact.

"Then you did call again?"

"Of course I called again. I'm supposed to call the police when I have information about a crime—you know, because of being a responsible citizen."

"Is it responsible to keep wasting the police department's time and resources?"

"It's not a waste of resources for them to investigate a crime. And how do you know anything about it anyway?"

"Last night was our bowling league tournament. And Louis was late because he had to pull out his report from the wasted trip he took to the school the other week and confirm that there were no signs of violent death in that auditorium. We almost had to forfeit!"

"Don't you think a murder investigation is a little bit more important than a bowling game?"

"It was the league championship, thank you very much."

"How'd you do?"

"We won."

"Congratulations."

"Thank you."

"So why are you still here complaining if my call didn't hurt anything?"

"Because—because—because there wasn't any murder!"

"What about the disappearance? A teacher came to Pennycross for an interview and he hasn't been seen since."

She rolled her eyes. "Oh, please. Louis told me all about it. The guy came for an interview at two in the afternoon. He met with the search committee for, like, an hour, then Principal Dahlgren and two of the other committee members—including the president of the PTO—walked him out. They were there when the guy drove away. They've also got a waitress who served him dinner at the River Inn several hours later."

"Why was he still in town? That's suspicious, isn't it?"

"Not really. He'd been driving around looking at neighborhoods where he might want to get an apartment. Apparently he was feeling pretty confident about getting the job."

"And he just told all this to the waitress?"

"Men do flirt with waitresses, you know. Apparently it was a slow night. They started talking and he asked her about living here. Since he wanted to know about specific apartment buildings, then yeah, he probably had just been riding around. When he left, he said he was heading back home to Medfield or wherever."

"Medford."

"Whatever. Anyway, he disappeared somewhere between the River Inn and Medford. It had absolutely nothing to do with Pennycross."

"Don't the police think it's suspicious that Irwin went missing on the same day, in the very place, that a murder was witnessed?"

"I'm sure they would if there was any evidence—any evidence at all—that somebody was actually killed at PHS. Because a call from a lunatic—"

"Excuse me?" I said frostily.

"Fine. A call from an eccentric does not count as evidence. The evidence they do have includes four witnesses that saw Irwin leaving PHS—Dahlgren and the teacher and parent who were members of the search committee, plus the candidate who showed up for his interview just as Irwin was leaving. They also have a waitress who served him at a restaurant some time after that time. What they don't have is anything that puts him back at PHS, a place he'd never been to before that day."

"Well, Sid knows what he heard, and he heard Robert Irwin being murdered—he's positive about his voice."

"How would Sid know—?" She held up one hand. "No, don't tell me. I do not want to know. But if you and Sid insist on playing Nancy Drew and Bones Benton, at least leave the police out of it. They've got better things to do than dealing with crank phone calls." She walked out of the room before I could argue with her and stomped down the stairs, calling for Madison to come on so they could get to work.

A minute later, I heard the front door close in not quite a slam. And a minute after that, Sid came into my room and said, "Bones Benton?"

"Don't you remember the Brains Benton mysteries I had when I was a kid? I loved those books, but they were old and obscure even then."

"Wow. She must have been saving up that joke for ages."

"Apparently."

"So, are you getting up now?"

"No." I rolled over and closed my eyes, waiting to hear the clatter as he left my room. It didn't happen. "Sid, are you still in here?"

"Yes."

"Why?"

"I just wanted to make sure that you're still going to investigate and that you still want me to help."

"No."

"No? What about our pinkie swear?"

"Oh, I'm still investigating. But you're my partner, not my helper."

"Oh. Then I'll let you go back to sleep."

"Thank you." This time I did hear the clatter, but before Sid left me alone, I felt the tiniest touch on the top of my head as he gave me a lipless kiss, which isn't nearly as creepy as it sounds.

15

When I finally did get up, much later that morning, I found a stack of paper waiting for me on the kitchen table. Sid had printed a copy of his database of PHS gossip. It was far too much to read at one sitting, especially with all the cross-references, but I kept reading a bit at a time through the day, when I wasn't doing my usual chores of grocery shopping, bill paying, essay grading, and clothes washing. To Sid's credit, he didn't rush me. He just kept looking at me expectantly and trustingly.

By the time Madison got home from working with Deborah, though thankfully not accompanied by her, I was thinking that Sid should have trusted somebody else. Maybe there was something useful in all that data, but there was just too much of it and too many suspects for me to logic my way through.

Finally, as I was taking some winter sweaters down to store in the basement, I saw a stack of old board games and came up with an idea for how to clear out some of the suspects.

After dinner—a roasted turkey breast that provided enough leftovers for several more meals—I said, "If the two of you have no objection, I declare tonight Family Game Night."

"Yu-Gi-Oh?" Madison asked eagerly. "I've got a new deck I've been wanting to test play."

"Pass. You blow me away every time, so it's not really a fair test of the deck."

"How about Operation?" Sid said.

"Definitely pass. You always win!"

"Is it my fault that I'm good with bones?"

"I could keep my hand that steady, too, if I didn't breathe. Anyway, I've got something else in mind. Do you two remember playing Guess Who?"

"I loved that game," Sid and Madison said in unison.

I'd played the logic game with both of them at different points in my life. The idea was for a player to pick a card with a character's picture on it. The other player had a board with pictures of a couple dozen characters and would ask questions to knock out possibilities. Is it a man? What color is his hair? Does he have glasses? And so on, until only one character remained. "I was thinking we could use that game's technique to eliminate some of our murder suspects."

"You lost me," Sid said.

"Okay, we're sure that the murder victim was Irwin, our missing job seeker. Since he had never been to PHS before that day, then it seems pretty likely that the killer is the one who's familiar with the school. Meaning a teacher or admin person or janitor—somebody who works at the school. Right?"

"Yeah, but I haven't been able to identify the voice," Sid said.

"I know, but maybe we can refresh your memory. I found a list of all the people who work at PHS in that stack of paper you gave me, and we're going to go through it together. I'll ask questions. Madison, you mark people off the list. And Sid, you try to remember what you heard."

"Got it!" he said.

I found the list and handed it to Madison, who got an orange highlighter pen to mark off the names.

"Okay, let's start with basics. The person who made the phone call had to be the killer. Right, Sid?"

"Right."

"So think about that voice. Was it a man or a woman?"

With neither eyes nor eyelids, Sid couldn't close his eyes to concentrate, so he had a habit of putting his hands over his eye sockets when he needed to focus, and he did so then. "A man."

"Excellent. Madison, cross off all the women. Unless any of the women teachers have particularly deep voices."

"Not that I've ever noticed," she said. We waited for her to mark off a lot of names. Well over half the people who worked at PHS were women. "That leaves eleven."

That was the easy part. Since Sid hadn't actually seen the murderer, I couldn't ask if any of the remaining candidates had a mustache or whether they wore glasses, the way I would have with the actual game, so I had to be creative with my next question. "Did he have a particular accent?"

He thought hard. "No, not really."

"Madison, you know the people at PHS better than I do. Do any of the men there have a strong accent?"

She looked at the list. "Yes. Mr. Little has a Southern accent, and Mr. Patel is from India."

"The guy didn't sound Southern or Indian," Sid said.

Madison crossed them off. "Mr. Neal's got a really soft voice, but not when he's mad."

"I think it's safe to say that the killer was mad, so we better leave him on the list." I thought for a minute, but was stumped until Madison said, "There might have been sports stuff that night."

"How can we find out?" Sid wanted to know.

"The calendar is online."

My laptop was still out from when I'd been grading papers, so I used it to go onto the Web and find the school's calendar, which conveniently listed practice times as well as games for that night. The baseball team had had the evening off, but the lacrosse and tennis teams had both had practice, and the track team had a meet.

"That lets out Coach Q, Coach Cullen, and Coach McLeod!" Madison crowed.

"Not necessarily. Couldn't one of them have slipped away?" Sid asked.

I checked the listings. "The track meet was in Springfield—I don't think Coach McLeod would have been able to sneak off long enough to drive to and from school. But we better keep Coaches Q and Cullen on the list for now."

Madison marked off the one name. "That gets us to eight. Any other activities that night that might eliminate a suspect?"

I looked over the calendar. "The Spanish club was in Spain that week and didn't get back into the country until late Friday. Madison, what teacher would have gone with them?"

"Senora Harper and Senor Benson. That makes seven."

"Okay. I don't suppose you remember whether any of the ones left were out sick that day."

"Yes! Well, he wasn't sick, but Mr. Bell went out of town for a family wedding during part of that week. Six."

"And isn't the librarian a wheelchair user?"

Madison nodded.

"Sid, could the killer have been in a wheelchair?"

"Absolutely not. There's no carpet in the auditorium, and I'd have heard it if he'd been on wheels. We've whittled it down to five."

We tried to come up with ways to eliminate more of the list, but finally admitted defeat. "Still," I said, "we're better off. Madison, if you promise to keep from being alone with those five men, I won't be so worried about you being in school. I mean, five suspects is a number we can handle."

"Well . . ." Sid said. "Maybe more than five."

"Who did we miss?" I asked.

"The thing is, if there's one thing I've learned while sitting in that locker, it's that there are all kinds of people in and out of that school. The families and friends of every student, teacher, and admin person. Delivery people, repairmen, other schools' teachers for meetings, sports teams and coaches from rival schools. Former students, former teachers. Other candidates interviewing for the job Irwin was trying to get."

"And Becca has brought some of her theater friends to help with acting exercises and sets," Madison added.

"Plus there are the male students," Sid said.

"You told me it was a grown man," I said.

"I *think* it was, but now that I've been around PHS so much, I've realized that some of those boys have awfully deep voices."

"Coccyx! So much for eliminating people. Now our suspect pool includes most of the town."

"Only men," Sid said cheerfully. "Let's try it from the other angle—now that we know who the victim is, that should help. I'll go online to see what I can find out about Mr. Robert Irwin." He gave us a big grin. "We're making progress!"

I was surprised Sid was taking it so well. It seemed to me that our only progress was backward. Then I looked at it from his perspective. As long as we were working on the murder together, he was making a significant contribution to the family. That was what he'd been craving.

Of course, that meant that if we ever did find out who the killer was, part of Sid would be disappointed that he wouldn't be helping anymore. Maybe a really big part of him.

16

My Sunday was filled with comfortingly normal activities: grading essays, cooking meals to freeze for later in the week, and helping Sid take a hydrogen peroxide sponge bath. Okay, maybe cleaning a skeleton with hydrogen peroxide wouldn't have been particularly comforting or normal for most households, but that's how we roll at the Thackery house.

Madison had a science project with a looming deadline that kept her busy, and once Sid was bright and clean, he devoted his day to working on what he called the Irwin dossier, which consisted of all the information he could dig up about Robert Irwin. He only ventured out of the attic to keep us company at meals.

Monday was just as normal: no bodies found or missing persons reported. I got home at my regular time and found Madison already there, playing Mario Kart on the Wii while Byron watched.

"Excuse me," I said, "but I seem to remember a no-video-game-before-homework rule."

"I'm already done," she said, waving the Wii controller around enthusiastically enough that I thought it safer to step out of range. "Rehearsal ended early because Becca had a dentist appointment, and I had a free period today."

"How did that happen?"

"Mr. Chedworth is still out. I guess he must really have hurt himself. Samantha said she heard he was going to have to have surgery on his foot or leg or something. Word is that he won't be able to come back to school for the rest of the semester."

"Poor guy," I said sympathetically, but then switched to practical-mother-of-a-college-bound-student mode to ask, "Why didn't they get a substitute?"

"They got a substitute, but I don't think he knows the material. All he did was tell us to read a section of the textbook, which took about ten minutes. After that, I did my homework, which is why—" She paused to put on enough speed to cross the virtual finish line. "Which is why I'm playing Mario Kart."

"They are going to hire somebody who can actually teach the rest of the course, aren't they?"

"I don't know if they can. Samantha said her mother called to ask, and they're not sure they'll be able to find somebody so close to the end of the year. So the good news is that I may have a free period every day!"

"Good news for your homework, maybe, but not so much for your test scores. Which are kind of important."

"I thought you didn't believe in SATs."

"Of course I believe in them—they exist. I suspect that what you meant to say was that I didn't agree with the way they're administered. Which I don't. I think it's ridiculous that so much of a person's future is dependent on a test score with no predictive validity other than a student's performance in the first year of college. They're a waste of time, energy, and money."

"So what's the problem?"

"A lot of things are a waste of time, energy, and money—like paying for gasoline and shaving my legs—but that doesn't mean I can afford to ignore their existence. As long as most colleges require the SAT, then I want you to get as high a score as possible so you can get into the college you want." *And maybe even get a scholarship,* I thought but didn't say out loud. Madison had enough on her plate without worrying about my shaky finances.

"Don't worry. I test well. And you can help me, right?"

"You remember what happened when I tried to teach you how to ride a bike? And the time you wanted help with a research paper?"

"Oh. Right."

According to her teachers, Madison was an excellent student, and according to peer review and student feedback, I was a good teacher. Yet when I tried to teach her anything more complicated than how to make a bed, we invariably lost our patience. Come to think of it, the bed-making lesson hadn't gone that well, either—I'd finally found a video on YouTube to show her how to make a hospital corner.

I made a mental note to call the school the next day and see what the situation was. "So what's the buzz today?"

"If you mean our so-called murder investigation, nothing."

"Can't a devoted mother ask her beloved daughter about her day without bringing murder into the conversation?"

"Sorry. Sid has been so focused, and it's kind of getting

on my nerves. I asked him to race me on Mario Kart, but he wanted to go up and work on his dossier."

"Sid can be pretty single-minded," I admitted. "So any non-murder-related news?"

"Some new faces at school today. Well, actually they're old ones. A bunch of former students showed up—they're on spring break from college. I totally don't get it. Don't they have something better to do with their time than to visit the high school they probably couldn't wait to get away from?"

"Nostalgia starts early for some," I said. "Besides, they want everybody to see how cool they are now. And some people like their teachers enough to visit them and tell them how they're doing."

"But none of these people had a teacher as awesome as Dr. Georgia Thackery."

"A fair point."

"Anyway, Tristan's big brother showed up at rehearsal, and he is nothing like Tristan."

"Is that good or bad?"

"Bad. For one, he's not too bright—he's on his fifth year of college. Tristan says he comes home and parties just about every weekend, which is why his grades suck. Plus the guy is a total creep. He kept joking about drama fags."

"Are you serious?"

Madison nodded. "Becca asked him to stop after the third time he said it, and he actually made a joke about it being her time of the month."

"I hope she let him have it."

"She was about to, but Tristan dragged him out of there even though rehearsal wasn't over. He was so embarrassed to have him around that he left early."

"I can only imagine."

Madison paused. "I know you and Aunt Deborah don't always get along, but did she—"

"No. Deborah never made fun of me in public. Or vice versa. We have always kept our sniping private, or at least only in front of immediate family members."

"Good. I mean, I didn't think she'd have done anything like that, but I'm glad to know she didn't. I just felt so bad for Tristan. How can his brother be so awful when he's such a sweetie?"

"How sweet is that, exactly?"

"Mom!"

"What? I can't ask about my daughter's new friend?"

"Yeah, I'm totally sure you were asking about him as a *friend*."

Maybe Sid wasn't the only single-minded person in the house—my interest was just different from his.

Since Madison was finished with her homework, I dragged her away from Mario Kart to help me broil chicken, steam broccoli, and mash potatoes. Sid came down just as we got food onto the table and started filling our plates.

"How's it going?" I asked.

He said, "I have Googled my phalanges down to nubs, but I cannot find anything that connects Robert Irwin to PHS. As far as I can tell, he'd never so much as driven through town before the day he disappeared."

"You look pretty perky for somebody who hasn't found anything useful."

Sid held up one finger, which looked as long as ever despite his early comment. "Good detective work takes time, my dear, but fortunately I have plenty."

"You've got about three and a half weeks," Madison said. "That's when we have our show."

"Don't worry about that," he said. "You can leave me in your locker for the rest of the school year—I don't mind."

The look Madison flashed me showed that she minded, even if he didn't.

Sid went on. "My next step will be tracking down information on the PHS Five."

"Excuse me?" I said.

"Those five teachers-slash-employees we haven't been able to eliminate yet. If they were ever so much as in the same town as Irwin, I'll find out about it. If I can't find the connection that way, I'll move on to other frequent visitors to the school. And then on to the rest of the town."

"Sid, you're talking about an inordinate amount of work," I said, exhausted just from hearing about his plans.

"True, but I'm not getting any older. I don't mind. Besides, I'm hoping my young apprentice can help."

Madison looked confused. "Do you mean me?"

"Who else would I mean? While I continue listening in during the day and hitting the Web at night, you can work on gathering data."

"Like what?"

"Like which students have deep voices, as a start. And has anybody ever lived in Medford or one of the other towns near there. I can get you a map of the area. Focus on the students whose parents are active in school functions, like Samantha. Her mother coordinates the monthly bake sales. And Jo's mother is helping her with the costumes for the play, so she's around a lot. Oh! Oh! There were two parent members of the search committee that interviewed Irwin— see if you can find out who they are!"

Madison had progressed to alarmed. "But, Sid, I can't—"

He patted her arm in what he probably meant as a gesture of comfort. "You'll do fine. Just remember to take notes about anything you find out."

"But—"

"Now if you two don't mind, I think I'll get back to it. Lots to do before school tomorrow!" He clattered up the stairs.

"Mom!" Madison said. "I'm not going to ask Samantha if her mother murdered somebody, or ask Mrs. Sinta if she had anything to do with a man disappearing."

"I know, I know."

"I've got the play, I've got homework and projects and Byron to take care of, and now I'm supposed to take notes about my friends? Even if I wanted to snoop around, I've got a life!"

"It's okay, sweetie. I'll talk to Sid and explain that you're already doing as much as you can." I paused. "But you do still believe he heard a murder, don't you?"

"Yeah, I believe it—I'm just not sure I believe we can do anything about it."

I was starting to doubt it myself, but I'd promised Sid, and I couldn't go back on that. "I'll talk to him," I said again.

It didn't happen that night. As soon as we were finished eating, I had work for the next day's class plus the seemingly never-ending stack of essays to grade. By the time that was over, all I wanted to do was sleep. And of course there was no time the next morning as Madison and I rushed around getting dressed and fed and so forth. I decided it wouldn't hurt to wait until that night.

But as it turned out, I didn't have to. After my morning class, I called Mr. Dahlgren at PHS to check on the situation with Madison's SAT prep class, and in the course of that, I got an idea that I was sure would take care of everybody's problems. We exchanged more calls and various e-mails, and by the end of the day, it was all set.

Sid and Madison were going to be so pleased!

17

Neither my daughter nor my skeletal pal was pleased.

"Mom! Have you gone insane?" Madison asked.

"She must have," Sid said. "Or maybe she's sick. Check her forehead for a fever, Madison—I'll go get the thermometer."

"I am not sick!" I'd waited until we were at dinner to share what I thought were glad tidings: while Mr. Chedworth was out on leave, I was going to be teaching SAT prep at PHS.

"Then Madison is right," Sid said. "You're insane."

"What is the matter with you two? Madison, didn't you tell me just last night that you don't have time to do detective work?"

"But I didn't mean for you to do it!" Madison protested.

"And Sid, didn't you say that you need somebody to gather data?"

"Yes, but—"

"So it makes perfect sense for me to take the job."

"You already have a job," Madison said.

"I won't be teaching at PHS full-time—just two classes for juniors on Tuesdays and Thursdays, where I have a gap in my schedule anyway." I'd taught SAT prep courses at Kaplan during dry spells in my academic career, and I had substitute teacher credentials dating back to a particularly awful dry spell. "Plus it'll only be for a few weeks, until the kids take the SAT."

I gave them another chance to applaud my ingenuity, but it wasn't happening. "Come on, guys. This is perfect. It gives us another set of eyes at the school."

"But, Georgia," Sid said, "you've barely got enough time to take a breath now. You're not like me, you need to breathe!"

"I breathe just fine, thank you."

"What about sleep? When was the last time you got a full eight hours? In a row?"

"I know, I know, I'm pretty busy—"

"Georgia, you know what you get when you work your fingers to the bone?" He waggled his at me. "Bony fingers!"

"Sid, you've spent the last week trying to hear something that'll clear this up, and you've drawn a blank."

"I'm doing my best!"

"I know you are." I patted his scapula. "You've been great, but there's a limit to how much you can do hidden away backstage and in lockers. We need somebody who can walk around and rattle cages. Madison can't, so it has to be me."

"Don't blame me for this crazy idea," Madison said.

"I'm not, I just—" I stopped. "Look, this was my idea and my decision, and since the last time I checked I was running this household. You two are just going to have to accept that."

It's funny—the two of them look nothing alike. Madison is curvy, with green eyes and strawberry blonde hair. Sid is, well, a skeleton. Yet when I looked at them, they had the exact same expression on their faces.

It was neither a happy expression nor an approving one.

The rest of the meal was not particularly convivial.

Once it was over, Madison pointedly announced that she'd be doing homework in her bedroom, though at least Sid hung around while I did the dishes and wiped down the kitchen.

It was only when I was starting to think about bed that he said, "Georgia, can I ask you something?"

"Sure."

"What do you think you can do that I can't?"

"I can actually ask questions instead of just waiting for somebody to say something worthwhile within my hearing. That ought to count for something."

"What are you going to ask? 'Excuse me, but did you perchance recently bash somebody over the head in the auditorium?' "

"Oh, let me write that down," I said. "I most definitely want to learn from your vast experience."

"I've got as much as you do."

"Again, I point out that I can ask questions, which is kind of what detective work is all about."

"Hey, I've been working hard!"

"I know you have been, Sid." I sighed. "Look, I realize that you're doing everything you can, but the only thing we've found out is who died. We have no idea who did it and we don't even know where the body is. Think about what that means."

"That I suck at this?"

"No! It means that the killer is smart. From what you heard, that murder wasn't planned. It's like somebody lost his temper and hit the guy—maybe he didn't even intend to kill him. Most people would freak out if that happened. But not this guy. No, he calmly calls for help to move the body and then cleans up any evidence. After that, he hides the body well enough that it hasn't been discovered. The police don't even believe that a murder has taken place!"

"He must have nerves of steel," Sid said.

"Exactly. And knowing that somebody like that has access to the school—has access to my daughter—scares me. I don't know that I can do any more than what you're doing, but I've got to try something."

"Okay, then. I didn't want you to think I was milking this for attention."

"Of course not. Who said anything like that?"

"Nobody, but you know Deborah—"

"Deborah! I love my sister, and her heart is in the right place, but she's not my best friend. You are."

He didn't say anything for a minute, and then it was just, "Well, I better go work on the Irwin dossier—I've found a new way to sort the information."

That took care of half my family problems, so it was time to see what I could do with the rest. Madison had left her door open, which was usually a sign that she was approachable.

She, her books, and her electronics were spread out on the bed, leaving just enough room for the dog to snuggle up against her.

"How's it going?" I asked.

"Mostly done," she said. "Just texting Samantha to see when the next test is."

"And maybe to complain about your crazy mother?"

She gave me half a smile. "Maybe a little. Nothing about the murder or Sid or—"

"It's okay. I trust your judgment."

That turned the smile up to three-quarters full, but after a minute, my message sank in.

"Oh. You're saying that I don't trust your judgment."

"Do you?"

"Yes, but—" She stopped herself. "Yes, I trust your judgment, but I do worry about you. Are you sure that taking the PHS job isn't going to be too much work? Or maybe even dangerous?"

"If it's too much work, I'll quit. If it's dangerous, then that's all the more reason for me to be there to keep you safe. That is my job, sweetie."

"Okay, I won't question your judgment again."

"Sure you will, but then you'll listen to my explanation. And we'll go from there. Okay?"

"Okay. Love you, Mom."

"Love you, too."

I gave her a kiss, and just to make sure everybody in the family was happy, I took a minute to rub Byron's tummy, too.

18

Principal Dahlgren had asked me to come to PHS Wednesday afternoon to fill out the inevitable paperwork, so I cut office hours short to take care of it. Mrs. Lynch, the school secretary, had a bundle of forms ready for me to fill out, and as many times as I've dealt with new-hire paperwork, it didn't take me long to whip through them. Then she showed me Mr. Chedworth's classroom, where I'd be teaching. Somebody had considerately emptied out a section of the closets lining the back of the room for me to use. I was touched—I'd taught at one college for three semesters without being given nearly that much storage space.

Mr. Dahlgren had also invited me to attend that afternoon's faculty meeting, and Mrs. Lynch sent me down to the auditorium as soon as I was done with everything else.

I realized I needn't have rushed through the paperwork. I was the first one in the auditorium, so I backed out into the hall. Every college I've worked at has its own customs for who sits where, and I didn't want to sit in somebody else's spot. Plus I couldn't help remembering what Sid had heard happen there. Madison had been in there any number of times since, but I hadn't, and it kind of weirded me out.

So instead, I read over a selection of essays on *Romeo and Juliet* that had been posted outside the nearest classroom. They weren't bad. A couple had cringe-worthy phrasing, but on the whole they weren't any worse than what I got in freshman comp.

A couple of minutes later, teachers started passing me on their way to the meeting. Most of them had two things in common. One, they were carrying coffee cups or water bottles, many of which had either the PHS lion or the apple motifs that mark most teacher gifts, and two, they gave me the hairy eyeball on the way past. Even the teachers I'd met through parent-teacher conferences for Madison just barely acknowledged my smile.

The only exception was Ms. Rad, Madison's favorite teacher. She was a perpetually cheerful firecracker of a woman, despite her specialty in Holocaust literature.

"Dr. Thackery! I heard you were joining our little family."

"Please, call me Georgia," I said.

"Well, I usually make a point of being more formal with my students' parents, but I'll make an exception in your case," she said with a wink. "Come on inside. Somebody should have warned you to bring your own refreshments. The budget in public schools doesn't lend itself to extras like I'm sure you're used to."

It wasn't the time to explain the usual status for an adjunct professor, or lack thereof, so I just smiled and followed her.

The faculty had scattered themselves throughout the auditorium, but there was one seat left empty in the front row, where Ms. Rad promptly sat. I'd been right in assuming people had accustomed spots. I took a seat in the row behind the rest of the teachers, figuring that would be safe. Then a foursome I recognized as math teachers wandered in, and I saw looks of extreme irritation on their faces before they pointedly took the row behind mine. Oops.

No one spoke to me during the year that followed—or maybe it was only three or four minutes—not even Ms. Rad, who was deep in a discussion of the latest YA book phenomena. I'd have been happy to join the discussion, but the unwelcoming backs of too many teachers separated us. Finally Mr. Dahlgren came in, his own coffee cup in hand. His had an apple wearing a top hat, whose significance escaped me.

I'd met him before, of course, but there's a difference between the way I look at a principal and the way I look at a new boss, even a temporary one. Dahlgren was a tall, thin man, with a definite but not overwhelming mustache. Though he usually sported suits for school functions, he stuck with khakis and button-down shirts for everyday wear.

He looked around, saw me, and said, "Ah, our new member is among us. A temporary member, it's true, but no less welcome. Dr. Thackery, would you stand?"

Since I was the only stranger in the room, it was a meaningless gesture, but I obediently stood. Very few of the teachers even bothered to look at me, and of those who did, the majority shot me hostile glances. I sat down as quickly as I thought polite.

"As you may know, Dr. Thackery will be taking over the junior SAT English prep classes for the next few weeks while Mr. Chedworth is out of commission. I trust you will offer her a warm PHS welcome."

Mr. Neal, a tall, dark man who taught Madison's algebra class, raised his hand and asked, "Is Dr. Thackery going to be proctoring the SAT in Mr. Chedworth's place?"

"We haven't discussed that, actually," Mr. Dahlgren said.

"I just wanted to remind you that I'm next on the proctor list."

Okay, I had to quickly decide if Mr. Neal was unhappy about being stuck with SAT duty or worried that I was going to get it. In that the SATs were administered by an outside company, and knowing roughly how much they cost, I was willing to guess that proctors got paid to do the job.

So I said, "It's fine with me if you take the proctor job. I probably shouldn't proctor tests for the kids I've been teaching anyway."

A scrawny woman with a dark gray cardigan gave me a baleful look. "I've always managed to proctor the students I've taught in SAT math."

Sometimes the only way out of an awkward situation is to just flat-out lie. "Oh, excellent. I'm glad to know that people who know the students proctor here. One of Madison's previous schools brought in the scruffiest bunch of people you ever saw to proctor their SATs, and one mother said—Well, that's neither here nor there, but I'm glad to learn that the policy here is more civilized."

The SAT math teacher looked mollified, but Mr. Neal said, "So you do expect to proctor the test?"

"I'm sorry," I lied again. "I don't have availability on Saturdays. I hope that won't be a problem."

Dahlgren said, "No problem at all. Mr. Neal, you can certainly take the job if you're next on the list."

With that settled, attention mercifully turned away from me, and I could sit in back looking interested-and-concerned as I jotted notes on my pad, only a fifth of which had anything to do with what was being said. Mostly I was doodling. Since most university staff meetings include only a few agenda items that affect me, I'd long since learned how to hold my pad so it's not easily visible to prying eyes.

After about an hour of serious doodling, the meeting broke up, and since I was fairly sure that nobody would want to chat with me, I was ready to beat a hasty retreat, when Ms. Rad came by. "Can you come over to my classroom for a minute? I want to introduce you to Lance."

"Sure." I followed her down the hall, up the stairs, and down a different hall to her classroom. The edges of the room were cluttered with mismatched shelves, all filled with books, and the walls were decorated with posters of authors ranging from Shakespeare to Jane Austen to Poe to J. K. Rowling.

Ms. Rad put her pad on her desk and picked up a plush lion. "This is Lance," she said, handing him to me with an expectant look on her face.

Fortunately, Madison had told me about Ms. Rad's mascot. "So this is the famous Lance." I ruffled his mane affectionately. "Looking good. And I love the shirt." He was wearing a miniature PHS Lions football jersey.

Ms. Rad seemed satisfied, so I put him down. I saw nothing wrong with talking to a stuffed lion. For one, like all mothers I'd had many a conversation with toys of all description, and for another, my best friend was a skeleton. Most people would have had an easier time accepting a Lance than a Sid.

"As acting English Department chair while Mr. Chedworth is out, I wanted to welcome you to PHS, even if it is just temporary." There was a slight edge in her voice when she said, "It is just temporary, isn't it?"

"Oh yes," I said firmly. "I don't have the skill set to teach high school students other than on a limited basis. It's a different ball game from college."

"Oh, I'm sure you'll do fine. Teaching is teaching." But I could tell that she had loosened up.

"Can I ask you something? Is that why people weren't happy to see me? Because they thought I was trying to take away somebody's job? Or was it the proctoring thing?"

"Well, proctoring is much sought-after because it's easy and pays over a hundred dollars for just a few hours. Here at PHS, we offer the PSAT once a year, the SAT twice, and some achievement and AP tests, too. So it adds up. I save my proctoring money up for Christmas shopping."

"But now that I've said flat-out that I won't be proctoring?"

"That will help, but the fact is that you're considerably more academically qualified than some of the other teachers in the English Department. Take Coach Q. Marvelous man, gifted teacher, but he's only got a master's, and his degree is in history, not American literature."

"Why is he teaching English?"

She shrugged. "He needed a job, and they needed an English teacher. So he did his homework and he's doing a wonderful job. Then there's Ms. Sullivan, who teaches computer science. Her degree is in English, and she's been promised a chance to move to this department when there's an opening, but again, she's only got a master's."

"So they're afraid of me because I've got a doctorate?"

She nodded. "I've got a doctorate myself, and so do a handful of the other teachers, but most of us don't. So when a real academic comes around, with published papers and such—"

"I haven't published anything worthwhile since grad school. Honestly. I'm a teacher just like you guys—I just teach at a different level."

"But with the whole tenure system, they're afraid you'll come in here and work for cheap because you can afford to."

"If I had tenure, the last thing I'd do would be to take on extra work. I'm an adjunct." I explained what that meant. "Do you think you could spread the word so people wouldn't hate me?"

"I could try," she said doubtfully, "but I'm not sure it would help. If they knew your job was that shaky, they'd be sure you wanted to come teach here."

"So I have a choice of them being jealous because they think I have tenure or being anxious because they think I want my job?"

"That's about the size of it!" Then she laughed at the expression on my face. "Don't worry, they'll get over it soon enough."

We went on to talk a little bit about expectations, and then I patted Lance good-bye and told Ms. Rad I'd see her the next day, when I taught my first couple of classes. Then I drove home and tried not to get depressed.

It wasn't concern about doing a decent job—I'd taught SAT prep before, and while it wasn't my favorite topic, I knew the material. Nor was it that I didn't feel particularly welcomed at PHS—I'd had that problem at any number of universities in the past. It was more that I didn't know how I was going to make excuses to talk to people when they were so hostile.

I just hadn't expected high school teachers to be so antagonistic of college professors. Then again, it went both ways. I remembered Patty Craft's funeral, and how that one adjunct had mocked the deceased woman's ex-boyfriend Bert for teaching high school. If Bert had worked at PHS, he'd probably have been just as suspicious of my motives as the other teachers.

Come to think of it, hadn't Charles said that Bert was looking for a job? Just like our missing murder victim.

I kept walking, but I was no longer paying attention to where I was going.

The missing teacher was Robert Irwin, and Bert was a nickname for men named Robert.

Could it possibly be the same man?

19

By the time I asked myself that question, I was in the parking lot and standing next to my car, though I wasn't quite sure how I'd arrived there. I also wasn't sure how I could find out if Bert was the same man as Robert Irwin, but Sid might. Deciding it would be as fast to drive home as to call him, I started the car.

But halfway home, I decided against telling him right away. His emotions had been so up and down, and I didn't want to get him all riled up over nothing. As it turned out, it was a good decision. There was more than enough excitement in the house already.

I heard the raised voices even before I opened the door, and I admit to being tempted to back up, hop in the car, and drive to just about anywhere else. I don't like arguments.

But since I was the only parent, I stiffened both my upper lip and my spine and went inside. The cacophony was coming from the living room, where I found Sid's skull on the couch with Madison standing in front of him, hands on her hips. Meanwhile, Byron was sitting a little too close for my comfort. He hadn't tried to gnaw on Sid in a while, but that didn't mean he didn't want to.

"This is none of your business!" Madison said to Sid.

"You knew I was in the bag when you started talking, and you know Georgia will want to hear this."

"I thought I could trust you!"

"You mean you thought you could sweet-talk me into keeping secrets from your mother."

"Ahem?" I said before they could continue their verbal blasting. "Can we use our inside voices?"

They stopped talking, but continued to glare at one another. Byron, at least, seemed glad to see me and even wagged his tail, though he had to realize it meant that his plans for a bony snack had been foiled.

"Dare I ask what's going on?" I said.

"Sid has been eavesdropping. Again. Still!"

"I'm supposed to eavesdrop. That's why I'm spending every day shut up in your locker!"

"You're supposed to be trying to find out about a murder, not sticking your nose into my business."

"I'm not sticking my nose in anywhere—I don't even have a nose."

"Let me extrapolate," I said. "Sid, you overheard Madison talking to somebody about something you think I should know, right?"

"She told Samantha that—"

"Stop. Does what you heard have anything to do with the murder we're trying to figure out?"

I think he tried to shrug, but since all he had to work with was his skull, he just wobbled a bit. "I thought we decided at the beginning of the investigation that there was no way to tell what facts and information could be useful."

"Okay, then, using your very best judgment—your honest judgment—what are the chances that what you overheard has anything to do with the murder?"

He mulled it over before finally admitting, "Maybe five out of a hundred."

"Not even!" Madison said.

I said, "If there's a ninety-five percent chance that the information has no bearing on the case, then I think you could keep it to yourself until such time as it proves to be important."

"It is important!" he protested.

"Until such time as it proves to have something to do with the murder. Okay?"

Sid's skull wiggled some more, but he said, "Okay."

Madison should have left well enough alone, but she had to add, "Nobody likes a tattletale, Sid."

"Now, Madison," I said, "I'm sure that if you have some information that is important to me, you will tell me yourself. Right?"

"It's no big deal."

"Glad to hear it. I'm sure I can trust you to tell me everything I need to know. That's how we work, right?"

The way she wouldn't meet my eyes told me that it was a bigger deal than she was willing to let on, but I wasn't going to order her to tell me. After a couple of long minutes, she finally said, "Okay, I blew a biology test."

"How badly?"

"Pretty badly."

"How much is it going to affect your grade this quarter?"

"I'll still get a B. I think."

"Make sure of it." I didn't insist on her getting straight As, but Bs were the minimum I would accept. "If you need extra help, I expect you to stay after school and get it."

"But Mrs. Hanson's only time for helping is during rehearsal, and Becca will drop me from *Hamlet* if I miss too many rehearsals!"

"Then you better make sure you learn the material during class."

"What do I need biology for anyway? I mean, have you used any today? This week? This year?"

"Do you have a career path already lined up?"

She looked blank. "No."

"Then how can you possibly know what you're going to need?" I thought it was a reasonable question, but I'm not a teenager and clearly she didn't follow my logic.

She said, "Whatever."

"Try that again."

She visibly swallowed what she wanted to say. "I'll do better."

"Okay, then. I trust you to take care of it."

"I should go get started on my homework."

"I'll call you when dinner is ready."

She took her backpack and dog upstairs, and I know she was working hard to keep from stomping.

"Um, Georgia," Sid said, "can I have a lift to the armoire?"

"Sure." I opened up the armoire and got Sid close enough to pull himself together. "So did you hear anything today that might fit into the whole murder plot?"

"Probably not," he said. "Just gossip, and some really raunchy jokes that are in terribly bad taste." He shared one, and I was appalled for a microsecond before we started laughing.

We were still laughing as we headed to Sid's attic, and

in retrospect, I wish we hadn't been, because the dirty look we got from Madison as we passed her door meant that she probably thought we were laughing about her.

I was thinking of that look when I sat down on Sid's couch and said, "Sid, you can't keep listening in on Madison's private conversations."

"I didn't do it on purpose—she was holding my bag when she told Samantha about that test."

"Yeah, okay, maybe this time you didn't mean to. What about the other times you've snuck around the house hearing things?"

He gave a full skeleton shrug this time. "It's an old habit. Besides, I kind of thought I could finally do something useful by letting you know."

"But I don't need you to keep tabs on Madison. She's extremely trustworthy. Besides which, you're not an employee, and you don't have to *do* anything. You're family. Okay?"

"Okay," he said.

Of course I could tell from his tone of voice and the precariously loose connections between his bones that it wasn't okay, but I patted his femur and went on downstairs. Sid closed the attic door firmly behind me, and Madison had her bedroom door closed, too. She'd even taken the dog with her, which left me by my lonesome.

I'd thought I'd had Sid and Madison all squared away the night before, but the peace hadn't even lasted a whole day. I would have loved to have somebody to talk to about the situation, but there wasn't anyone I could call to grouse with. The only ones who knew about Sid were my parents, who weren't in the right time zone, and Deborah, who I didn't think would be sympathetic or supportive. There is no Facebook group for blended families like mine.

20

As soon as my eight o'clock class was over the next day, I headed for the adjunct office. I didn't have to be at PHS until noon, and I wanted to talk to Charles first. When I didn't see him around, I went to my mother's office and tapped on the adjoining door to my father's office. A minute later, Charles answered.

"Good morning, my dear," he said cheerily. "I've just brewed some fresh coffee, if you'd care to join me."

"Coffee sounds great."

I waited for him to stop fussing with the cups and a selection of honest-to-God digestive biscuits before I said, "I have an odd question for you."

"I would be honored to answer if I can."

"At Patty Craft's funeral, somebody mentioned her ex-boyfriend. A man named Bert something?"

"Yes, Robert Irwin."

I managed not to spill my coffee, but it was a close thing.

Just to make sure I'd heard it right, I said, "Patty Craft used to date Robert Irwin?"

"For some time, actually. I didn't realize you knew him."

"I don't—I've just heard the name."

"Ah. I thought perhaps you had worked with him."

"Isn't he a high school teacher?"

"He is currently, but he started out as adjunct faculty. That's how I met him, actually. Patty, Robert, and I were all together at Tufts for a fall and spring semester."

I was so going to have to smack Sid for having missed that when he was compiling his Irwin dossier. "Have you heard about what happened to him?"

"Has he finally turned up? I really was surprised he didn't attend the services for Patty."

"According to the paper, he's missing, Charles, and has been since right around the time Patty died."

"Really? That's rather shocking, isn't it?" He took a swallow of coffee.

I waited for him to express sympathy for the man, but there was nothing. "Do you know him well?"

"I'm acquainted with him," he said shortly.

"You don't like him, do you?" Charles was so scrupulously polite that for him to say no more than he had almost certainly meant that he hadn't approved of the man.

"I'm afraid I never warmed to him—I felt he'd led Patty down an unsavory path, and my feelings about him were forever cemented after she was diagnosed with cancer and he immediately cut her from his life. He said he couldn't handle it."

"What a selfish sleaze! I know it's hard to be with somebody going through cancer treatment, but how could he live with himself knowing that he'd abandoned her?"

"Frankly, had he shown up at the funeral I would have been forced to cut him dead." That was about as strong a measure as I'd ever seen Charles take against somebody.

I took a bite of biscuit. "Him disappearing around the time of her death is an odd coincidence, don't you think?"

"I suppose it is," he said, but went no further.

"Do you suppose that 'unsavory path' you mentioned had anything to do with his disappearance?"

"If it did, then he has only himself to blame."

"Was it something dangerous?"

He actually shrugged—Charles never shrugs. Then, with an air of finality, he said, "I am sorry if Robert has come to a bad end. Now, if you'll excuse me, I have some tasks I must attend do."

I tried to prod a little more while I helped him clean up, but Charles is discreet to a fault. It was the only time I'd ever wished that he, or in fact any living person, were more like Sara Weiss.

I did a little work from the privacy of my mother's office, then met with the students who wanted advice on the assignment due the next day. Some hadn't even done the reading about which they were supposed to be writing: one of my favorites, a meaty article about the effect of comic books on modern culture. Still, knowing that some of them were going to have to pull an all-nighter to catch up, I tried to treat them gently. It's just that being diplomatic was harder than usual because I was still trying to figure out what it meant that my murder victim—probably—was connected—however tenuously—with a recent death—that could have been either suicide or an accident. I was just glad I didn't have to parse out a sentence that convoluted for any of my students.

After I shooed off the last student, what I really wanted to do was go talk to Sid. Unfortunately, according to my watch it was going to be several more hours before that happened. So I did something desperate—I went looking for Sara Weiss.

21

Luckily, Sara was at her desk in the adjunct office—from her active use of a red pen, I assumed she was grading papers. I resisted the impulse to smile when I saw her because she knows she's not my favorite person and would instantly suspect any direct attempt to engage. Instead I tried to act normal, in that I ignored her presence as I went to my desk and opened up my laptop so I could pretend to Web surf. Then I muttered, "Robert Irwin, Robert Irwin," as if I were trying to remember something.

"Robert Irwin?" Sara said, turning in my direction. "Did you know Robert?"

"I was just reading an article about a man who went missing," I said, "and his name is ringing a bell but I'm not sure why. No, wait. The article says he was a high school teacher. That might be it—maybe he taught at a school Madison went to." I acted as if the matter was settled as far as I was concerned.

But Sara was just warming up. "You could have worked with him. He used to be an adjunct."

"Really?" I made a show of looking through the article. "It doesn't say anything about that here."

Sara said, "He switched to teaching high school. Robert and I were at UMass Lowell for a semester years ago, but I knew he wasn't cut out for the life."

"Why do you say that?"

"Didn't have the brain for it, no real feel for biology. He was one of those who tested well, but couldn't do the work."

"The person who created standardized tests has a lot to answer for," I said. "I wonder what happened to the guy."

"No idea, but I seem to remember there was something not quite right about him."

With anybody else, I'd have said something to prompt her further, but I knew I could count on Sara to keep dishing dirt.

After a short pause, she said, "He always had more money than he should have. I mean, it's not like we didn't all get paid the same."

"Maybe he had a side gig."

"If he did, he never talked about it." To Sara, that was an automatic indictment—she thought she was supposed to know what everybody was doing. I wondered what she'd think about my part-time work at PHS.

I was waiting for her to come up with more, when the mail cart went past the door and Sara jumped up. "Mail call. I'll get yours while I'm up!"

She was outside the room before I could object, and was gone an undue amount of time to just grab our mail. She was almost certainly flipping through mine, but since I was still hoping to pick her brain for information about Robert Irwin, I let it slide.

When she came back and slapped mine onto my desk, I said, "Thanks. So, about Irwin . . ."

But she was looking through her own mail. "Damn."

"What's wrong?"

"I sent a note to the Sechrest Foundation, and they haven't even bothered to reply."

I remembered that that was the group that Yo had been wary of. "A grad student I know got a letter from them, and it sounded suspicious, so maybe you should be grateful."

"Some of us can't afford to be picky," she said. "We don't all have friends in high places, like you and your parents."

My parents were a source of irritation to Sara, or at least the fact that they were both tenured faculty rankled. Never mind that they'd been on sabbatical the whole time I'd been at McQuaid, and I'd gained very little benefit from their officially still being on staff. She was incredibly jealous that I got to use my mother's office, and she was sure I was getting other perks as well, almost certainly to culminate in their handing me a tenure-track position.

I cast around for a subtle way to move the conversation back to Robert Irwin, but the best I could do was, "So, this missing high school teacher—"

Before I could complete my lame gambit, Sara said, "Well, I've got no time for idle gossip. I've got a class to teach." She bundled her things together with an insufferable air of superiority and flounced out of the office.

Since I didn't have anybody else there to talk to, and there were still hours to go before I could talk to Sid, I put the murder and/or missing person case completely out of my head and concentrated on work. Well, I tried to, but I honestly wasn't at my most productive. I kept trying to guess what terrible things Robert Irwin and Patty Craft could have been involved with.

I grabbed an early lunch at McQuaid's Campus Deli before heading to PHS for my first SAT prep class.

22

My classroom—or rather, Mr. Chedworth's classroom—was occupied when I got to PHS, so I stayed out in the hall until the bell rang. Then I played salmon-swimming-upstream as the students flowed outward. Madison was one of the students caught in the tide, but we only had time for a quick wave before she was carried away.

The teacher in charge of the classroom was a substitute brought in to keep the kids quiet—he had no experience in teaching the SAT. Despite my earlier concerns, since Madison was a freshman and wouldn't take the PSAT until fall of her junior year and then the SAT the following spring, it really wouldn't do her any harm to have the study hall. The two classes I was teaching, however, were juniors and they would be taking the SAT in May, so it was considerably more important that they be ready.

I made nice with the substitute, then got myself settled in. Since I've never had a permanent classroom in any of the colleges where I've taught, I'm used to getting myself ready to teach in just a few minutes. So when the bell rang to start the class, I was ready and raring to go.

The students in the class, however, seemed to be neither. Fortunately, years of teaching sections of a required course had left me uncommonly prepared for the situation. I have a standard first-day-of-class wake-up speech committed to memory and only had to change the particulars to match. So after I introduced myself, took attendance, and explained that I'd be taking over for Mr. Chedworth—which they already knew—I said, "The SAT is a joke."

As usual, the students looked confused.

"It's an arbitrary test and its predictive validity—" I stopped, remembering this was high school, not college. "And the only thing it predicts with any accuracy is how well a student does during the first year of college. Not if you ultimately do well, not if you graduate, nothing vital. Just how you do your first year. So yeah, it's a joke."

I definitely had their attention.

"But taking the SAT is required for a large percentage of the colleges to which you'll be applying. That's not because college admissions people are stupid—they know the limitations of the SAT as well as anybody. They use it because it's a way to differentiate between the vast number of students applying each year. When you realize that each of you will be applying to six or more colleges, you can see why admissions people need something to help them figure out their best candidates. And what they've got is the SAT.

"So if you want to maximize your chances of getting into the college you're dying to attend, then you're going to want to get the best score you can on this test. And I'm here to help you do that.

"You know I'm not here long term and I get paid no matter what. That means the only one who will pay the price if you fall asleep during this class is you." I clapped my hands together to simulate enthusiasm. "So let's get started!"

It worked as well as it usually did, which is to say that I got about seventy-five percent of the class ready to do the work. As for the rest, they were welcome to nap as long as they didn't snore and disrupt the class.

Mr. Chedworth had prepared a seating chart, which I appreciated mightily. After years of adjunct life I'm good at memorizing student names quickly, but a cheat sheet never hurts. Since the kids were two years older than Madison, I didn't recognize many of the names, but a couple were familiar from Madison's stories about Drama Club, including Fortinbras, Laertes, and the boy playing Rosencrantz to Madison's Guildenstern.

The period went by quickly, again thanks to Mr. Chedworth. He had the students in fairly good shape already—about all I'd need to do to make sure they were ready was to lecture on test-taking strategies and administer a few more practice tests.

The second class went pretty much the same, except that it included the student playing Hamlet. I wasn't sure if he was perpetually emo or was using the Method to prepare for his rendition of the melancholy Dane. Whatever it was, it was certainly drawing the attention of several of the female students.

I wasn't overly surprised when Ms. Rad happened to wander by after the class was over—she took her role as acting department chair seriously.

"How'd it go?" she asked.

"Pretty well. They seem invested in the process, which is good."

"SAT prep is an elective, so nobody is in the class if they're not college bound. Other than a couple whose parents want them to be college bound, of course."

"I've seen a few of those pushy parents on college campuses, too. They expect college instructors to call them with their kids' grades—they don't realize our students are presumed to be adults."

"That's nothing compared to what we get around here. You'll see on parent-teacher conference night."

"I will?"

"Of course. Mr. Dahlgren mentioned it at the meeting yesterday?"

"I didn't think that applied to me. I mean, I'm only part-time and I'll only have taught a few classes by then. Plus I'll be meeting with Madison's teachers."

"Don't worry about that—you can catch up with Madison's teachers any workday. But parents will want to meet you."

"But—"

She was looking at me, somehow implying I wasn't taking my teaching job seriously. Which I wasn't exactly, given that I had another reason to be hanging around the school, but I still owed it to PHS to give it my best shot.

I swallowed a sigh and said, "Of course I'll be there."

She offered to explain the procedure for the evening, and though I'd intended to walk around a little and see what I could snoop into, I couldn't very well turn her down. Afterward we walked out to the parking lot together.

Since Madison didn't have rehearsal or choral ensemble

that day, I'd told her that she could pile her bike into the backseat and catch a ride home with me, but she'd told me she wanted the exercise and was already gone. I'd wondered if she was still disgruntled about my taking her to task about her biology grade, and soon got the answer. By the time I got home, she'd already grabbed Byron and retreated into her room with the door closed and her music turned up louder than usual. Definitely disgruntled.

I had several options. I could try to jolly her out of it, but that wouldn't be supportive of her feelings. I could patiently explain my reasoning to her once again, but that might undermine my parental authority. Or I could wait her out— she was a teenager and sooner or later she'd want food. I went with that one.

At least she'd helped Sid regroup before secluding herself, and he'd gone up to his attic.

I knocked at the door.

"It's open," he yelled down, and I climbed up to find him at his computer playing Facebook games.

"Oh, it's you," he said with a distinct lack of enthusiasm.

"Who were you expecting?"

I could just tell that if he'd had eyes, he'd have rolled them. So he was in a mood, too. But since I didn't have to be supportive of his feelings, I had no parental authority to exert, and I sure as sacrum couldn't wait for him to get hungry, I was free to snark back at him. "Okay, then. I was going to tell you what I found out about Robert Irwin, but I can see you're in the middle of a game." I started back down the stairs.

"Stop, stop, stop!" He managed to get ahead of me, probably because he wasn't afraid of bruising or even capable of it, and blocked the door. "Please, Georgia, come have a seat and visit. I'm dying to hear about your day. Or I would be, if I hadn't already . . . you know."

"If you're sure I'm not interrupting . . ."

"I've always got time for you." He smiled winningly, which is harder than one might think for somebody who smiles 24-7. "Please, have a seat. Would you like me to go get you a cold drink? A snack?"

I was tempted, but I decided I had let him squirm enough. "No, thanks, but I would like to chat."

"Then pull up a chair and spill."

I did so. "You know the first body the police found, the one we thought was our murder victim at first?"

"The woman who died of an overdose? Yeah."

"When I went to her funeral, a couple of people were saying they were surprised her ex-boyfriend wasn't there—they'd been broken up for a while, but it was pretty serious for a long time."

"So?"

"So her ex-boyfriend was Robert Irwin."

"Oh, my sternum! So you think he—I mean, maybe she—" Sid scratched his skull, though I was quite certain it couldn't itch. "I don't know what this means."

"I don't either," I admitted. "But remember how I told Deborah that having two bodies found in one week in Pennycross was just a coincidence? Now I'm thinking that maybe it wasn't a coincidence at all. Maybe the deaths are linked."

"But how? And how did you find out?"

"I had a hunch yesterday, but—"

"You realized this yesterday and didn't tell me?"

"First off, I wasn't sure. Second, with you and Madison going after each other hammer and tongs, and not exactly showing me any love, I kind of got distracted."

"Fair point."

"So why didn't you tell me that Irwin had been an adjunct? Was it not in the information you found?"

"Of course it was, but it was years ago," he protested, "and I couldn't find any link between those years and anybody at PHS."

"Okay, that makes sense. Anyway, I had this hunch yesterday, and then I talked to Charles today to confirm it." I recounted the conversation and added the little I'd learned from Sara.

Sid said, "I know Charles is a quiet kind of guy, but that was sort of a mild reaction to finding out that a guy he knows has gone missing, wasn't it?"

"A bit. I think he disliked Irwin a lot, so either he was just being too reserved to say 'I hope the guy is dead' or he feels guilty for not realizing it before."

"Maybe, or . . ."

"Or what?"

Sid looked at me, eye sockets wider than usual, which was impossible but pure Sid. "Georgia, how well do you know Charles?"

"I've been friends with him for years. You know that."

"Yeah, but I just had an awful thought. What if the McQuaid gossip queen was right and he really was dating Patty Craft?"

"He never said one word about them dating."

"Did he tell you they weren't?"

"Not explicitly, but he said they weren't close until she got ill, and he hasn't been acting like a bereaved boyfriend."

"Okay, so they weren't dating, but he did do a lot for her, right? He must have cared for her."

"He's a very loyal friend."

"So what if he blamed Irwin for Patty Craft's death? I mean, the louse dumped her after she was diagnosed, which is pretty low. And suppose Charles saw Irwin while he was driving around town looking for a place to live once he moved to Pennycross? Might he have wanted to avenge her?"

"You think Charles killed Irwin?"

"You said yourself that he said he'd have cut him if he'd been at that woman's funeral."

"Cut him dead, not cut him with a knife. Besides, why would Charles and the guy have gone to PHS? And how would they have gotten in?"

"No ideas on the why, but from what you've said, Charles is pretty good at getting into places where he shouldn't."

Sid was one of the few people I'd told about Charles's unusual living arrangements. Of course Charles must be good at sneaking into buildings. How else would he have managed to squat in colleges all through New England?

"No, wait," I said. "Patty Craft's body wasn't found until the day after Irwin went missing, so Charles couldn't have known she was dead and wouldn't have had a motive."

Sid paused, but not for long. "The police seem to think it was a fifty-fifty chance that the death was suicide instead of an accident, right? And she wasn't found immediately after she died, was she?"

"That's what Deborah got from her pal on the force."

"So maybe it was suicide, and Charles found the body and a suicide note. But, not wanting his friend's memory besmirched, he took the note. So there he is, feeling hurt and angry that his friend has killed herself, and he sees the man he blames. For all we know, Irwin could have been mentioned in the note!"

"By that reasoning, your theoretical note could have blamed George W. Bush!"

"But Bush wasn't murdered that very day. Irwin was."

"Okay, fine. Even if your murder-in-retribution-for-causing-suicide idea is right—which I'm not saying I think it is—doing something like that doesn't fit Charles at all. Maybe he'd destroy a suicide note, but he wouldn't leave his friend's body alone like that without at least calling in an anonymous tip. It would be . . . unseemly."

" 'Unseemly'? That's your defense of the guy? That he wouldn't do anything unseemly?"

"Fine, then. You heard the killer's voice. Did he sound anything like Charles?"

"I didn't hear him that well," Sid said.

I just looked at him.

"Okay, no, he didn't sound like Charles, but he didn't sound enough unlike him to rule him out. Who knows what Charles sounds like when he's angry?"

"Then who did Charles call to help him hide the body?"

"No idea. That should be the first line of investigation."

"We are not investigating Charles!"

"You're that sure he didn't kill Irwin?"

"Yes." But I usually try to be honest with Sid, and I had to say, "Okay, not one hundred percent sure. I suppose anybody could be a killer under the right circumstances. And I can see him confronting Irwin if he really thought he'd caused Patty Craft to commit suicide, but I don't see him murdering the guy."

Sid snapped his finger bones. "I've got it! What if Patty Craft was murdered, too?"

"Oh, come on, Sid. You can't have Charles killing Irwin to avenge Patty if he killed Patty himself!"

"But what if Irwin killed her?"

"Now you've lost me."

"If Patty Craft's death was fuzzy enough that the police can't be sure it was suicide or accident, then how can they be sure it wasn't murder? Irwin could have played games with her meds so that she took more than she intended to—"

"Wait, wait. Why would Irwin want to kill her?"

"I don't know. Maybe he has a hot new girlfriend he's planning to bring to Pennycross with him, and he didn't want his old girlfriend hanging around like the ghost at the feast. Maybe he just didn't like her anymore. What about life insurance? He could still be her beneficiary." He casually waved any objections away. "Whatever the reason, if he killed Patty and Charles found out, Charles could have confronted him over that and had it escalate to murder. At which point he decided he didn't want to go to jail because he'd have to wear those tacky orange jumpsuits, so he hid the body. It could be in any of the college buildings where he's squatted over the years."

"I'm not buying any of this," I said.

"You're just mad because I came up with a theory that explains all the facts and you didn't."

"It doesn't explain anything!"

"It sure explains why Charles won't talk about the unsavory thing Patty did."

Sid had a point, though I wasn't willing to tell him that. "Charles is my friend, and I trust him. Are you that desperate to make progress? Or are you jealous of me spending time with him?"

"Please. Check how many Facebook friends I have and then look at how many you have. If anybody has a reason to be jealous of friendships, it's you, not me."

I managed to resist pointing out that Facebook friends weren't anything like real friends—since Sid couldn't really have other real friends, that would have been mean. But I didn't keep myself from saying, "Then you go investigate all your friends, and leave mine to me."

It was not my proudest moment, and I hope Sid felt as bad about some of his retorts as our conversation devolved to early junior high school levels. He finally stomped over to his computer—at least, he tried to, though all he could really manage was really loud clattering—and I went downstairs to work.

At least I tried to.

I didn't want to believe Charles was involved in Robert Irwin's death, and I kept dismantling all of Sid's theories in my mind. There was just one thing I couldn't get around. If Patty Craft's death was connected to Irwin's disappearance, and I was sure it was, then the only known link between them was my friend.

23

As I'd expected, Madison did venture out of her room at mealtime, but also as expected, none of us were feeling particularly friendly toward one another that night. So we dealt with it in time-honored New England fashion. We acted as if nothing was wrong.

Over dinner, Madison asked me how my first day teaching at PHS had been, and we shared tidbits about her classmates. Sid recounted an amusing story about a student who'd spent fifteen minutes trying to get his locker unlocked only to realize that he was at the wrong locker. Nobody tried to get out of cleaning the kitchen or taking out the garbage, and we agreed on a show to watch on TV without any argument. In contrast to our feelings toward one another, we all lavished Byron with affection. Well, Madison and I did. Sid did go as far as he ever went with the dog, which is to say that he handed him a pizzle stick every time Byron looked like he might possibly be considering the idea of chewing on any part of Sid.

It was perfectly polite and perfectly peaceful, and I hated every minute of it. I was pretty sure that Madison and Sid felt the same way as I did, but nobody knew quite how to thaw out the situation. I was fairly sure that as the head of household, more or less, I should be the one to make the first move, and if it had just been me and Madison, I would have. Had it just been me and Sid, we'd have fussed at each other and then gotten over it, as we had many times in the past. The dynamics of the three of us had me flummoxed.

Fortunately, by Friday morning, things had improved. Nobody came out and apologized, but the tension was definitely loosening up. Our "good mornings" were genuine instead of forced, and Sid joined us for breakfast instead of squeezing in an extra few games on Facebook.

It didn't hurt that when Madison was stuffing books into her backpack she pulled out what looked like one of Sid's bones and said, "I almost forgot. I got this at school."

"Sid, I told you to leave the rest of yourself at home," I said.

"That's not mine!" he said.

"It is now," Madison said, handing it to him. "One of the dads gave this out Wednesday at career day, and I thought you'd like it."

Now that it was closer, I could see it was a bone-shaped ballpoint pen. "Let me guess. Doctor?"

"Pharmaceutical sales rep," she said.

"Cool!" Sid said, twirling it around. "Thanks, kiddo!"

"You didn't tell me it was career day," I said.

"I forgot."

"I could have come to talk to you guys."

She rolled her eyes. "Might I remind you that last time you came to a career day, you spent three-quarters of the time talking about the benefits that adjuncts don't get?"

"Oh yeah. That was the week I found out I'd been turned down for tenure." Technically, one of the weeks. "I could have stuck to the positive aspects of my work."

"They already know what a teacher does, Mom. They spend their whole day with teachers."

"What about the joys of academic research?"

"We're in the middle of science fair projects—how many kids do you think would like the idea of doing research forever?"

"Good point. And what could be as exciting as being a pharmaceutical sales rep?"

"I asked Aunt Deborah if she wanted to come, but she had a conflict. I'll get her next year."

"Oh boy," I said, "Mr. Dahlgren will love it if she teaches all the kids how to pick locks!"

"Maybe she can get lock picks to hand out," Sid suggested.

Madison rolled her eyes at us, but it was definitely an affectionate roll. Any mother of a teenager would know the difference.

"Come on, Yorick," she said to Sid. "We've got rehearsal this afternoon."

She held out the bowling bag, and Sid popped off his skull to put it in, dropped in his right hand, and zipped up the bag with the left.

That was no more impossible than most of what Sid did, but then the skull-less, one-handed skeleton started walking up the stairs. From the sound of it, he got all the way to the second floor before the rest of his bones fell apart.

"Hey!" I said. "Since when can you do that?"

"We've been practicing," Sid said from inside the bag.

Madison was grinning. "Cool, huh?"

"Definitely, but Sid, are you sure you want to leave the rest of your bones on the floor with Byron around?"

The dog had just risen from his favorite spot by the back door and was starting in that direction.

"Coccyx!" Sid yelled. "Somebody get me out of here!"

Hilarity ensued, at least for me and Madison, while I grabbed hold of the dog and Madison retrieved Sid's skull and took it upstairs so he could pull himself back together. Then he ran into the living room, jumped into the armoire, and yelled, "Madison, come get my skull. And keep that fleabag away from me!"

It was, in other words, a normal morning at the Thackery house.

My workday was also on the normal side, though not from my lack of trying to do a little investigating.

First off, I tried to get more out of Sara Weiss, but she had her own fixation. Once my classes were over, I headed to the adjunct office so I could try to ease the subject over toward Irwin, but as soon as I walked in, she said, "Enough is enough! I'm approaching this scientifically."

"Approaching what scientifically?"

"The Sechrest Foundation!" she said, as if it were painfully obvious. "So yes or no: have you received an invitation from them?"

"No."

"Okay." She turned to her laptop and typed something.

"Is that a spreadsheet?" I asked.

She ignored me. "Ray and Esteban told me they were invited, and I saw invites in Andrea's, Matt's, and Sunil's mailboxes. So that's physics, math, and biology represented. But Audrey was invited, too, and she's in English, so it's not limited to the sciences." She tapped her finger on the desk. "The gender split looks even, and the minority sampling is actually better than McQuaid as a whole. Maybe I should cross-reference with where people got their degrees. Should I tabulate undergraduate, master's, or doctorates? Or all three?"

"They're inviting grad students, so advanced degrees couldn't be the main criteria." Okay, I was sucking up—a little—but it was for a good cause.

"Good point. I only have to track undergraduate degrees. Where did you get yours?"

I told her, then said, "So, have you heard anything more about that guy you used to know who went missing? Robert something?"

"He's still missing," she said shortly. "Could there be some sort of subtle class-system thing happening? Where people were born, or towns of residence . . . ?"

I thought about suggesting eye color or shoe size but was afraid she'd take me up on it. Clearly she wasn't going to talk about Robert Irwin until she'd figured out why the Sechrest Foundation was snubbing her. Given the choice of waiting her out or helping her get it out of her system, I went for the slightly lesser of two evils. "Can I see the list of people who've received the invites?"

"It may not be a complete list," she said. "Not everybody gets their mail here."

I ignored the implicit confession that she looked through other adjuncts' mail—it was no secret that she spent more research hours on the lives of her fellow faculty members than on biology—and took the intricately formatted report she handed me. At first glance, I didn't see a pattern, either—she'd tabulated all the most obvious factors. I was actually getting intrigued enough by the problem to suggest that she look at research projects, but realized that would also leave out grad students, most of whom hadn't had a chance to publish much. In fact, of the people listed that I knew personally, none of them had been in academia long enough to amass publications. They were all fairly young. . . .

"Age!" I said.

"What?"

"Age. Everybody on this list is young."

"Ageism? How could I have missed that? I could sue for ageism!" She grabbed the report out of my hand and started going through it. "No, wait. Marie didn't get invited, and she's younger than Audrey, who did."

"Really? I thought Marie was older. Must be her clothes." Marie's style was a lot like Sara's, come to think of it. "Audrey wears—" I was about to say that she dressed like most of the rest of the faculty but thought Sara might take that amiss. "Then maybe it's looks. Which is obnoxious, and probably illegal as well."

But Sara shook her head. "They sent a letter to Matt."

"Ah." Matt was a nice guy, and a solid scholar, but I could imagine no world in which he would be considered pretty. "Still, all the ones they picked look young, even Matt. That was true with the grad students, too." Yo's goth style would have blended in with some of my students at PHS.

"You may have something there." She looked me up and down. "That certainly explains why you weren't invited. Even if you weren't past their target age, having a teenager adds years to a woman's age."

"Thanks for the self-esteem boost, Sara."

"Don't blame me! I'm not the one who's only inviting the young-looking ones. Charles's girlfriend would have fit right in."

Great, we were back to Charles's hypothetical—and probably fictional—relationship with Patty Craft. "I don't think they were—"

But before I could finish the sentence, there was an alarm from her computer. She said, "Time to get to class. We can't all spend the day lounging around the office." And off she went.

Since I wasn't in a lounging mood, I went to my mother's office to work and also to try to buttonhole Charles to see if I could persuade him to tell me more about Robert Irwin and his nefarious dealings, but he didn't answer my knocks on his door. Either he was really busy or he was avoiding me. Given Sid's suspicions, I was really hoping it was the former.

After a couple of hours of reading freshman papers about the cultural influence of comic books, and not hearing Charles, I packed up to head home. I didn't get a lot more done there than I had at McQuaid, but it was so much more comfortable to grade homework while sitting on my couch, and nobody was going to catch me when I dozed off over my work. Well, Byron, of course, but since he was curled up next to me, I figured he wouldn't rat me out.

24

I woke up when the front door opened, and tried to rearrange myself so it wasn't completely obvious I'd been sawing logs. I was just checking for drool when Madison walked in. With a boy.

Byron greeted the former with his usual enthusiasm, and the latter with a touch of suspicion. Akitas are protective by nature.

"Hi, Byron," Madison said. "This is Tristan. Tristan, this is my dog, Byron."

Tristan held out a hand for Byron to sniff and apparently passed inspection.

"Mom, this is Tristan McDaniel. Tristan, this is my mom."

"We've already met," I said, remembering him from my SAT class.

"Hi, Ms. Thackery."

"Hi, Tristan. You're playing Rosencrantz, right?"

He nodded awkwardly. He was kind of awkward all over,

really. He hadn't quite grown into his height and had a cowlick that he hadn't figured out how to disguise with the right haircut, plus bigger feet than any normal person should need. But his eyes were a pretty blue, his smile was nice, and I suspected Madison would have described him to her friends as "totes adorb," which translated to "totally adorable."

"Rehearsal ended early, so we thought we'd practice our lines here, and then work on a biology project," Madison said. "Didn't you get my text?"

"I must have missed it." I really had been out if the phone's "you have a text" tone hadn't woken me. "Why don't you fix yourselves a snack before you get started? I'll move upstairs and get out of your way."

"Cool," they said in unison and then beamed at one another.

They were both totes adorb.

Madison had casually left Sid's bowling bag on the floor by the front door, and I just as casually picked it up on my way up the stairs. I was pretty sure Sid realized we had company, but still, I waited until we were all the way up in the attic before unzipping the bag and pulling out his skull:

"What did you bring me up here for?" he said as I put his skull and hand onto the couch. "You should have put me into the armoire with the rest of me. Don't you want me to listen in to make sure those two aren't up to anything?"

"No, Sid, I do not want you to eavesdrop. Madison and Tristan both know I'm in the house—do you really think they're going to try anything radical?"

"Didn't you hear them? A biology project? Boy, you don't remember what it's like being a kid, do you? Like that time you and Reggie—"

"Don't go there, Sid. And besides, I need to talk to you

about something a little more serious than some innocent necking."

"So you think they're going to neck?"

"Sid! I trust Madison!"

"But what do we know about Tristan?"

"We know Madison likes him and that she's a pretty good judge of character."

"You're not going to let me spy, are you?"

"Nope."

"You used to let me spy on Deborah."

"I was in little-sister mode then—annoying Deborah was part of my job description. In fact, you could spy on Deborah now if you wanted to. But when it comes to Madison, I'm in parental mode, which means I'm supposed to be mature."

"Parental mode sucks."

"I kind of like it. So what did you hear at school today? Anything useful?"

"Bubkes. Though a kid from one of your SAT classes said he thinks you're hot."

"You're making that up."

"No, seriously."

"Huh. I don't know if I should be flattered or disturbed."

"What you should be doing is telling me that you got some good dirt at McQuaid. Did you manage to get anything else out of Charles?"

"Nothing," I said. "I never even saw him."

"Interesting," he said.

"Not interesting. He's just busy."

Sid didn't say anything, but I knew, sure as sacrum, that if he'd had eyebrows, he'd have been lifting one of them significantly.

"Anyway, for once I couldn't get any gossip out of Sara Weiss. At least, I couldn't get the right flavor of gossip. She's got her panties in a twist about the Sechrest Foundation."

"The Sechrest Foundation?"

"Didn't I tell you about that?" I explained the letters offering grants. "I wouldn't mind something like that myself so I could hit a conference or two, but I definitely don't have the look they seem to be going for. I wonder if they can be sued for age discrimination."

"Maybe somebody did," Sid said. "That name is ringing a bell for some reason. Something I read on the Web."

He booted up his computer and went online, but after a few minutes he said, "Not finding anything but a bare-bones Web site."

I thumped his skull.

"Sorry. Anyway, it looks like they took a stock layout and just added their contact info. I mean, is that a lame logo or what?"

"Big talk for somebody who only discovered the Web six months ago."

"You learn quickly when sleep is not an issue."

I yawned, demonstrating that I didn't have that particular advantage. "Is it just the one page?" There was a brief, vague paragraph about the aims of the foundation, which were apparently to help academics reach their goals, and an e-mail address. No street address, and no names or pictures of the people involved. "I think I was right to tell Yo to run from this group. And if Sara were smart, she wouldn't be bothering to chase them down, either."

"I admit I've only encountered the woman briefly, but has she ever shown any sign of being smart?"

"I don't know about her work as a biologist, but she is an excellent snoop—that should count for something. I just wish I could get her back on the subject of Robert Irwin."

"I don't think I ever added what she told you before to the Irwin dossier."

"Is it even worth adding?"

He shrugged noisily. "Maybe not. I hate to say this, Georgia, but I'm getting kind of discouraged."

"Hey, I've only taught the two classes at PHS so far, and I still haven't had a good chance to snoop around. We're not beaten yet."

"Are you sure?"

"If it was easy, the cops could handle it," I said in as lighthearted a tone as I could muster.

After that, Sid caught up with Facebook while I went back to grading homework. Eventually, I figured I'd better go downstairs and see what Madison and Tristan were up to. In deference to their privacy, and my own sensibilities, I made as much noise as possible walking down the stairs. If they were sharing any unauthorized smooches, I didn't want to know about it.

As it turned out, they were seated decorously, with Madison on the couch in the living room and Tristan on the easy chair. Books were open, papers were spread far and wide, and, if the empty plates, bowls, and potato chip bags were any indication, half the food from my kitchen had been consumed. I didn't think they'd have had time for making out.

"How's it going?" I asked.

"Mom, tell me I'm never going to need to know about cell mitosis to succeed in this world!" Madison pleaded.

"You'll need it long enough to get through this year of

biology," I said heartlessly. "Tristan, I was thinking about getting dinner started, and I wanted to see if you could join us." Assuming that there was enough food left in the house.

"No, thanks, Ms. Thackery. My dad is going to pick me up any minute. I better start packing up."

I'm always impressed by just how much stuff teenagers manage to fit into a backpack without it coming apart at the seams. It reminded me of the time I'd made too much stuffing at Thanksgiving but insisted that I could get it all into the turkey. It had been a poor choice.

The doorbell rang as Tristan was in midstuff, and when I answered it, I found a nice-looking man who looked like a mature version of Tristan. He had the same eyes and smile, but none of the awkwardness, and if he had a cowlick in his blond hair, he'd used just enough product to tame it. "Hi, I'm Adam McDaniel. I'm here to pick up Tristan."

"I think he's getting his things now. Come on in." I pushed Byron aside to make it possible. "I'm Georgia Thackery."

McDaniel stepped in with his hand stretched out for a handshake. "I've been wanting to meet you, Dr. Thackery. I understand you've joined the PHS faculty."

"Only temporarily," I said.

"That's what I hear. You see, as part of being PTO president, I'm part of the school search committee, and normally we have to vet all new hires. Naturally Mr. Dahlgren had to move quickly this time, what with Mr. Chedworth's injury. We're just lucky that somebody with your background was available, and grateful that you're willing to fill in."

"I know how important the SATs are." I felt marginally guilty that my reason for taking the job had almost nothing to do with the SATs, but only marginally.

"I managed to get my older boy through them, but it took some doing. Bright boy, Adam Jr., but not great with tests. Tristan, here, is a different story. Tristan has this thing down cold, don't you?"

"I guess we'll see," Tristan mumbled.

"You bet we will," McDaniel said and tousled his son's hair, making the cowlick even more pronounced. "I'm not worried about you at all."

Madison, who'd come over to see her guest off, said, "Hi, Mr. McDaniel."

"Hello, Madison. You making sure Tristan gets his lines right?" To me, he said, "I met your daughter during career day this week."

"That's right, she told me. Pharmaceutical sales, isn't it?"

"That's me." He reached into his pocket and pulled out a couple of bone pens like the one Madison had given Sid. "Here's a little thank-you for having Tristan over. Hope he didn't eat you out of house and home."

"Well, the house is still here," I said, taking the pen. McDaniel and I smiled, and the kids rolled their eyes simultaneously. It was a nice bonding moment right until the extended car honk from out on the street.

Tristan made a face, but McDaniel forced a laugh. "Speaking of Adam Jr., I think he's impatient to get going."

"It sure sounds like it," I said loudly so I could be heard over the sound of the horn.

"Thanks again for letting Tristan come over, and for taking over that class."

Mercifully, Adam Jr. stopped honking as soon as his father opened the door. From the look on the man's face, I was pretty sure Junior was going to get a well-deserved talking-to as soon as his father got into the car.

"I told you he was a jerk," Madison said.

"No arguments here."

"So did I hear you say something about dinner?"

I looked pointedly at the mess in the living room. "It depends on if I find any food left."

"No problem. We left all the boring stuff," Madison said and started gathering up snack-related debris. Then she took Byron for a walk while I fixed dinner.

The two-teenager horde had missed the hamburger meat I'd set aside for sloppy joes, and though we no longer had the chips I'd intended to go on the side, I filled in with oven-baked French fries. Once I retrieved Sid's skull and hand from the attic and got him connected with the rest of his bones, he was happy to keep us company, and even managed to resist interrogating Madison about Tristan's intentions.

After dinner, Madison texted half of the Western world in order to arrange a trip to the movies for her and a bunch of her friends, and when I learned somebody else was going to drive, I gave her my blessing and the requisite cash. Sid and I divided our evening between watching TV and my letting him thoroughly defeat me in several games of Operation.

By the time Madison got back from the movies, I was yawning, so the breathing members of the family went to bed while the nonbreathing minority headed to his attic.

I woke up with a skull looming over me in the darkness, and even after years of living with a skeleton, I couldn't hold back the yelp of alarm. "Sid! What's wrong?"

"Nothing! I found something."

I sat up and checked the clock. "And you had to tell me at three in the morning?"

"I couldn't wait."

"Okay, tell me."

"I decided I better add that stuff that Charles and Sara Weiss told you to the Irwin dossier, even though I was pretty sure the whole thing was a waste of time."

"It wasn't a waste of time—"

"I know that now. Because I found something in there I'd forgotten. Robert Irwin used to work for the Sandra Sechrest Foundation!"

25

"What? Are you sure? Why didn't you tell me that before?"

"Irwin worked for the Sechrest Foundation. Yes. And because it was in a cache. Did I miss any?"

"You missed explaining what cash has to do with anything."

"Cache—c-a-c-h-e. Which in this case means a Web site that doesn't exist anymore."

"It's three in the morning, Sid. My brain doesn't exist right now."

"Okay, let me break it down for you. Four years ago, Robert Irwin was puffing up his profile on his college alumni site."

"As one does."

"I prefer a bare-bones approach myself."

"Don't we have a no-puns-until-dawn rule in this house?"

"No."

"We do now."

"Anyway, Irwin put all this fluff into his profile: fancy titles and obviously expanded job descriptions. And he said he was an associate with the Sandra Sechrest Foundation. Two months later, he went back in and deleted all references to the Sechrest Foundation. Everything else was the same."

"If he deleted it, how do you know about it?"

"This is where the cache comes in. You see, just because you delete something from the Web, that doesn't mean it doesn't exist anymore. The original version is put into a special storage area—the cache—and then the locator IDs—"

"Three in the morning."

He sighed. "Pretend it's pieces of paper. He wrote stuff on a piece of paper and put it into a file folder. Then he made a photocopy of that piece of paper, cut out the stuff about the Sechrest Foundation, and put the new piece of paper into a new folder and hid the old folder. But that old folder still exists, if you know where to look for it."

"And you found the old folder?"

"That's right. And I added that information to my big stack of papers—"

"I've got it now."

"Okay, then. I added the info to the Irwin dossier, which is why the foundation's name sounded familiar when you mentioned it earlier."

"So let me see if I have this right. Irwin said he worked for the Sechrest Foundation, but then took the information off his profile for some reason. When we looked at the Web site for the Sechrest Foundation, it looked suspicious. Irwin got Patty Craft involved in something that Charles thought was unsavory. Which adds up to . . ." I rubbed my eyes. "Add it up for me, Sid."

"Irwin got his girlfriend to work for the Sechrest Foundation, even though the foundation was—and likely is—doing something immoral and/or illegal. They were both killed within a day of each other. Therefore their deaths likely had something to do with the foundation."

"But what could the foundation be up to? Wait, do we know how old Irwin was?"

"Thirty next month."

"Do you have any pictures of him? Especially from when he supposedly worked with the Sechrest Foundation?"

"Sure! Come up to the attic and I'll show you."

I just looked at him.

"Or I could go get them and bring them to you." He hopped off my bed and I tried not to fall back asleep while he was gone. Fortunately, he was swift and came back with a stack of pictures in under a minute. "Okay, these are from his Facebook page, and these are from archives of the schools where he taught."

I looked through them, realizing that I'd never even thought about what he must look like. In the earlier pictures he was slim, with a full head of blond hair, and looked awfully young for his age. By the time he disappeared, the hair had thinned and his comb-over aged him to the point where he actually looked older than he was.

"He sure used to fit the pattern of the people at McQuaid who've been getting letters from them," I said.

"So what is Sechrest doing? Making a 'campus guys and girls gone wild' tape? Full-blown porno? Prostitution? What would require people who looked young?"

"I have no idea." I yawned again. "Tell you what—let me sleep on it." I settled back down under my comforter.

"You're not going to be able to sleep now, are you? Won't this keep you up?"

"I'll risk it. Turn the light off on your way out, will you?"

He wasn't happy about it, but he complied. At least I think he did. I was asleep before the light went out.

The situation seemed just as confusing in the morning. Madison was off for her workday with Deborah, which gave Sid and me plenty of time to discuss the options, but we never did come up with a better theory than pornography or prostitution, but why would anybody recruiting for either of those professions focus on the halls of academe?

"What we need to do," Sid finally said, "is score an interview with the foundation."

"How's that going to work? I don't look nearly young enough, and, well, you look dead."

"I prefer to think of myself as well preserved."

"Still, not quite what they're looking for."

Sid and I kept talking while we tackled the weekend chores, but we didn't get anything out of it but clean laundry, which was of more interest to me than it was to Sid.

When Madison came in, I was dreading Deborah coming in with her to rail at me for taking the job at PHS. But it appeared Madison hadn't told her, or maybe she had better things to do with her time than criticize me or she'd realized I had good reasons for doing what I was doing. Nope, I knew my sister. The only reasonable explanation was that Madison hadn't told her.

The rest of the weekend went by without excitement or progress. It wasn't that we'd forgotten the murders, of course, but there wasn't anything we could do until Monday.

I did call Charles and invite him over for dinner Saturday, but he said he had other plans. I couldn't talk him into coming on Sunday, either. Sid, of course, thought this was highly significant. I didn't want to think that way, but it was hard not to.

I was just hoping something would break on Monday to get us moving again.

26

By the time I got home from work on Monday, I was thinking that nothing was ever going to break. I didn't see Charles all day, and, despite consulting Sara's database of people who'd received a letter from the Sechrest Foundation, I couldn't find a single adjunct who'd actually gone in for an interview with them. We adjuncts might be a little bit desperate, but apparently we're even more paranoid. Though I admired my fellow adjuncts' caution, I wished one of them could have been more like Sara, who would apparently have had a face-lift if she could have gotten an invite.

Added to that, so many students showed for office hours to discuss their grades on the essays I'd just handed back that I ended up staying at McQuaid for an extra hour.

So by the time I got home, I wasn't in a happy mood.

Sid and Madison were waiting for me in the living room.

"Just in time!" Madison said. "I think we've got it now, Mom."

"Got what?"

"Show her, Sid."

"Stay here," he said and clattered upstairs. I heard the attic door shut. Then I heard him coming down again, but clumsily. A second later, I saw why. Sid, on the other hand, saw nothing. He'd left his skull upstairs.

"Wow," I said. "I'm trying to decide if this is amazing or deeply disturbing."

"I know, right?" Madison said, clearly delighted.

From the attic, Sid yelled, "Aim me back in this direction, would you?"

"Sure!" Madison called back. She took the skeleton by the hand, turned him around, and guided him toward the first step. Haltingly, the skeleton climbed up. "Isn't that great?" she said.

"I guess. It's just that . . . Sweetie, I'm not sure you should push Sid so hard."

"How else is he going to know how much he can do? You always taught me to try to exceed expectations or I'd never know what I was capable of."

"I know, but that's because you make sense. Sid doesn't. The only thing—the *only* thing—keeping him alive is his will to be alive. I'm afraid that if he starts thinking too hard about how he's able to do what he does, he won't be able to do anything. He'll just go away."

"Huh?"

"You know who Descartes was, right?"

"Sure. 'I think, therefore I am.'"

"There's an old joke about him. Descartes walks into a bar, and the bartender says, 'Can I get you a beer?' Descartes says, 'I think not,' and disappears in a puff of logic."

"And you're afraid Sid will disappear in a puff of logic?"

"Yeah, kind of." I heard Sid coming back down, so I left it at that.

As soon as he was in the room, Sid said, "Madison, are you going to do your homework down here?"

"I was planning to. Why?"

He looked distinctly uncomfortable. "This is awkward, but I need to talk to your mother."

"I'm listening," I said.

"I mean, alone. Just the two of us."

"Excuse me?" Madison said. "Is this about our investigation? Because I know I haven't been all that active this past week or so, but I am still involved, aren't I?"

"Of course you are. Maybe Sid wants to talk about something else." I looked at him questioningly.

But he shook his head. "It's murder related, but I really think this is best left to adults."

"Mom!" Madison said, turning to me.

The joy of having only one child was never having to worry about sibling rivalry, just as the joy of being a single parent meant nobody to second-guess my decisions. So how had I managed to find myself in a situation where I was dealing with both? There was no way that both would be happy.

I carefully said, "Madison, let's assume that Sid has a good reason for wanting to talk to me without you around. I can fill you in later if it's appropriate."

"Fine! I guess I'll go take Byron for a walk if that's *appropriate* for a child like me." Her footsteps as she got the leash and called Byron may have been louder than was strictly necessary, and the manner in which she closed the door behind them definitely was, but I didn't really blame her.

"Thanks bunches, Sid," I said. "Now Madison is mad at me, and I'm not sure if I deserve it or not."

"You don't," he said emphatically. "This is definitely not for her to hear." He pulled me over to the couch. "You know today was the day that theater troupe came and performed *Great Expectations* at PHS, right?"

"No, but okay."

"So just about everybody in the school was in the auditorium all morning long, and I was getting pretty bored."

"I can imagine." Actually, I couldn't imagine being a disembodied skull sitting on a locker shelf all day, but I thought it sounded nicer to say that I could.

"About an hour after the show started, I heard footsteps. A minute later, there was a second set. Somebody said, 'Just where do you think you're going?' It was a male voice." He looked at me significantly, but I didn't see any significance yet. He went on. "The other one was a girl. She said, 'Oh, I just need to get something.' He goes, 'You know you're supposed to be in the auditorium with the other students,' and he sounds really mad. She apologizes and says it'll never happen again, but he says, 'I think we're just going to have to make sure it doesn't. You've been a very bad girl, and bad girls need to be punished. Isn't that right?' And she starts telling him she'll be good, that he doesn't have to punish her—and get this—that he doesn't have to punish her 'again'! But he says he wants her to come to his room that afternoon after school. She says she can't because she has cheerleader practice, so he says she can come tomorrow, but she better be there on time. Because she knows what happens to girls who don't obey!"

"Oh, my gosh! Did you see who it was?"

"I couldn't see the girl. She had this real babyish kind of

voice, but I didn't recognize it. But I saw the man through the vents in the locker. It was Madison's algebra teacher."

I felt sick. "Mr. Neal?"

He nodded.

"No wonder you didn't want to say anything in front of her."

"I know!"

Neither of us wanted to have to tell Madison that one of her favorite teachers was sexually abusing one of the school's cheerleaders.

"What do we do?" Sid asked.

"Well, it has to be reported, but I don't know how. I mean, you're a witness, but you can't exactly go to Mr. Dahlgren and tell him. It's the same problem we had with the murder."

"Not to mention the fact that the murder might be connected."

"Did you hear anything—?"

"No, nothing about the killing, but it just seems like a teacher might go a long way to hide that kind of activity. What if Irwin saw something he wasn't meant to, and Mr. Neal decided to get rid of him? The girl might not even know about it, or what kind of man she's dealing with."

"Okay, then the first thing we have to do is find out who she is, and preferably in a way that will be reportable. Did they set a time for their . . . ? For tomorrow?"

We began planning, and though we were fully engaged when Madison came back in with Byron, we stopped immediately before she could hear anything. She was going to find out eventually, but there was still the barest chance that Sid had misconstrued what he'd heard. So it was really for her own good that we stopped talking.

I don't think she saw it that way. She sniffed disdainfully and said, "Come on, Byron. We're not wanted here."

She was still a little distant at dinner, but I didn't blame her for resenting being kept in the dark. I remembered plenty of times when my parents had kept things from me when I was a kid, and at the time, I'd thought it was rank unfairness. Things looked different from the parent's side.

Sid had heard Mr. Neal tell his cheerleader victim to be at his room at three, which was forty-five minutes after the end of the school day, meaning the halls would be deserted. Neal's classroom was on the second floor, the same as mine, but it was down at the far end of the hall, separated from other rooms by a storage room and a stairwell. Fortunately, since that area was out of the way, there were some empty, unused lockers. I got Madison to put Sid, his hand, and his phone in one of them first thing in the morning, and though she was still grumpy about not knowing what was going on, she went along when I promised to tell her the story as soon as I could verify it. She even left the other piece of equipment Sid needed, though she was clearly mystified.

Of course, I still had my morning class at McQuaid to tend to and then I had to teach my SAT prep classes at PHS, but they went by quickly. Finally the bell rang, and we could put our plan into motion.

Sid and I had speculated that the girl might not show if she thought there was still anybody around, so when I was sure nobody was looking, I turned out the lights in my classroom, locked the door, and sat in a chair where I couldn't be seen from outside the room. I checked my phone and found a text from Sid.

Waiting . . .

I responded in kind and watched the minutes tick by, resisting the impulse to try to catch a glimpse of the girl myself.

At three, my phone vibrated with another text.

She was right on time.

Couldn't see her face.

Blonde ponytail & jacket over cheerleader outfit.

Ew.

I responded:

We'll give them 10 minutes.

Nine and a half minutes later, which was as long as I could make myself wait, I texted:

Getting into position now.

Taking a deep breath, I opened the classroom door and faux-casually ambled down to the water fountain near Mr. Neal's classroom. Then I leaned up against the locker where Sid was hiding and pretended to take a phone call, knowing Sid could hear me. I couldn't hear anything from the classroom, but my imagination was lurid enough.

Just as I was about to text Sid to get on with it, a voice boomed through the hall. *"Come out of there right away. Leave that girl alone!"*

It was so startlingly loud that I didn't have to pretend my

shock. Sid had taken a megaphone with him, and the empty halls, the locker, and Sid yelling as loud as he could combined to create a tumult on the Richter scale.

I heard scrambling from Mr. Neal's classroom, and a minute later, he came out looking angry and frustrated. I felt smug at having interrupted him until his partner came out.

She was wearing a letter jacket with her hair pulled back into a ponytail with a bright ribbon around it, but it wasn't a student. Nor even a girl, really. It was a woman, a grown woman. One I knew. It was Ms. Zale, the SAT math teacher.

Sid and I hadn't interrupted a sexual predator—we'd interrupted a bit of role-play.

Mr. Neal and Ms. Zale looked around furiously, but of course there was nobody to be seen but me and obviously I wasn't the one who'd spoken.

I quickly stammered, "What in the world was that racket?"

"Did you see anybody near here?" Mr. Neal demanded.

"Not a soul," I said, which was true. I knew where Sid was, but I couldn't see him. "Maybe somebody was messing with the intercom. What did they say, anyway? I couldn't understand it."

They looked slightly relieved at my pretended ignorance. "I've got no idea," Ms. Zale said. "You're probably right. Some joker messing with the intercom."

"Teenagers!" I said ruefully. "You two are brave to deal with them all day long. Well, I better be going. You two have a good rest of the day."

I walked away as quickly as I could, hoping that I hadn't betrayed any knowledge of anything they were doing, which I really wished I didn't know about anyway. I could feel my cell phone vibrating in my hand, but didn't dare look at it for fear of not being able to keep a straight face. Instead I waited until I was out the door and in my car with the doors firmly locked.

After all that, all Sid had texted was:

Never mind.

That summed it up for me, too.

27

Madison was still at rehearsal, and I'd promised her a ride home, but I didn't want to go home only to have to turn around again and come back an hour later. Nor did I want to hang out in my classroom, where I might see—or hear—Mr. Neal and Ms. Zale again. Instead I went to see how the play was shaping up.

I paused as I stepped inside the auditorium. Normally I sit way in the back during a rehearsal so as not to disrupt anything, but I just didn't like the idea of sitting so close to where a murder had taken place. So I went about halfway down the aisle before sliding into a row of seats.

My timing was good. I recognized the scene being enacted onstage as the conversation between Polonius and Ophelia that comes just before the first appearance of Rosencrantz and Guildenstern. I resisted the impulse to pull out my phone so I could video the kids, even though it went against my maternal instincts.

Once Polonius and Ophelia finished their discussion of Hamlet's inexplicable behavior, Becca the director called a halt and started to give the actors in that scene notes about their performances. I was impressed by her technique, which had the proper ratio of positive to negative comments.

She was working with Ophelia as Adam McDaniel the elder came down the center aisle of the auditorium, and when he saw me, he raised his eyebrows at an empty seat beside me. I nodded for him to join me.

"You're just in time," I said quietly. "Madison and Tristan will be making their entrance in the next scene."

"Wonderful. How are you doing with your classes?"

"Pretty well. Mr. Chedworth left things really well organized for me, which makes it easy."

"Nothing gets past Chedworth."

It looked as if the actors were about to get started again, so we quieted down. Unfortunately, a young man I didn't recognize picked that moment to come traipsing through the auditorium, talking on his cell phone. Since he bore a striking resemblance to McDaniel as well as to Tristan, I felt safe in assuming that he was Adam Jr., still living up to his jerky reputation.

Becca turned to glare at him, but before she could say anything, McDaniel gestured sharply at his son and said, "Hang up right now!"

The boy gave him a look of annoyed disbelief, but said a few words and obeyed. Then he slung himself into a chair on the opposite side of the aisle from us, making his displeasure plain, and immediately switched to texting. McDaniel mouthed, "Sorry!" at Becca, who nodded curtly and got her actors started again.

"Teenagers," McDaniel whispered to me, and I nodded

sympathetically. Tristan seemed nice enough and McDaniel himself was perfectly pleasant, so maybe Adam Jr. took after his mother. I glanced at the ring finger on McDaniel's left hand. It was bare.

Before I could speculate further, Madison came onstage, and while her appearance was brief and light on dialogue, I thought it was arguably the best rendition of Guildenstern I'd ever seen. Admittedly, I might have been biased.

The scene was a long one, and Becca stopped the actors about halfway through to work on blocking, which McDaniel took as permission for us to continue our conversation. "The play seems to be going well."

"Don't say that," I said in mock horror. "Actors are notoriously superstitious. You might jinx them."

He chuckled. "I suppose Shakespeare is old hat to you in your line of work."

"Only as a fan. My specialty is contemporary American literature, but mostly I teach writing."

That led to a discussion of the College Board's recent decision to make the essay portion of the SAT optional, which carried us through until the kids continued with their scene.

Madison once again gave a remarkable interpretation of Guildenstern, though I was willing to admit that Tristan made a fair to middling Rosencrantz, too.

At the end of the scene, Becca had more notes, so McDaniel and I went back to our conversation.

"Is Madison's father in academia, too?" he asked, and I knew he'd checked out my bare finger, too.

"Yes, but he's not in the picture."

He nodded and did not seem displeased.

"So how did you get into pharmaceuticals?" I asked.

"By accident. I started out majoring in biology, but when

I looked at the job prospects, switched to business. It turned out to be just the background I needed. And I can work anywhere, which is a big plus. The boys and I really needed a change of scenery after my wife and I split up, which is how we ended up here."

Interesting how he'd smoothly managed to both ask about my marital status and establish his own.

I said, "So you don't have to travel?"

"Not much. There are plenty of nearby hospitals, clinics, and doctors to deal with." He went on a little too long about how great it was to meet people, sell miracle drugs that would save the world, and enjoy perks like bonuses and vacations when he exceeded his quota, which he did frequently. He must have sensed that he was losing me, because he dialed it back and added, "Of course, there are downsides, too. Every time I go to a party, people have to ask if I have any free samples. Just joking, of course, but still, it gets old."

"The one I always get is, 'You teach at a college? You must be really smart.'"

"But you are really smart," he said with a winning smile.

"Now, don't you start."

We chuckled companionably until there was a loud snort of derision from Adam Jr., who was apparently unimpressed by our playful banter.

McDaniel shot him an angry look, but fortunately the actors onstage began to run through the scene again, from the beginning, so we were suitably distracted. After that, Becca let everybody go and, after telling me how nice it had been to talk to me, McDaniel went to collect his younger, more polite son. I called out to Madison that I'd meet her at our car and headed for the parking lot.

28

A few minutes later, Madison banged impatiently on the passenger-side window of my minivan and I unlocked the door for her.

"Great rehearsal."

She grunted, and I wondered if she was still upset with Sid and me. "Did you get—"

She waved the bowling bag at me. "He's right here."

"Good." I started the car and began driving.

"So do I get to know what you were doing now or not?"

Okay, she was still peeved. I opened my mouth to answer just as Sid mumbled something from inside the bag. "Unzip the bag, will you? Then we can explain."

Looking slightly mollified, she did so.

"I have never been so embarrassed in my entire lack of life," Sid said. "Except for that time I was hiding in the armoire when Deborah brought a date home, and she didn't know I was there, and—"

"Ahem!" I said.

That reminded Sid that Deborah might not appreciate him sharing her past exploits with Madison, so he switched to, "And they started kissing. Just kissing."

"Oh, that's convincing," Madison said. "Just as well you're only a prop in *Hamlet* with those kind of acting chops."

"Anyway," Sid said, "this was nearly as embarrassing as that."

"*What* was nearly that embarrassing?" Madison wanted to know.

I said, "Okay, this is more than a little uncomfortable to talk about, but yesterday Sid heard something that led him to believe that one of the male teachers at PHS was having—" I mentally ran down a list of euphemisms. "Was having an affair with of one of the students."

"Well, that's what it sounded like!" Sid said.

"What did they say?" Madison asked.

"Never mind," I said. I didn't have any euphemisms handy for that. "Anyway, we knew what teacher it was, but Sid didn't see the student. We couldn't go to Mr. Dahlgren without more information, so we set it up so we could see who it was who met Mr.—Who met the male teacher. And it turned out not to be a student after all. It was another teacher."

"Who?"

"I'd rather not say. They're both unmarried adults, so it's really none of our business, though they really shouldn't be doing anything like that on school property. I hope being interrupted teaches them a lesson."

"Come on, Georgia, it wasn't that kinky," Sid said. "Compared to some of the Web pages I've seen, this was tame."

"Sid!" I said. "I cannot unhear it when you say things like that."

"Georgia, are you saying you didn't know there was—gasp—naughty stuff on the Internet?" He and Madison both started snickering.

"Laugh it up, and I'll start telling you more than you want to know about my sex life."

"What sex life?" Sid said. "You haven't had a date in months."

"I have a child—obviously I have had sex at least once. Plus I had a long labor. Want to hear about that?"

In unison, they put their hands over their ears—well, just the one hand in Sid's case—and started loudly singing, "We can't hear you. La la la la!"

I let them keep it up for a few minutes, though I knew Sid could have heard me fine with only one ear hole covered. Finally they got tired of it, for which I was grateful. I love them both, but neither of them are famed for their singing voices.

"Anyway," I continued, "since both parties are single adults, I don't think their activities have anything to do with our murder. Why would they care if they were found out? Embarrassed, perhaps, and maybe they'd get in trouble for indulging themselves on school grounds, but I don't think that would be worth killing for."

"If it had been two guys, that might have made a motive," Sid said speculatively.

"Please," Madison said. "What is this, the nineteen hundreds? Nobody cares about gay teachers."

"Some people aren't as modern in their thinking as you are," I said, but I was proud of her, and of Pennycross, too. We had lived in towns where people would have had problems with it, and I was glad PHS didn't have those kinds of hang-ups.

Sid said, "What if one of them has a jealous boyfriend or girlfriend?"

"Sounds iffy," I said, "but I can check around with the other teachers and see what I find out."

"Or I can check their Facebook pages, see whether they've got relationships listed."

"Or you could ask me," Madison said, "since I spend every day at PHS."

"I don't want to name names, sweetie. I'm afraid it'll be awkward for you."

"Yeah," Sid said. "You don't want to know which of your teachers are doing the nasty with each other."

"Sid!" I said, but it was too late. Madison had caught the essential clue.

"So it's one of my teachers?" Madison said. "Or more? Do I have both of them for classes?"

"I'm not saying," I repeated. "Sid, keep your mandible shut."

He did so, but Madison wasn't giving up that easily.

"Okay, you guys wouldn't tell me anything last night, and last night you only knew who the guy was, so that means he's definitely one of my teachers. Right?"

Neither Sid nor I responded.

"I have three guy teachers. One is gay, and one is married, so that leaves Mr. Neal." She looked at us for confirmation, but I kept my face as blank as I could. Fortunately Sid has a permanent poker face.

"If it was Mr. Neal, then the woman was probably Ms. Zale."

"How did you know that?" Sid said. His face was made for poker, but not his mouth.

"It's no secret. They've been seeing each other for a while. They don't do PDAs in front of us or anything, but everybody in the school knows. One guy swears he saw them last Halloween, going at it in vampire costumes, and Samantha saw Ms. Zale buying his-and-her elf suits before Christmas. What were they dressed up as this time?"

So much for protecting my innocent child. "I'm not telling you. Yes, it was them, but I don't want details of this particular encounter getting out because then they'd suspect me of spreading rumors."

"I wouldn't tell anybody," Madison said. Then she said, "On second thought, don't tell me. It would be tough to keep it to myself if it was anything really juicy."

"Anyway, if everybody at school knows about their affair, I think we can safely take them off the suspects list," I said as we drove into our driveway. I was almost hoping that one of them would contradict me, because if the two teachers were out of the running, then we were back to square one. Again.

29

After that, I was not at my most cheerful that night. I grumped my way through dinner and cleanup, enough so that Madison retreated to her room. I was so low that I pulled out the vacuum cleaner—I hate vacuuming, but I figured it couldn't make me any more miserable than I already was. It didn't, except that when I'd finished the living room, I remembered that I still had homework assignments to grade, and that did the job.

I briefly considered just going to bed and playing hooky the next day, and only the knowledge of how much havoc that would wreak on the week's schedule convinced me otherwise. So I brewed a pot of coffee and went to work, but had only made it through the first half by midnight. The coffee was long gone, and I could barely keep my eyes open. I've always been a good catnapper, so I set an alarm on my computer then moved to the couch for a half hour's nap.

I woke up with Sid gently shaking my arm. "Time to get up, Georgia."

I'd been dreaming of a handsome adjunct I'd dated once, and to see Sid's bony countenance was kind of a letdown. Then I realized it was daylight. "Coccyx! My alarm didn't go off," I said, pushing off the afghan I didn't even remember putting on.

"You never went upstairs to set it."

"No, the one on my computer. I was only going to sleep a little while."

"Oh, I turned that off."

"Sid! I was supposed to finish grading last night!" I grabbed the pile of papers next to the computer, but realized that the one on top had a score written on it. So did the next, and the next. They'd all been graded. "What the—?"

"I hope you don't mind. I figured you needed the rest. Did I do okay?"

"You did great. A lot better than I would have, considering how beat I was last night," I said, flipping through one of them. "Thanks, Sid. I owe you."

He looked pleased. "You better go wake Madison. I'll get breakfast ready."

"You don't have to do that." It didn't seem fair when he couldn't eat any himself, but he was already rattling around in the kitchen before I got upstairs.

I still wasn't at my best—I'd only had six hours of sleep, after all—but I was infinitely better off than I would have been without his help. So I decided to pretend the previous day's investigative debacle hadn't happened and to refocus on what the Sechrest Foundation was up to. Since I still couldn't find a single adjunct who'd met with them, I thought

I'd check with Yo and see if she knew of any grad students who had.

We'd exchanged phone numbers over our lunch a few weeks back, so I texted her and asked her to meet me at the same place for lunch. She sent back a warm and gracious acceptance of my request, consisting of:

'K

I already had a table at Hamburger Haven when Yo arrived, and we started by getting our food and then prepping same.

"So what's up?" Yo asked. "Another skeleton to examine?"

"No, one skeleton is plenty for me," which was truer than she knew. "I was wondering what you decided to do about the letter from the Sechrest Foundation."

"After our talk? Nothing."

"What about the other students you know who got that letter? Did any of them go meet the people?"

"Not after I spread the word that the offer smelled rank."

"Coccyx!"

"Say what?"

I didn't even bother to make up an explanation. "It's just that I was hoping to talk to somebody who'd met with them."

"Why for?"

"It's kind of complicated."

She raised one pierced eyebrow.

"A friend of mine may be involved with them, but he won't tell me what's going on." I didn't really think Charles had done whatever it was that was being done, but 'involved' was a fuzzy enough word that I was being truthful. More or less.

"And you're going to get all up in your friend's business to try to save him from himself."

"Sounds kind of stupid, but that's basically it."

"Stupid," she agreed, "but my kind of stupid. If I knew anything, I'd share, but I've got nothing."

I thought, *Coccyx!*, but at least I didn't say it out loud.

As we started in on our burgers, an idea popped up. I considered it for a good ten minutes before saying, "I don't suppose you'd be willing—"

"To what? Call them and see what I can find out? Maybe meet with them?"

"You did say it was your kind of stupid."

"Maybe I'd be stupid for my friends, but your friend? He's not mine. What's in it for me?"

"If I'm wrong, and the foundation really can help you pay for a conference or two, then that's a win. If I'm right, you've helped a really nice guy."

She didn't look convinced.

"Then how about this? You're going to be applying for jobs and postdoctoral fellowships soon, right? Here on the east coast?"

"Yeah."

"I've been an adjunct at colleges for fifteen years, and maybe I'm not in your department, but I bet I can wrangle connections in almost any college you'll be looking at."

"So? Can an adjunct get me a job? A real one, not the stuff you have to put up with."

"If any adjunct could do that, he or she sure wouldn't give it to you. What an adjunct can do is get you dirt. Which profs are good to work with and which ones claim your hard work as their own? Which ones treat you like a human being and which ones don't? Which ones should you avoid being alone with in a lab? Other profs won't tell you that, and other grad students might have their own axes to grind. We adjuncts have nothing to lose, and we love to talk. Access to insider information like that ought to be worth a few hours of your time."

She thought it over for a minute, then nodded. "I've probably still got that letter in my bag, so I'll give them a call. Can I assume that you're going to want to listen in?"

"If you don't mind."

She started rummaging around in the black-and-white-checked backpack she carried. In a surprisingly short time, given the amount of stuff crammed into the bag, she pulled out the letter. Then she pulled out her cell phone and made the call.

"Good afternoon," she said, "this is Yolanda Jacobs. I received a note with an invitation to call to speak with Ethan Frisenda."

I blinked. Had I not been watching, I never would have believed those cultured tones and scrupulously polite phrases would have come out of the Yo I'd come to know and kind of like.

She went on with her side of the conversation. "Wonderful. Your offer of funding for conference attendance most definitely caught my attention, and I'd love to know more. . . . Certainly. Getting together in person would make it much more pleasant. When and where should we meet? . . . Yes, I believe I know where that is. . . . Five o'clock? Perfect. I look forward to it. Thank you very much for your time." She hung up and said, "Eager beavers. We're meeting today. Five o'clock at the Pennycross Hilton."

"Wow. You give good phone."

"Whatever."

"You're not going to meet him in a hotel room, are you?"

"Do I look like a complete moron? No, we're meeting in the bar in the lobby."

"Good." I hesitated. "Look, I don't really think that this is dangerous or anything, but—"

"But you want to play Mata Hari and spy on the meeting. Yeah, I expected that, and as ideas go, it doesn't suck." Since I thought my actually appearing with her would blow the gaff, we made plans for me to get to the bar half an hour before she did and watch while pretending not to know her. "After the meet, we leave separately and intersect at Bertucci's downtown. I'll tell you what I've found out, and you can buy me dinner. Deal?"

"Deal." I just hoped, for the sake of my wallet, that Yo would be a cheap date.

Once Yo and I went our separate ways, I called Deborah at work and asked if she'd take care of Madison's dinner while I went to an unexpected dinner meeting. Then I texted both Madison and Sid, so they'd know the real story, and fended off Sid's entreaties that I stop by the house and pick him up to take along as backup. After that, I even had time to do some of my real work.

As arranged, I got to the Pennycross Hilton at four thirty, a half hour before Yo was due to meet the mysterious Ethan Frisenda. The Hilton is only nominally in Pennycross—it's way out of town along the highway, and in my suspicious frame of mind, I wondered if it had been chosen as a meeting place to facilitate a fast getaway. Of course, it also had the advantage of being so far from McQuaid that there probably wouldn't be anyone else from the college there.

The bar was in the middle of the lobby, and I picked a table in the center so I'd be able to keep an eye on Yo and the man she was meeting, no matter where they sat. I was hoping I could set up my laptop and pretend to work without having to buy an overpriced drink. Unfortunately, the waitress was either bored or conscientious, because she brought me a complimentary bowl of snack mix right after I sat down, and asked what she could get for me. I bowed to the inevitable and ordered a Coke, figuring I could nurse it for as long as I needed to.

The bar had been empty when I arrived, but three parties arrived before Yo. Since one was a woman alone with her laptop, and the second was two men talking earnestly, I was betting on the third, a man on his own. He looked older than I was, maybe in his mid-forties, and was wearing a classic academic outfit—gray slacks, tweedy jacket with patches on the elbows, and button-down shirt without a tie. He put a notepad and an iPad on the table in front of him and watched the door expectantly. When Yo arrived at five on the dot, he stood and waved at her.

After her impressive phone manners, I wasn't as surprised as I might have been otherwise to see that she was dressed much more conservatively than I usually saw her, in creased black slacks, a silver-gray shell, and a trim charcoal blazer. The muted colors left her hair as the only pop of color, and it was styled more neatly than I'd ever seen it.

Yo joined the man at the table, which fortunately was in my line of sight so I didn't have to try to switch seats inconspicuously. I wasn't quite as happy with the acoustics in the bar, which all echo even without the music playing, but at least I could watch them. In fact, as soon as they started talking, I held up my phone, pretending to check messages, so I could snap several pictures of the two of them.

They ordered drinks and spoke for a little over forty-five

minutes. Just from the body language, I'd have said that if it had been a job interview I was spying on, it wasn't a slam dunk but that Yo had definitely scored a second interview. They parted with a handshake and professional smiles, and Yo left without even looking in my direction. Her companion stayed only long enough to pay the check, then he started for the door, also not looking at me.

I'd already paid my tab and packed away my laptop so I was right behind him, hoping he'd get into a showy car of some description, but it was just a silver sedan in a parking lot half-filled with silver sedans. There were no parking decals, company names, or even bumper stickers. I did snap a blurry photo of his license plate, though I had no idea of how I could use it to track him down.

He turned out of the parking lot and, as I watched, headed for the highway, so presumably he didn't live in Pennycross. I went the other direction to meet Yo at the restaurant, immensely curious to hear what she had to say.

By the time I got to Bertucci's, Yo had fluffed her hair up enough that she looked like herself again. She'd already grabbed a table and was looking at the menu when I sat down opposite her.

"Food ordering first, question asking after," she said.

"Fair enough." I'd been there enough times that I didn't need to look at the menu, and the waitress took our order right away.

"So what happened?" I prompted.

"It was weird. I mean, this was supposed to be some sort of grant to fund me going to a conference, right? So I'd have thought he'd want to know all about my research. And he asked about it, but I could tell he didn't care. Didn't bother to take any notes, and it's kind of obscure, you know."

"What did he want to know about?"

"My standardized test scores."

"You mean your GREs?" I asked. Most grad schools required applicants to submit scores from Graduate Record Examinations—GREs—as part of the admission process.

"Those, and he wanted to know about my SAT, too. I mean, who even thinks about SATs once you're in college, let alone grad school? Unless you're one of those losers who brags about hitting ninetieth percentile because you haven't done anything worthwhile since."

"So you didn't remember your numbers?"

She grinned. "Sure I remember. I rocked that thing. Ninety-third percentile."

"Was he impressed?"

"He definitely wrote that part down, I can tell you that."

"And that was it?"

"No, he asked about my plans, whether I had anything lined up post grad school, stuff like that. He made some kind-of-but-not-really jokes about student loans and how rough they are, and how hard it is to pay off the debt load."

"Sounds as if he was trying to see how hungry you are."

Appropriately enough, our salads and rolls arrived, and we took a few minutes to appreciate them before Yo said, "I got that same feeling."

"What did he say about the grant?"

"He made some noises about putting my name up to the committee and how he'd get back to me within a week if I was still in the running. Oh, and he gave me his business card." She fished it out of her pocket and handed it to me.

Ethan Frisenda, Sandra Sechrest Foundation. There was no street address, just a phone number and e-mail address.

"I asked him who Sandra Sechrest was, and he claimed

she was some rich woman who'd left all this money for educational grants. It was BS. I Googled her on my phone while I was waiting for you, and found nada. What kind of rich woman doesn't show up on Google?"

"An imaginary one."

"That's what I thought. I Googled Frisenda, too, and got nothing. So if he calls back, I'm not returning the call. I don't trust him. He smelled off, and I'm a big believer in trusting my instincts. We're still set for the info network thing, right? Even if I don't talk to the guy again?"

"We're set," I confirmed. Given what had happened to Robert Irwin and Patty Craft, I sure didn't want Yo spending time with a guy who smelled off.

My chicken Parmesan and her lasagna arrived, and as we ate we went step-by-step through the meeting again, but didn't come up with anything that explained what it was Frisenda really wanted. Eventually Yo got impatient, so I paid the check and we left.

30

Sid was watching TV in the living room when I got back, but shut it off as soon as I came in the door.

"Well? Well? You could have texted me something, you know!"

"Nothing worth texting," I said glumly. "Where's Madison?"

"Up in her room with the dog. Deborah brought over Thai food and did her best to pick my brain about what you were up to, but she got nothing from me!" He stuck one finger bone through his left eye socket and rattled it around. "See? Nothing to pick."

"Don't do that," I said, wincing.

"It doesn't hurt."

"I know, but . . . Ew."

"So what happened with Yo the cold handed?"

I told him what she'd told me, and when I produced the

business card, he grabbed it and promised to do his very best to track the man down.

"Yo already Googled him."

"A three-second Google search on a phone!" he said disdainfully. "I think I can do better than that."

"Well, knock yourself out. I've got response papers to grade." Then I yawned so widely my jaw cracked.

"Why don't you give them to me? I can do them overnight and still have plenty of time to track down Frisenda and the Sechrest Foundation on the Web."

"Don't tempt me."

"I don't mind helping. You said yourself that I'm great at grading."

"I know, and you really are, but my students are paying for a Ph.D. professor, not a gifted amateur."

"What difference does it make who does the work as long as it's good?"

"Sid, you know my parents. They are academics to the core, and they raised me to never plagiarize or take credit for somebody else's work."

"They let grad students grade papers for them."

"True, but you don't even have a B.A."

"Well, excuse me for dying before I had a chance to graduate!"

"Sid! I'm sorry—I didn't mean it like that." I should have been able to come up with a better apology, but all I produced was another yawn. "Look, I really appreciate your offer, but I'll just let them wait until tomorrow."

Of course, I still couldn't go straight to bed. I had to empty the dishwasher and refill it with accumulated dirties, check the mail, and make sure I had clothes set for the next day. Plus I spent a whole half an hour of quality time with Madison.

Then I made sure the house was locked up with lights turned out, and I got ready for bed. As I crawled between the sheets, something Sid had said floated up into my consciousness.

I sat up. What difference does it make who does the work as long as it's good? Why had Frisenda been so interested in Yo's test scores? How could Patty Craft have prostituted her talent, and why was the Sechrest Foundation only interested in younger-looking grad students and adjuncts?

I finally thought of an answer that made sense.

If I could have pulled the same trick on Sid as he had on me Friday night—looming over him in his sleep—I would have, but he doesn't sleep. The best I could do was throw on my robe and pad up the attic stairs to where he was working.

"Georgia, what's wrong?" he asked when he saw me.

"I think I've got it. The Sechrest Foundation is faking standardized test scores. Frisenda wanted to hire Yo to take the SAT for somebody else!"

31

I stood waiting for Sid's gasp of realization, which I expected to be followed by sounds of admiration, but what I got was, "That's it?"

"What do you mean, 'That's it'? It's fraud, Sid."

"I know it's fraud, but I was expecting something a little more . . . I don't know. More dramatic. Cheating at tests is kind of penny ante, isn't it?"

"Dude, you need to Google the College Board and see how much money they rake in for standardized testing. Even though not all colleges require those tests, almost every college-bound high school student takes the PSAT and then the SAT at least twice. Bear in mind that the SAT is around fifty bucks a pop! A lot of kids take multiple AP exams and SAT Subject Tests, too. Then there are the ACTs, GREs, LSATs."

"Are those tests or alphabet soup?"

"Then you've got the companies that pay people like me to teach kids how to improve their scores, and the publishers that produce guidebooks to the tests. Standardized testing is a huge business, Sid."

"Well, yeah, the people giving the tests make money, but how much money would there be in a cheating-for-hire scheme?"

"Plenty. Think of how much is riding on those stupid tests. Admission to a lot of colleges depends on them, plus any number of scholarships. I read that people have been paid two to three grand to take the SAT in someone else's name."

"Seriously?"

"You can look it up later, but I remember a case a few years back when a bunch of students at a high school in Long Island hired other kids to take their SATs. It got a lot of press, and colleges all up and down the east coast were worried they'd admitted these students on the basis of those phony test scores. My parents checked to see if they'd accepted any students from that school at McQuaid, and they hadn't, but you know what else they found out? Nothing happened to the kids who cheated."

"You're kidding."

"The SAT people wouldn't even release their names—they said they couldn't because of privacy laws. But they sure prosecuted the people who actually took the tests. And afterward they hired high-powered security gurus to look into their procedures so it couldn't happen again."

"But apparently it is happening?"

"If there's one thing I've learned while working in academia, it's that you can't ever stop all the cheating."

"I get that. I'm just not seeing how this leads to murder."

"I'm not sure, either, but money and fraud seem like pretty good pieces of the puzzle. If I'm right, that is."

"How do you find out if you're right?"

"Tomorrow I'm going to find Charles, and I'm going to make him tell me the truth."

"You won't be alone with him, will you?"

"Sid, Charles is not going to hurt me."

"You don't know that."

"I have known Charles for years. He's slept in this house!"

"Georgia, if you don't take me with you, I will call Deborah right now and tell her."

I blinked. I'd never known him to make a threat like that. If he felt strongly enough to go for the nuclear option, I had to accept it. Even if I didn't like it. "Fine, you can come."

"All of me this time, not just my skull."

"You know that means the suitcase."

"I know. Actually, after all that time in the bowling bag, the suitcase is starting to sound almost roomy."

Sid's usual mode of transportation for leaving the house was an old hard-sided suitcase with a decorative pattern that was advertised as Antelope, but which looked like bacon to me. All of his bones would fit in, just barely, and since it was wheeled, it made it easier to move him around. He only weighed twenty pounds or so, but that was more than I wanted to carry in addition to my usual load of stuff.

Sid must have been worried that I'd try to sneak off without him. He was downstairs waiting for me when I got up Thursday morning, with his suitcase by the front door.

"What's with the bacon bag?" Madison wanted to know. "It's not going to fit into my locker."

"Sid's coming with me to McQuaid today." I had a detailed explanation prepared for why, which wouldn't have been a lie but which shouldn't have alarmed her, either, but I didn't need it.

She said, "Okay. No rehearsal today anyway."

Having had a bad experience with leaving Sid in the adjunct office once before, I gave Sid the choice of waiting in my mother's office or coming to class. He voted for class, of course, which made more work for me. On the other hand, it spurred me to give a really good lecture because I knew he was listening.

After my eight o'clock class ended, I hotfooted it for the adjunct office. No Charles in sight, so I didn't stop, just kept going until I got to my mother's office. Moving as quietly as I could, I went inside and put my ear against the door to my father's office.

"He's in there," I whispered to Sid. "I can hear him moving around."

"Unlatch my suitcase, just in case."

It was easier to agree than to argue, so I laid the case down on its side, next to a wall, and left it open so Sid could get out if he needed to.

Only then did I rap at the door between the two offices.

The movement stopped instantly. Then I heard tiny little sounds as if he were tiptoeing.

I made similar noises myself as I snuck to the door that led to the hall, getting there just in time to see Charles sneaking out of his office.

"Dr. Peyton!" I said in a loud and cheery voice. "Just the man I wanted to see. Might I have a moment of your time?"

Two professors happened to walk by at that moment, and since Charles apparently didn't want to cause a scene, he said, "Of course, Dr. Thackery. I was on my way out, but I can certainly spare a few minutes."

"Thank you so much."

I kept the false smile on my face right up until I closed the door. Sid had originally wanted me to keep it open, but

I'd pointed out that if Sid needed to intervene, it would be better for all involved if nobody else saw him.

"Have a seat."

"I really can't stay long, as I was on my way out."

"Charles, you have been avoiding me. I don't know why, and right now I don't care. But I've got to ask you some questions, and I expect you to answer."

"What sort of questions?"

"About Patty Craft, and what she did that she was ashamed of."

"She revealed those matters to me in confidence."

"I understand, and I know better than most how good you are at keeping confidences." He'd performed more than one favor for me in the past and had never asked for an explanation or told anybody what he'd done. "But I'm not asking just to be nosy. The fact is, I'm suspicious about her death."

He cocked his head to one side. "Is there a basis for your suspicion?"

"There is, but it sounds pretty nutty. A friend of mine—a friend who was somewhere he shouldn't have been— overheard two men talking before Patty's body was found. He thinks they were talking about murdering somebody, and the only body that has been found in Pennycross in the recent past is Patty's." Okay, it wasn't anything like the whole story, but it was mostly true.

"Has he notified the police?"

"He left an anonymous tip, but couldn't give details."

"Because of his being where he should not have been?"

"Exactly. Which is probably why the police didn't take him seriously. My sister has a friend on the force and according to him, the police think my friend is a crackpot."

"Could he in fact be a crackpot?"

"Oh, he's definitely a crackpot," I said, "but he's also truthful, and he's really worried that somebody has gotten away with murder. I don't think he's slept a full night since hearing those men talking." Of course, Sid didn't ever sleep, but it sounded more pathetic this way. "He only told me because he thought I might have known Patty Craft from when she worked here at McQuaid, but of course I didn't. You did."

"Yes, I did." Charles took a deep breath, leaned back in his chair, and clasped his hands over his stomach to ponder the matter. I just waited. After maybe five minutes, he said, "Under those circumstances, and in case your friend is right, I think I'm justified in revealing some of Patty's secrets. But only if you keep it all sub rosa."

"Of course, unless it had something to do with her death."

"Granted. I cannot imagine that she'd want her killer to get away with a crime, just to protect her reputation. Which, sadly, was not the best anyway."

"Was she not a good instructor?"

"She could have been excellent," he said, "but money woes were a powerful distraction. She had quite a debt burden because of student loans, like so many of our young academics."

Everybody in academia—and most parents with a child approaching college—knew there were people graduating from college with two hundred thousand dollars or more in debt, with no job in sight and no way to keep from defaulting on their loans. I lived in fear that Madison would be in the same boat in a few years.

Charles went on. "In order for Patty to keep up her payments, she took on too many classes and as a result, the quality of her teaching suffered. That led to her getting fewer and fewer classes, which meant that it became harder and harder for her to meet her living expenses, let alone make loan payments. Then she heard of a way to earn extra money. Had I realized what she was going to do, I'd have tried to stop her, but by the time I found out, she had already dishonored her academic gifts."

"She was taking the SAT for other people, wasn't she?"

"How did you find out?"

"It's a long story, and I can't tell you all of it anyway."

"That's no matter. You are correct. She was paid to take standardized tests while in the guise of a variety of high school students. So not only did she commit fraud but, in doing so, she enabled others to commit fraud as well."

"And her then-boyfriend Robert Irwin was involved, too?"

His face darkened. "Irwin was the one to draw her into the scheme. I understood her succumbing, given her situation, but he had no particular financial burden. It was pure greed on his part."

"Greedy and willing to dump a sick girlfriend. What a guy! Did Patty ever tell you how the operation worked?"

"I fear not. She never shared the details of the dreadful scheme with me, and I never asked."

I'd expected that, actually, though I wouldn't have minded if he'd had more information for me. "One other question. Why have you been avoiding me? Pretending you weren't in your office and all that rigmarole."

He looked abashed. "Oh, that. Well, it seems as if our colleague Sara Weiss has been heard making disparaging comments about my 'girlfriend,' and I was afraid that if she had been misconstruing our relationship that egregiously, others may have been, too. I thought maintaining a little distance would preserve your reputation."

"Charles, dating you would not hurt my reputation. You're a great guy."

"There is quite an age difference between us."

"Which nobody cares about." I held my hands up. "And no, I am not suggesting anything. You're a great friend, and I'm very happy with our relationship just as it is."

"I feel the same," he said.

"Good. At any rate, the girlfriend Sara has been referring to isn't me. She's got it in her head that you and Patty Craft had a thing."

He drew himself up. "How dare she insinuate anything untoward about my feelings for that child?"

"The same way she dares insinuate stuff all the time."

"Still, this must not be allowed to continue. I will speak to her immediately."

"Good idea." I didn't think it would make the slightest bit of difference in Sara's behavior, but if it would make him feel better, I was all for it.

Charles marched off to right wrongs, and I locked the door behind him so I could let Sid out of his suitcase.

"Okay, Georgia, go ahead and say it," he said.

"Say what?"

"Say 'I told you so.' You know you want to."

"Nope. You were looking out for my welfare and drawing my attention to a blind spot I had about Charles. I can't tease you about that."

"Really?"

"Really. Unless you want me to say it—"

"No, thanks. I'm good. So why didn't you tell Charles about the Sechrest Foundation?"

"I was afraid to. If Charles knew they were the ones Patty was working for, and that they were recruiting here at McQuaid, he'd go all Don Quixote and go after them. I don't want him to end up dead, too."

32

I spent a couple of hours revising lecture notes and catching up on journal reading, then drove by Wendy's to grab a chicken sandwich for lunch before I had to be at PHS for my SAT prep class. Sid insisted on coming along for that, too, but not to protect me this time. He just didn't want to get bored sitting in the car. To avoid student questions about the suitcase, I stuck him in the storage closet that had been emptied for me and cracked open the door and unzipped the case enough so he could hear what was going on.

While I was eating, Sid had asked how much I knew about security for the SAT, thinking that it might help to figure out how the Sechrest people could circumvent their procedures. In fact, I didn't know a whole lot. It had been a long time since I'd taken the test myself, and the textbook I was using in the class didn't go into the details. But since Ms. Rad was a regular testing proctor, I hoped she'd be willing to fill me in.

I'd planned to scoot over to her classroom right after the last class of the day, but a few minutes before the bell rang, an older man hobbled in on crutches.

"Mr. Chedworth!" one of my students said.

"Dr. Thackery?" he said in a voice so rough he could have used it as sandpaper. "Sorry to interrupt your class, but I was passing by on my way home from physical therapy, and I thought I'd drop by."

"No problem at all. I'm glad to see you're feeling better." I rolled my desk chair over to where he was standing, and he sank into it gratefully. Then I quickly wrapped up the class and let the kids visit with their teacher. You can tell a lot about a teacher by how kids react to a visit from him or her. About half the class seemed happy to see Chedworth, while the other half couldn't care less, which I took to mean that he was liked by those who respected a tough teacher and disliked by those who wanted an easier road. It was a balance of which I approved.

When the bell rang, there were kids who still wanted to chat, so I said, "If you don't mind, Mr. Chedworth, I need to speak to Ms. Rad about something. I'll be back in a few minutes to lock up the classroom."

"Take your time," he said. "I may as well get some journals from the cabinet while I'm here so I can get caught up on my reading while I'm stuck at home."

"Sure thing." I went downstairs to Ms. Rad's room, glad to see that she hadn't left.

"Ms. Thackery," the other teacher said with a welcoming smile. "Everything going well?"

"So far, so good. Have you got a minute?"

"You mean you're giving me an excuse to take a break from grading tests? Twist my arm!"

I pulled one of the aqua blue plastic student chairs closer to the desk and did so. "I've got a question about the way the SAT is administered."

She instantly flipped from friendly to wary. "I thought you said you didn't want the proctoring job."

"I don't—I promise." I'd weighed several different approaches for getting the information I wanted because I figured that if I asked her directly, she'd be suspicious, and what she'd just said confirmed that. Then I thought about bringing up the idea of parents trying to skew tests in favor of their kids, but I was worried that she'd think I wanted to help Madison cheat. So I was just going to go with a simple, plausible lie. "Some of the kids are a little confused about the procedure for the day of the SAT. It's been a long time since I took mine, and I gather it's a trickier setup now."

"It hasn't changed since they took the PSAT," Ms. Rad said, sounding baffled. "And it's on the Web site and the registration materials."

"That's what I told them, but they're anxious."

"Well, that's the last thing we want. Okay, they should remember that when they registered online, they had to send a picture of themselves—just a head shot. That picture will be printed on the entry ticket each one will need to get into the test."

"The ticket will be e-mailed to them?"

"Right. So when they come to the testing location they have to bring the entry ticket and a photo ID to present to the proctor at the door. And of course the photo ticket and the photo on the ID will have to match their actual face—not a big deal, because most students take the test at their own school, and we don't have such a big student body that we wouldn't recognize them. If they are using a different location for some reason, you might warn them not to do anything radical with makeup or jewelry."

"Good idea. I wonder if anybody was ever kept out because of a recent nose job."

"It's an interesting question, but fortunately one that hasn't come up on my watch. Let's see, what else? They have to keep their phones turned off and put away, and it's probably better if they just leave them home, if they can stand to be apart from them that long. And remind them to bring their two sharpened number two pencils. Of course all the proctors have spares, just in case, but you'd think they'd have that part down pat."

"Will do."

"Anything else that has our scholars worried?"

"One of them said something about the picture being on the test results or something like that?"

"That's right. The test results that are sent back to the student's school have the same picture as on the entry ticket. So if I were to get blonde, blue-eyed Suzie's test scores with a photo of a brunette with black eyes, I'd know a mistake had been made. That's not anything they have to worry about."

"I wouldn't think so," I said. "I'm not sure what her issue was."

"Who knows? Anyway, you can tell them not to worry just because their whole future depends on this one test."

"I'm sure that will make them feel so much better—just remember that you're going to be the one proctoring if anybody has a meltdown in the middle of the test."

"It has happened," she said, "but most of the time, it's just me sitting at a desk with a stopwatch, trying to stay awake."

I thanked her for her time and headed back up to my classroom. Mr. Chedworth was gone, so I got Sid from the closet and left. The second I shut my car door, Sid yelled, "Georgia, let me out!"

"Okay, okay!" I unzipped the bag, and Sid's skull popped halfway out. "What's the matter with you?"

"I know who the murderer is! It's Mr. Chedworth!"

33

" A re you sure? You recognized Mr. Chedworth from his voice?"

"Well, no, not exactly. He sounded different today than he did at the murder, but—"

"But what? Was he the killer or not?"

"Okay, I'm not absolutely sure he was the killer, but I know something's not right with the guy."

"Like what? Did he say something suspicious to one of the kids?"

"No, just the usual things. He asked them how they're doing, and they caught him up on what's been happening here at school. It was what happened after they left that got my attention." He paused dramatically. "I heard him walking around."

"Okay. So what?"

"I heard him *walking* around."

"Yes?"

"As in, without his crutches."

"You mean he's faking his injury?"

Sid nodded vigorously enough to rattle his jaw. "After the kids left, I heard the classroom door shut and lock. Then Chedworth came over to the cabinets in the back of the room, clump-clump-clump from the crutches, and started rummaging around. But I heard him grunting like he couldn't quite reach something, and he muttered, 'The hell with it.' And he leaned his crutches against a desk."

"He can probably limp for a few steps, or hop, or whatever."

"Not like that. Take it from a champion eavesdropper—the man was walking normally. Maybe with a little bit of a limp, but he was walking."

"I can't believe that guy! He's getting paid for disability leave when he's not disabled!"

"Who cares about that?" Sid said. "What I'm thinking is that if he's lying about his foot, then he's staying away from PHS for another reason."

"Getting paid for doing nothing seems like a pretty good reason to me."

"At any other time, maybe, but the timing of this 'fall' looks kind of suggestive."

"I don't know, Sid. Chedworth's accident—"

"You mean his alleged accident."

"Okay, then, his alleged accident was over a week after the murder."

"Then perhaps I should remind you that Chedworth was part of the group that met with Irwin," he said.

"You're right! And he was a regular proctor for the SAT and other tests here at PHS." That reminded me that I was still at PHS—I hadn't started the car yet. I did so. "You're right, Sid. You definitely have something." I didn't know what, but I was awfully interested in finding out.

Sid spent the rest of the evening concocting theories for why Chedworth was staying away from PHS, most of which involved increasingly elaborate ways of hiding and/or disposing of Irwin's body. I let him natter on without paying much attention because I was doing my own concocting. I wanted a reason to go to Chedworth's house. Sid was so disappointed when what I came up with was entirely prosaic.

34

"I still don't like you going in there alone," Sid grumbled the next afternoon. I'd kept him home from school again, and after I taught my classes at McQuaid, I'd canceled office hours and run home to grab him for backup while I went to see Mr. Chedworth at his home.

"Sid, there is no costume on earth we could use to hide your bony physique, and no matter what else Chedworth is, he's old. I don't want seeing you to give him a heart attack."

"What if I—"

"Besides," I said, talking over him, "it will be safer for me if you're out here in the car, listening in on the phone. If I give the word, I want you to tell him you're watching the house and will call the police if I don't come out immediately. Okay?"

"Don't turn your back on him!"

"I won't."

"And don't eat any food or drink he offers."

"I won't."

"If he picks up an ax, run!"

"You bet."

"And . . . And . . . And don't get hurt!"

"I'll do my best not to." I leaned over to pat his shoulder blade.

Given the circumstances, all of Sid had come along with me rather than just his skull and hand. I'd carried him out to the car in a clothes basket with a blanket on top, and he was currently crumpled on the floor of the front passenger seat, with the blanket hiding him.

"Okay, I'm going in." As my last precaution, I dialed Sid's cell phone number before I got out of the car.

"Georgia? Can you hear me?" he asked from under the blanket.

"I haven't gotten out of the car yet. Of course I can hear you."

"Sorry."

I carefully put my phone in a side pocket of my purse, making sure not to accidentally hang up on Sid. "I'm leaving the keys in here with you, just in case." I wasn't sure if Sid could drive, or what kind of panic he'd cause if he did, but I wanted him to have some sort of exit strategy. "Lock up as soon as I get out, okay?"

"Okay. But don't get hurt!"

"Words to live by." I climbed out of the car quickly, before he could point out that he wasn't technically living by those or any other words. The door locked behind me.

Mr. Chedworth had a small but neat house in the older part of Pennycross. The yard was nicely tended, and there was a gravel path to the front door. I rang the bell and waited.

I'd gone back and forth between showing up unexpectedly and warning him I was coming and had finally decided it would be better to set it up ahead of time. Otherwise, I ran the risk of him being away from home or just refusing to let me in. So I'd asked Mrs. Lynch at PHS to call to arrange a meeting to discuss the topic Sid had found so hopelessly mundane: student progress for the classes I was teaching in his place. Since the parent-teacher conferences were scheduled for the following week, it was a solid excuse.

Chedworth was slow to answer the bell, but that fit his role of old-man-with-an-injury. When he opened the door, I had to admit I was impressed by his devotion to the character of invalid. He wasn't using the crutches, but he was leaning heavily on a sturdy-looking cane, and he was wearing a blue zipper cardigan Mr. Rogers would have loved. "Dr. Thackery, good to see you again. Come on in," he said. He gestured for me to go ahead of him and he closed the door firmly behind me.

Great. Two seconds in, and I was already breaking my promise to Sid by turning my back on Chedworth. Despite the imminent peril, I made it down the hall and into the living room unscathed.

It was a cozy room, heavy on upholstery in warm colors. An ottoman was ostentatiously placed in front of a comfy-looking armchair, and while I took a seat on the couch, Chedworth made a production of settling himself in the chair and putting his foot up.

"I didn't want to bring it up in front of the students yesterday, but you're Madison's mother, aren't you?"

"That's right."

"So which hat are you wearing for this visit? Mother or teacher?"

"Teacher. Unless you have something you need to tell me about Madison . . ."

"She's doing fine. Smart girl."

"Okay, then. You know Monday is parent-teacher

conference night, and I've never dealt with one from the teacher side of the desk. It's not really an issue in college."

"That's a relief. There's so much talk about helicopter parents that I assumed they were worrying instructors at your level as much as they are at ours."

"Not yet, anyway," I said. "I don't know how many of the parents are going to want to talk to me since I'm so new to the class, but I thought I better be prepared."

"The first thing you need to know is that the parents who are most likely to come are those whose children are doing poorly or particularly well. The parents whose kids have problems are split down the middle—either they want to know what the problem is so they can fix it or they want to make excuses for their little darlings, which will likely include blaming you. The parents whose kids are doing well are mostly there to hear their kids praised, though you get a few of the helicopter variety who want to know how to raise their kid's grade from a ninety-nine to a hundred. You want to know how to treat the different types?"

"Sure."

"Treat them all the same, that's my advice. Start by introducing yourself and shaking hands. Then say something nice about the kid, even if it's a stretch to think of anything. He's a hard worker; she always pays attention; he's always prepared for class; she's got a great sense of humor. Then review the test scores, so they'll know exactly what grade their kid earned. Point out attendance or behavior problems if there are any. End with something else nice about the kid. Shake hands again, and usher them out. You're not supposed to spend more than five minutes per meeting, so keep it short and sweet.

"You've got their test scores, of course, but those only

show how the kid is doing, not why, so let me fill in the gaps. You may want to take notes."

I took the hint and got out my laptop. He was good—off the top of his head, he gave me a quick rundown on every single student in the two classes I was teaching. In fact, he was so fast I had to ask him to slow down a few times because I couldn't keep up with him, and I'm not a slow typist. I got so caught up that I almost forgot why I'd come in the first place, but eventually I remembered I was supposed to get him to somehow reveal that his foot wasn't really injured.

Sid had suggested all kinds of gambits: spilling a hot drink on him so Chedworth would jump up screaming; knocking something valuable off a shelf so he'd hop up to save it; leaving the room while music was playing so I could run in and catch him twerking. Only Chedworth hadn't offered me anything to drink, he didn't have anything on his shelf worth throwing oneself on the floor to rescue, and he just didn't seem like the twerking type. Soon we were on the last student, and I was running out of time.

Chedworth finished his rundown on that final student, and once I'd finished typing up the information, he said, "So is there anything else I can help you with?"

"Just one question," I said, putting my laptop into my bag in case I had to run. "Why are you pretending that you're hurt when you don't even limp anymore?"

He stared at me, mouth open, for a solid minute before he started to chuckle. Then he broke into a full-throated laugh that grew into a roar of hilarity.

To say that I was nonplussed would be putting it mildly.

He actually had to pull a handkerchief from his pants pocket to wipe his eyes before he could speak again. "I sure didn't expect that," he said. "I can't believe you held it in for all this time. I knew I shouldn't have put the crutches down at PHS yesterday, but they're such a pain to use all the time. My underarms are never going to be the same."

"So you admit there's nothing wrong with your foot?"

"What are you, a lawyer? I'm not admitting, I'm saying. My foot is fine. Well, not fine—I broke a small bone and sprained things that don't like being sprained, so it still hurts, but nothing that Advil won't take care of."

"I'm confused. You're pretending to be more hurt than you are, and I've found out, but you aren't even bothering to deny it."

"Why should I? What are you going to do about it? I've been teaching in the Pennycross school system for as long as you've been alive. So who do you think Dahlgren is going to believe: you or me?"

"All he'd have to do is talk to your doctor."

"And the doctor would tell him that my symptoms are entirely consistent with a man of my age who fell the way I did. That quack thinks everybody over sixty has one foot in the grave already—it would never occur to him that a man who runs every day and works on his feet might recover faster than a couch potato with a desk job. He told me I should stay out of work for eight weeks, and that's what I'm doing. I've got more sick time stored up than I'll ever use anyway."

I honestly didn't know what to say. My lever was useless, and if Chedworth was the killer, he was too smart for me to catch. Fortunately, he was also curious.

He said, "Dr. Thackery, I know you're not stupid enough to come over just to accuse me of malingering when it's none of your business—you thought you were going to get something out of it. So what do you want?"

If he could be blunt, so could I. "I'm trying to find out

what happened to Robert Irwin. He disappeared after his interview at PHS and hasn't been seen since."

"Is he a friend of yours?"

"Never met the man."

"Then why do you care?"

I smiled. "None of your business."

He chuckled again. "Tit for tat. I like that. If I knew anything about Irwin, I might even tell you. But I don't. The first time I met him was when he showed up for that interview, and I'll be just as happy if it's the last time."

"You'd have seen him a lot if you'd hired him."

"What? Did Dahlgren say we were going to hire that idiot?"

"I don't know about Mr. Dahlgren, but Irwin told the waitress at a restaurant where he ate that night that he was sure he was going to get the job. In fact, he spent the afternoon looking at apartments here in Pennycross."

"He was fooling himself if he thought we'd hire him."

"Was he not qualified? He had a lot of experience."

"Plenty of experienced teachers are useless. I know people at the last school he'd worked at, and I called them and got the real story, not the pabulum they put in the official record. The man had no feeling at all for literature—he taught the most obvious interpretations to every work he covered, and woe unto any student who dared to utter an original thought in class. And he came into that interview thinking he was God's gift because he'd taught at universities. No offense."

"None taken."

"And here's the kicker. We'd asked candidates to submit a sample lesson plan for teaching *The Crucible*, and he told us he was planning a multiple choice test."

"For *The Crucible*? No essay questions? Not even short

answers or character descriptions? What kind of teacher would do that?"

"An inept one," Chedworth said, nodding approvingly at my reaction. "I wouldn't have hired that man to run a study hall."

"And you're sure the other committee members wouldn't have outvoted you?"

"Ms. Rad thought the same thing I did, and the parents are just advisory."

"What about Dahlgren?"

"He knows better than to hire anybody for my department without my approval."

"He hired me."

"He talked to me first," he retorted. "I checked you out with some of the professors at McQuaid, and they said you're a skilled classroom teacher and your research has been solid. Apparently the main reasons you're not in a tenure-track position are politics and money."

"Really?"

"Don't get too excited. They also say you need to publish a lot more papers."

"Let them try to write papers while teaching five sections of freshman comp every semester!"

"Don't bark at me! You want the job, you've got to do the work. Which Irwin wasn't willing to do for PHS, I might add. All he wanted to do was talk perks, and whether he'd be able to proctor standardized tests."

"I've come to understand that proctoring is a sensitive issue," I said.

"Extremely, and Irwin should have known that it would go to teachers with seniority. He wasn't even applying to teach SAT prep or AP-level classes, so I don't know why he was going on and on about how having the right person handling testing was so important. He even asked the parents on the committee how their kids had done. Why didn't he just ask them to lie outright? Parents will tell the truth about their salaries sooner than they will their kids' test scores. To hear parents tell it, no child in this country ever made less than eightieth percentile."

"Unless they're delicate flowers who don't test well despite their obvious genius," I suggested.

He chuckled. "So is there anything else you want to know about that pitiful excuse for a teacher?"

I was grasping at straws, but I said, "I don't suppose you've ever heard of a group called the Sechrest Foundation, have you?"

"Can't say that I have."

"Then I guess I'm done."

"Good enough. Now, why don't you stop worrying about my foot and missing idiots and make sure you get my kids ready for the SAT."

"If you're that concerned, why don't you come back and teach them yourself?"

"No, thanks," he said with a satisfied grin. "I think you've got it covered, and I've still got reading to catch up on."

Since I was in on the gag, Chedworth walked me to the door without crutches or cane and only the tiniest of limps.

Sid didn't say a word when I got into the car and started the drive home, but about the time we got into our driveway, he said, "You know, now that I've had a chance to listen to more of his voice, I'm pretty sure that Chedworth isn't the killer."

35

Madison had Byron out for a walk when we got home, and as soon as they got back, she said, "Mom, can I go out tonight?"

"Where, when, and with whom?"

"Over to Chelsea's house, whenever, with a bunch of people."

I waited.

"Okay, yes, Chelsea's parents will be there. Samantha, Liam, Colleen, Nikko, and Serena are definitely coming, and I think Tristan might come over, too."

"And that supplies the why," Sid said with a smirk.

"That's fine," I said. We negotiated drop-off and pick-up times, and since I hate the idea of any other parent having to feed six teenagers without outside help, I let her have a package of Oreos that I'd been saving for a gloomy day.

After making and eating grilled ham and cheese

sandwiches for dinner, I delivered Madison and the Oreos and came back feeling a bit disgruntled. After the afternoon I'd had, I could really have used those cookies.

Sid was waiting for me. While I'd been gone, he scrounged some Hershey's Kisses, arranged them on a plate, and put them out on the coffee table along with a frosty glass of Coke. *Strictly Ballroom* was already in the DVD player, and I'm pretty sure he'd fluffed the sofa cushions. He'd even given Byron a chew stick. It added up to an amazingly welcoming picture.

I said, "Well, I was planning to grade papers responding to a reading on the appeal of reality TV and be depressed, but now you've blown that."

"Eat your chocolate and watch your movie."

"Only if you'll watch with me."

It's really hard to stay discouraged with a skeleton like that around.

By the time Paul Mercurio and Tara Morice had paso-dobled across the ballroom floor and into each other's hearts, I was willing to view the day's events in a more positive light.

"You know, talking to Mr. Chedworth wasn't a total loss. He gave me all that information on the students in my classes, so now I'm all set for parent-teacher night."

"True," Sid agreed.

"And there was that bit about Robert Irwin having zero chance of being hired, even though he thought he had it in the bag. That's interesting, isn't it?"

"Definitely."

"And we got so distracted by Chedworth that we've never really talked about what I found out from Ms. Rad about how the SATs are administered." I told him about the procedures, ending with, "I've been trying to think about how the Sechrest people can get around all that, but it's got to be possible. The impostors must be taking the tests at different schools from the ones the real students attend."

"That makes sense."

"So maybe they're bribing proctors to look the other way when they show up with the wrong IDs. Not Ms. Rad, of course, and I don't think Mr. Chedworth would be susceptible to bribery, either, but I don't know the other teachers at PHS well enough to say."

"Good thought."

"Or maybe they're doing something with the photos. It's supposed to be fairly easy to fake an ID, and if the kids are using school IDs instead of something like driver's licenses, that's even easier."

"Wow, you're right."

I looked at him. "Sid, you've given me chocolate, you showed me one of my favorite movies, and now you're agreeing with everything I say. Stop it! It's making me nervous."

"Just making sure you're not giving up."

"Don't be a bonehead!"

"Hey, it's not like I have a lot of choices here." He rapped his hand against his skull, making a surprisingly loud noise.

"Granted."

"So what do we do next?"

"Well, we've linked Patty Craft's death to Robert Irwin's and connected both of those murders to the Sechrest Foundation. And . . . And that's where we're stuck. It all goes back to them, and we don't have an in there."

"Could we get Yo or one of the adjuncts to take a job with them?"

"No, I couldn't put anybody in that kind of situation. Not only could it be dangerous, but it could also damage somebody's career if it were to come out. And make no mistake, the Sechrest Foundation is going down. I know we're not absolutely sure they had anything to do with the murders—"

"Of course they did!"

"I think there's some connection, but even if there isn't, I'm going to make sure that the people who run the SAT find out exactly what Frisenda and company are up to."

"Really? As much as you hate the SAT? Wouldn't it be satisfying to see them get conned?"

"It's not that simple. The SAT is flawed, and I can't stand the fact that somebody's future can be so influenced by a single test, but cheating just makes things worse. I mean, there are kids who are good at taking tests, and if it gives them an advantage for scholarships or whatever, they should be able to benefit from that. Those scholarships shouldn't be given to kids who are bad at tests just because their parents can afford to pay somebody to take the tests for them."

Sid reached over and gently slugged my arm. "I love it when you get all idealistic and stuff."

"Bonehead!"

"Meat puppet!"

We went on in that affectionate way for an interval until I said, "Fun times aside, we still need a way into the foundation."

"I know what we can do. Mail me to their office, and put a box cutter in the box with me. Then I cut my way out and search the office for clues."

Rather than argue with the logistics of the plan, I said,

"I don't have a street address for them. Just the e-mail and Web site."

"Yeah, and you know what they say. On the Internet, nobody knows you're a dog."

"Say that again."

"On the Internet, nobody knows you're a dog. It means that—"

"I know what it means. It's given me an idea."

"We're going to send Byron after them?"

That I just ignored. "Instead of hoping for them to approach me, I'm going to approach them."

"How?"

"Get me my laptop, and I'll show you."

After nearly an hour of careful writing and rewriting, which would have gone faster without Sid's help, I had what I hoped would be a tempting letter to send to Ethan Frisenda.

Dear Mr. Frisenda:

It has come to my attention that the Sandra Sechrest Foundation is actively recruiting specialists in testing strategies. Though I am not within the ideal demographic for test specialists, I do have special expertise and access that would add value to your organization.

I've been an adjunct faculty member for almost two decades, and have worked in eight different institutions, which has helped me form an extensive network of contacts.

I work part-time tutoring high school students in taking standardized tests such as the PSAT and SAT, so I would be able to identify students who might benefit

*from hiring a test specialist and whose parents would
have the financial assets to afford such a service.*

*I would very much like to discuss opportunities
within the Sechrest Foundation.*

> *Regards,*
> *Jean Schulz*

"I think that's got it," I said with more than a little satis-
faction. "It's both pompous and slimy—perfect for the
Sechrest Foundation."

"I still think you could shorten that second bullet item
if you—"

"English is my department!"

"You misspelled 'students.'"

"Coccyx!" I fixed it. "Now for your part. You're sure you
can create an e-mail address that they won't be able to trace
back to us?"

"Of course. I've read a dozen articles about how it's done
and what services to use. It's simple if you know how."

"Okay, then, if you're sure."

"Sure as sacrum."

Since it was late Friday night, we didn't expect an answer
until the next morning at the earliest, and we weren't even
surprised at not hearing anything over the weekend. Still I
had high hopes of getting a response on Monday.

I did, but it wasn't what I'd been hoping for. Despite Sid's
best efforts, by lunchtime the Sechrest Foundation had
tracked the letter back to me.

36

I'd finished up with my morning classes at McQuaid and was reading while eating a ham sandwich, which is undeniably rude but since I was alone, I figured it wasn't going to offend anybody. Unfortunately, it meant that I wasn't paying attention to my surroundings at the Campus Deli and didn't notice that I had company until a man slid into the other side of the booth. I looked up and was suddenly glad I'd already swallowed or I might have choked.

Ethan Frisenda, the man from the Sechrest Foundation, was sitting across from me.

Logically, I should have realized that there was nothing he could do to me in public, but I couldn't stop myself from stiffening as if he'd pulled a gun on me.

"Ms. Schulz?" he said politely. "Or should I say Dr. Thackery?"

I nodded.

"We received your note this weekend and found it extremely

interesting." He smiled thinly. "I thought it might save us all a great deal of time and effort if I were to come talk to you. I can be difficult to find, whereas you were easily located."

"Is that a threat?"

"No, of course not," he said. "Merely an observation."

I wasn't convinced. He clasped his hands on the table between us, which also seemed vaguely threatening. Admittedly, at that point I'd have been alarmed by a sneeze.

"At any rate, now we have a chance to talk," he said. "We were very surprised to find out how much you know about the business of the Sechrest Foundation. I'm hoping to find out how that came to be."

I suddenly realized that Frisenda must have seen too many movies and TV shows, because he sounded just like a Hollywood villain, with his euphemisms and vague warnings. Having seen those same movies and TV shows, I knew exactly how I was supposed to respond: "How did you find me?" And in an ominous tone he'd say he had his ways, and I'd point out that I wasn't without resources myself, and he'd say that he hoped unpleasantness could be avoided, and I'd say . . . Screw it. I'd been asking people discreet questions for weeks, and I was tired of it.

In a clear voice, I said, "You mean how did I find out about you guys committing fraud? Arranging for parents to hire people to take the SAT and other tests on behalf of their kids? Is that the business you're talking about?"

I saw his knuckles whiten, as if he was squeezing his hands too tightly, but he tried to stick to his script. "I have my ways of learning these things."

"Well, obviously, or you wouldn't be here."

Frisenda blinked. "Then you have been taking an interest in the foundation?"

"Duh!"

He blinked harder, and I knew he was trying to remember his next line. "I do hope we can avoid—"

I held up one hand to stop him. "Why don't we cut to the chase? I despise your business. It's dishonest and immoral and more than a little tacky. I wouldn't work for you guys if I was starving." Okay, I'd do it if Madison was starving, but that was a moot point.

"You seem to know a lot . . . You have a great deal of knowledge . . ." He paused, then triumphantly added, "For a disinterested party."

"I said I'm not interested in working for your crummy business. I *am* interested in what happened to Patty Craft."

I'd gone so far off script that he actually had to start making up new lines for himself. "I thought Patty killed herself."

"Is that what you thought? I've got reason to suspect otherwise." Coccyx, now I was starting to sound like a TV villain. "She was murdered."

"You're serious?"

"As a heart attack."

"And you think I had something to do with it? Hey, I liked Patty. Even after she went through chemo and couldn't fool anybody into thinking she was a high school student, I used her for other work until last year, when she got too sick to do even that."

"She must have needed money pretty badly after that. Did she maybe call and threaten to go to the police if you didn't pay her?"

"You mean like blackmail?" he said.

"That's what blackmail is."

"That's crazy. How could she turn me in without getting herself in trouble?"

"People get immunity for testifying against others."

"Sure, but it would have ruined her career, right? What school would have hired her once word went out about her being involved?"

That hadn't occurred to me, but I didn't want to admit it to him. "What about Robert Irwin?"

"What about him? I haven't used him since he started losing his hair and showing his age. He couldn't even fake being a college student for the LSAT anymore."

"He's missing, probably dead."

He blinked. "For real? This is the first I've heard of it."

"So Irwin wasn't blackmailing you, either?"

"Same answer. He couldn't have said anything without losing his job. To tell you the truth, both Patty and Bert had as much to lose as I did."

"Then were you blackmailing them?"

"Of course not! Patty Craft had cancer—what kind of an a-hole do you think I am?"

Maybe I was nuts, but his mingled shock and offense sounded utterly sincere.

He pulled himself together and assumed his oily, urbane tones again. "I assure you, Dr. Thackery, I am simply a businessman providing a valuable service. I treat my contractors with utmost respect."

I believed him. Not about the simple businessman, valuable service, or utmost respect parts, but that he didn't know what had happened to Patty Craft or Robert Irwin. Given the amount of trouble he'd gone to in order to confront me, I figured I could at least let him finish the scene closer to his original vision. So I said, "Very well then. I have no further interest in your activities, though I suggest that in the future you utilize universities other than McQuaid for your recruiting efforts."

He nodded regally and stood. "I think I can guarantee that. I'm gratified that we were able to resolve this without any unpleasantness." Then he moved away smoothly.

I waited until he was gone before I started laughing. He'd gone off with a napkin stuck to the bottom of his shoe.

37

After the hilarity wore off, I realized that it was really no laughing matter. Okay, the napkin on the shoe had been guffaw-worthy, but now I was even more at sea than I'd been before. Instead of the shadowy crime kingpin I'd been expecting, I'd encountered a Netflix addict. Frisenda was a crook, but he wasn't a killer.

So where did I go next?

I took a deep breath, tossed out my trash, and headed for my mother's office. I still had a job to do. Two, in fact. As soon as I'd finished up with office hours at McQuaid, I had to run home, make sure Madison had something for dinner, and zip back to PHS for parent-teacher conferences.

I really wasn't expecting many parents to care enough about a part-time SAT prep teacher when I hadn't had their children as students for long and wouldn't keep them for much longer, but there was a line of a half dozen parents waiting when I opened my classroom door at five o'clock to get things started.

Ms. Rad had told me that there were no set appointments for the parents—it was first come, first served. The evening would end at seven thirty, though it was considered polite to continue meeting with parents if they'd joined the line before then.

First up was a father.

"Hello, I'm Jarod Kingston. My son is Frank."

"Of course. I'm Dr. Thackery." I shook his hand, waved him to a desk, took my own chair, and pulled out my laptop with the class records. I didn't see much resemblance between the lanky red-headed boy in my class and this man, balding and dressed in regulation Brooks Brothers from head to toe, but maybe Frank took after his mother.

Kingston said, "You know, Mr. Chedworth is great, but I'm really excited to have the opportunity to talk to somebody who teaches at the college level. I was wondering if you'd gotten a good picture of Frank yet."

I wasn't sure what he was asking for, so I went into the spiel Mr. Chedworth had coached me on. "He's a great kid, always cheerful and on time, and he seems to have an excellent grasp of the material. We've only had the one practice quiz so far, but he did very well on that, and Mr. Chedworth's records show that he's made straight As all quarter."

"Good, good. Do you have any suggestions for positioning Frank?"

"Positioning him?"

"For his college applications." I must have continued to look blank because he added, "His college admissions hook.

His grades are solid, and as you know, he tests well, but we're still struggling to find his 'wow factor.'"

"Wow," I said weakly.

"I did have one thought. Frank is an excellent magician, particularly with card tricks, and I thought we could do something with that, have him perform at a children's ward in the hospital or maybe at a senior citizens' home. I'm just not sure which would be better."

"I'm sure people would enjoy either."

"But which would look better on the application? Sick kids or old people?"

I belatedly realized what I was dealing with. I'd heard rumors in the academic community about how parents hired consultants to help their kids get into college, but I'd thought it was something confined to people who had more money than they knew what to do with. Though I doubted Kingston had that much money—his suit was Brooks Brothers, not Armani—I could tell he'd either spoken to somebody or absorbed a boatload of articles about student positioning.

"Which group of people does he prefer being around?" I asked.

"Does that matter?"

"Absolutely. If he's not really dedicated to magic or performing for one group or the other, admissions people are going to know he's just being 'packaged.'"

"But I thought—"

"I know, you thought that positioning wasn't the same as packaging, and there's something in that, but you still can't fake it."

"Oh," he said. "What about music? Like playing the xylophone? That's unusual, right?"

"Does Frank play the xylophone?"

"I could get him lessons over the summer. Hey, then he could combine magic and music. Like playing a song, then making the xylophone disappear!"

What I really wanted was to make Kingston disappear, but I hated the idea of the guy forcing his kid to spend all summer learning an instrument when it wouldn't do him any good.

"My best advice is for you to figure out what Frank already enjoys. That's all the positioning he needs."

"I see," he said, nodding. "Thank you for your insight."

I could just tell that he was going to start disregarding my advice before he got to his car.

About half of the rest of the parents were a variation on that same theme. No matter what I said, they were sure there was a trick to getting their kids accepted at a good college, something beyond good grades, high test scores, and a well-written personal essay. Some of the exceptions wanted to tell me how stupid they thought the SAT was, which I agreed with, and a few actually wanted to know how they could help their kids do better on the test. I wished I could have talked to them all night.

Two parents were waiting when the announcement came that the evening's conferences were over, so I took the first and told the second to warn off anybody else who tried to get in line. So naturally, when I opened the door again, I found that two more parents had shown up and were waiting with an air of determination. So I bit the bullet and spoke to each of them, though admittedly I was talking as fast as I could.

As I was ushering the last one out, I saw a woman walking quickly in my direction, so I firmly closed the door and locked it. Ms. Rad had warned me that there might be latecomers, and my best bet was to wait in the classroom until they were gone. So I took my time gathering my things, straightening the room, and making sure all the cabinets were locked before I peered out through the door's inset window into the corridor.

The woman was standing right outside.

I texted Madison that I was stuck at school for a little while longer, checked e-mail on my phone, and peeked again.

She was still standing by the door.

Okay, if I let her in, it would take five minutes to get my stuff back out so I could access her child's records and probably fifteen minutes of conference. So it was a choice of twenty minutes of work or an undermined amount of time waiting her out. Plus, if I did talk to her, it would encourage her to come late next time—maybe it wouldn't affect me, but it would be a pain for other teachers. So I waited.

At nineteen minutes, I was about ready to throw in the towel. But then I heard the welcome sounds of her stomping down the hall toward the stairwell. Victory was mine!

Just in case she was lying in wait downstairs, I waited another five minutes before turning out the lights and locking up. By that time, it was nearly eight thirty, and apparently all the other teachers had managed to avoid being ambushed. I didn't see another soul as I went toward the exit.

As I walked, I texted Madison again, to let her know I was really on the way this time, and got a message back:

Don't forget Sid!

"Coccyx," I said loudly, immediately regretting it because of the way it echoed through the empty building.

It had been Sid's idea to stay at school during the meetings, hoping he'd hear a familiar voice or something juicy as parents wandered to and fro. Of course, what he'd really wanted was a chance to make up for his misstep in setting up the supposedly untraceable e-mail address that Frisenda had used to find me.

Now I had to go get him out of Madison's locker, which meant backtracking down a corridor that seemed longer than usual.

I know it's nuts for somebody who's spent most of her life in the halls of academe, but I still get creeped out when those halls are empty. A school without students or teachers is just unnatural, and since PHS teachers were regularly reminded to turn out their classroom lights when they left, to save power, every doorway was ominously dark. Though I was annoyed I'd have to get Sid, I was just glad I was going to have him for company on the drive home. What could be more cheering than a talking skull?

Just as I turned the corner of the hall where Madison had her locker, the lights went out. "Coccyx," I said again.

I felt along the wall at the corner where I was fairly sure I'd seen light switches, but my triumph at finding them was quashed when I flipped all the switches and nothing happened. I had no idea if it was a busted fuse or a security timer, but either way, I was stuck in the dark.

I reached into my purse for my phone and managed to find the flashlight app. Having only a streak of illumination was almost worse than being in darkness, but not quite, so I used it to make my way to the right locker.

"Sid? You okay in there?" I whispered. There was no reason to whisper, of course, but I didn't want more echoes.

"What's going on out there?" he said. "What happened to the lights?"

"Don't know, don't care. I just want to get out of here." Then, of course, I had to find the text Madison had sent me with the combination, and that took what seemed like two or three hours of fumbling around. Once I had it, I had to hold the phone in one hand while twisting the ossifying knob on the ossifying lock with the other. Meanwhile Sid was humming the theme to *Jeopardy!*

When the lock's shackle finally let go, I swung the locker door open and snarled at Sid.

He was grinning at first, but then his eyes got impossibly wide. "Georgia, behind you!"

Without thinking, I threw myself to the side and onto the floor and heard the swish of something going over my head and the earsplitting crash of something slamming against the row of lockers.

38

I'd dropped my phone as I hit the floor, and the light showed only a pair of sneakered feet standing behind where I'd been a second before.

"Help! Police! Help! Fire! Help! Police! Help! Fire!" Sid yelled.

The person in sneakers hesitated, probably trying to figure out who was making all the noise. Then he—or she— turned to go. I stuck my foot out, hoping to trip him, but he dodged it easily and ran down the hall.

"Help! Police! Help! Fire! Help! Police! Help! Fire!"

"Sid! Sid, he's gone."

"Are you okay?"

"I'm fine." I took a moment to make sure I was telling the truth, but while I might find a bruise later, nothing seemed to be broken or bleeding. "I'm fine," I said again and got up from the floor.

"Call 9-1-1!"

"Already on it."

An hour and a half later, I almost wished I hadn't bothered. First off, the woman answering the phone sounded all too familiar—I was pretty sure she'd been the one who answered the phone when I'd called in my anonymous tip, and I was afraid she recognized my voice, too.

To add to my paranoia, Deborah's friend Louis Raymond was one of the responding officers, but if he was suspicious about my being attacked after having been involved in a bizarre murder case a few months before, he kept it to himself.

Principal Dahlgren, on the other hand, couldn't quite hide his feelings. While he said all the right things, I couldn't help but pick up the impression that he thought the incident was most peculiar. He kept asking why I'd stayed at school so late, even after I explained that I was dodging a tardy but overly persistent parent. I couldn't tell if he thought I was stealing school supplies or if I'd been doing something illegal and/or immoral on school property.

He insisted that they'd never had violence at the school before, and when Officer Raymond reminded him of Irwin going missing after his interview there, he came just short of snapping when he insisted that Irwin's disappearance had nothing to do with PHS. What he really wanted was for the police to confirm that I'd been attacked by a random stranger coming into the school.

The police weren't buying it. For one, my attacker had known how to temporarily disable the hall lights. It turned out that it hadn't been a fuse—it was something much simpler. There were switches on both ends of the long hall, and the lights had been turned off using the panel farthest from me. Plus the switches had been left halfway between on and off, so they couldn't be turned back on from the end I was on. It was an old trick, but it showed that my attacker was familiar enough with the building to know where the light switches were and how to rig them. Moreover, the police found that he'd left behind the weapon that had hit the locker instead of my head. It was a baseball bat clearly marked as PHS property. Dahlgren had no rebuttal for that.

The police started out by focusing on any kids I might have flunked out of my class, or possibly arguments with their parents during the night's meetings, but I kept telling them that it was a pass-fail course and nobody was failing. Then they asked about my personal life, and I had nothing to tell them about that, either.

Eventually they concluded that they couldn't conclude much of anything. It could have been random or it could have been personal, but they were having a hard time reconciling either scenario with somebody finding out that I'd be at school late and alone, knowing how to deal with the lights, and being able to locate the baseball bat.

Of course, I couldn't explain why I thought I'd been targeted, and I certainly couldn't tell the real story of how he'd been scared off. I'd had Sid back in his bag before the police and Dahlgren arrived, and if anybody wondered why I was carrying a bowling bag, they didn't mention it.

Finally everybody agreed that there was nothing else that could be done. The police took the bat with them to check for fingerprints and escorted me to my car to make sure I got there safely.

Sid managed to contain himself until we were out of the school parking lot, but then he started thumping on the inside of the bag and kept at it until I was stopped by a red light long enough to unzip the bag.

"Are you sure you're okay?" he asked immediately.

"Yes, Sid, I'm okay. Thanks to you."

"Thanks to me? If it hadn't been for me, you wouldn't be involved in this crazy mess!"

"Stop that!"

"You know it's true."

"And you wouldn't have gotten us involved if Madison hadn't forgotten you at school, and Madison wouldn't have had you at school if I hadn't let her take you. So that makes it my fault."

"That is the worst logic trail I have ever heard."

"Okay, then blame Deborah. That's always fun."

"Seriously—"

"Seriously, Sid, you had my back. As always. And literally this time."

"But—"

"But me no buts until you grow one of your own."

"Hey! I have a very shapely tailbone."

"If the shape to which you refer is a point, then sure you do."

"You're just jealous because I'm prettier than you are."

"Speaking of looks," I said, happy to have moved the subject away from the blame game, "I don't suppose you got a look at the face of the guy who tried to hit me, did you?" The police had responded so quickly I hadn't had a chance to ask before. That and the fact that I might have been too much in shock to think of the obvious.

Sid said, "I'm sorry, but I didn't. It was so dark, and his face was in shadow. All I saw was somebody behind you, and then him raising his arms."

"All I saw was his feet, and of course he wasn't wearing anything distinctive, like sequin-covered Uggs or limited-edition Converse high-tops. Just plain white sneakers."

"Were the police any help at all? It sure didn't sound like it from what I heard."

"They were trying. I mean, they searched the school, but didn't find any signs of him or any forced entry, just the baseball bat."

It was when I said "baseball bat" that it got to me. Somebody had actually swung at my head with a baseball bat. He'd swung so hard he'd left a visible dent in the locker he'd hit instead.

"I'm sorry," I said stiffly, "but I need to stop for a minute." I guess there was no traffic because nobody honked when I suddenly pulled over to the side of the road and threw the car into park before my shaking got so bad I couldn't drive anymore.

"Oh, Georgia," Sid said. His hand reached out from the bowling bag and took mine in a firm clasp. I know it sounds incredibly creepy, but he meant it to be comforting, and I was in fact comforted. He murmured the kinds of things I used to say to Madison when she'd fallen and hurt herself, and eventually I remembered that the older version of Madison was waiting at home.

"I'm okay now," I said firmly and took my hand back to put the car back in gear. I must have been somewhat better, at least, because this time I remembered to check for other cars before pulling out onto the road.

For the rest of the drive home, I tried to come up with a way to tell Madison what had happened without making her freak out. It was wasted mental effort. My sister had gotten to the house ahead of me.

39

Deborah and Madison were at the door when I walked in, and my daughter immediately grabbed me with the desperate hug of a frightened child. Even if I hadn't seen her face first, I'd have known she'd been crying. Meanwhile Deborah took Sid's bag out of my hand, opened it to pull out his skull, and said, "Spill it, bone boy—everything that happened, not just what Georgia wants us to know."

Sid did so, leaving out nothing, but at least not making it sound any worse than it had been.

When it was all over, Madison looked as if she was about to start crying again.

"Sit!" Deborah said, pushing the two of us toward the living room. "Take bone boy with you."

We went to sit on the couch, with Madison so close beside me that she was nearly in my lap. Sid was on my lap. Even Byron seemed to sense something was wrong, because he was keeping watch. Or maybe he was hoping to run off with some part of Sid.

A few minutes later, Deborah came in with mugs of milk, a stack of ham sandwiches, and the package of Oreos I'd bought to replace the ones Madison took to her friend's house. "Eat."

Those of us who were in the habit of eating did so, and after the first half of her sandwich, Madison lost that about-to-break-down look. I felt a lot better, too—I'd nearly forgotten how hungry I was.

Only when we'd eaten our way through all the sandwiches and a ludicrous number of cookies did Deborah say, "Okay, then. Let's recap. Did Sid leave anything out?"

"Nope, he told you everything I know—which is next to nothing—and what Officer Raymond told me. Which reminds me. Isn't it against the rules for your bowling buddy to tell you about police investigations?"

"It wasn't Louis who called me," she retorted. "It was Mr. Dahlgren. He wants me out at the school bright and early tomorrow morning to see about replacing the locks, and he wants recommendations for updating the security system."

"I'm impressed. From the way he was talking, I thought he'd convinced himself I was making it up or that I was using the school as a lair for my gang of hoodlums."

"Hoodlums? Not hooligans?" Deborah asked with one eyebrow raised. "Never mind. The point is, no matter what Dahlgren believes happened, or wants to believe happened, he has to take measures to make sure it doesn't happen again. He's smart to get things moving before parents start finding out."

"Dahlgren!" Sid said with a sniff. " 'Oh, it couldn't be one of our students. Our students are perfect angels.' If he'd heard some of what I've heard the past couple of weeks, he wouldn't even try to say that. Can he really be that naive? Or is it denial?"

"Maybe it was something else," I said. "You couldn't see his feet from the bag, could you, Sid?"

"Of course not. Why?"

"He was wearing white sneakers."

Madison said, "Mom, now you're freaking me out. Look, I think it's great that you've been trying to find out who killed those people, but this is getting too scary. You have to stop doing this before you get hurt."

I'd been afraid that was coming. "I'm sorry, Madison, but I'm more convinced than ever that the killer is somehow attached to PHS, and I'm going to get that ossifying piece of sacrum out of your school!"

I was expecting Deborah to chime in, which she did, but not the way I would have predicted.

"Georgia," she said, "when are you going to learn how to cuss like a grown-up?" Then she turned to Madison and in a matter-of-fact tone said, "Here's the thing, kiddo. Your mother is already a target, and the only way to change that is to catch the killer. The police can't do it because they don't have the same information we do and we can't give it to them in a way that they'll accept. So from this point on, you guys are going on red alert. You don't go anywhere alone, you keep your cell phones charged and close to hand, and we work this problem until it's solved. Madison, you are not to ride your bike to school—either your mother or I will take you there and pick you up again. As for walking the dog, both of you go or you let him do his business in the yard. A couple of days without walks isn't going to hurt Byron."

"Wow. Deborah, I'm impressed," I said.

"Me, too," Sid said. "She made a *Star Trek* joke."

She reached over and thumped him a good one before giving us more instructions about everything from making sure we all had GPS enabled on our electronics to changing the password on the home alarm system.

The only sticking point was when she tried to mandate that Madison immediately quit all of her extracurricular activities.

"No way," Madison said. "I could stall on choral ensemble, but the play is next week, and I am not leaving the club high and dry."

"She's right, Deborah," I said. "Remember when you were in drama in high school and two people dropped out of the cast right before tech week? *Twelve Angry Men* suddenly became *Ten Really Angry Men*."

So we compromised. Madison would attend rehearsal every afternoon of tech week—the last few days before the Friday and Saturday night performances—but she promised not to so much as leave the auditorium without accompaniment.

"And I'll be there with her!" Sid said.

"I might be, too," Deborah said. "I wonder if your director could use a little extra help backstage."

"I've never known a student production that couldn't," I said. "Are you okay with that, Madison?"

"Sure," she said. "Becca has been going crazy trying to do everything herself, and Jo is still finishing up costumes, so I'd be glad for the help even if things were normal."

We worked out a few more details, and then I realized how late it had gotten. After testing the burglar alarm she herself had installed, Deborah left for home and Madison and I went to bed.

Normally I hate it when Deborah tries to pull big-sister

rank on me, but for once, I didn't mind a bit. Not only was it good to have her help and expertise, but I was more than a little gratified that she was assuming that I could find the killer. I just wished I was as confident in my abilities as she seemed to be.

40

I got two e-mails from PHS the next day: one because I was the parent of a student and one because I was a member of the faculty. Both had the same message. In the most vague terms imaginable, Mr. Dahlgren described the attempted attack on me, emphasizing that I had not been injured and that it was likely a random occurrence. Then he invited the entire PHS community to attend a meeting that night in which questions of safety would be addressed.

The letter to parents referred only to "a member of the faculty," but the teacher letter did give my name, so I was wondering what kind of welcome I'd get when I showed up at PHS. Would the teachers share Mr. Dahlgren's opinion that I'd brought trouble to the school?

I got the answer as soon as the bell rang at the end of the day. Almost as fast as my students poured out, teachers poured in, with Ms. Rad leading the pack.

"Georgia, I heard what happened, and I am so sorry. I should never have told you to let parents keep you late!"

"It's okay, I'm fine. It's not your fault."

Then Mr. Neal and Ms. Zale gave me a box of chocolates and the quartet of math teachers who'd been so irritated at my sitting in their row during the faculty meeting said they'd take turns walking me to my car after school. It went on from there. Some people had questions about what had happened, but it felt like honest concern, not morbid curiosity, and nobody even hinted that it could have been my fault. I'd never have gotten out of there if Madison hadn't come in, wanting her ride home.

On the way, Madison and Sid both said that gossip had been flying ever since the morning announcements, when Mr. Dahlgren notified the students about the upcoming meeting. But while they'd both kept their ears open—well, Madison's ears and Sid's ear holes—neither had heard anything useful. Dahlgren may have been too circumspect when talking to the students—the rumors were far more alarming than the real story.

Since Deborah was also going to the meeting at PHS because of her job, we met up for pizza at the house first and took one car. It turned out to be a good choice—it looked like the entire town had shown up, not just the people with ties to PHS. I managed to squeeze my minivan into one of the last spaces in the parking lot.

I may have been overly sensitive, but given the number of people who glanced in my direction, I figured the word was out about who'd been attacked. We stopped by Madison's locker to leave Sid—who'd insisted on coming just in case—and then filed into the auditorium. Normally I would have sat with Madison, but since the faculty had been asked to gather together in the rear of the auditorium, Deborah took Madison with her while I sat in the seat Ms. Rad had saved for me.

I've never attended a school meeting that started on time, and this one was no exception. It was ten after seven before Mr. Dahlgren came onto the stage, accompanied by the head of the school's guidance department, the Pennycross police chief, Mr. McDaniel in his role as head of the PTO, and Mr. Chedworth, still on crutches. The actual meeting portion was fairly brief. Mr. Dahlgren didn't say much more about the attack than what he'd put in his e-mail, and when people pushed for details, he would only say it was an ongoing police investigation. As soon as he could, he moved on to what the school was doing to prevent similar incidents in the future: added security cameras, more secure locks, and extra care in adhering to policies already in place. Then he opened the floor to questions. After the first ten minutes of those, my eyes glazed over.

I understood people being worried about their children's welfare—I shared that worry—but I'd never figured out why it manifested itself in asking the same question that has been asked several times before. Though Dahlgren had plenty of experience with parent groups, I could tell he was starting to lose patience, and finally he shut it down despite the dozen or more parental hands still waving for attention and asked anybody with more questions to contact him later. Then he had us teachers distribute handouts outlining everything he'd said.

The auditorium was so full it took forever for everybody to filter out, especially when people were clumping in the least convenient locations possible to rehash the situation. The other teachers, more experienced in such matters, had zipped out before Dahlgren finished and were long gone, but I had to wait for Madison and Deborah. Then we three had to inch through the crowd to get to Madison's locker, dislodge a man who was leaning against it, and retrieve Sid before we could get back to the minivan. By then, the parking lot was a gridlocked wonderland.

And once again, Sid was banging against the inside of his bag. "Let me out! Let me out!"

"Madison, let him out," I said, still stuck in traffic.

"But for Pete's sake, don't let anybody see him!" Deborah said.

"I heard him! I heard the murderer!" Sid said.

"He was there? Are you sure?" I asked.

"I'm sure!"

"Who was it?" Madison wanted to know.

"I don't know."

"Let's go back a step," I said. "You're sure you heard the murderer's voice?"

"Yes, but I didn't see him. Too many people were around, and one guy leaned up against the vent of the locker, so I couldn't see for most of the time. It's a good thing I don't breathe, or I could have suffocated."

He was so indignant I didn't bother reminding him that if he could breathe, his skull wouldn't have been in a locker in the first place. "So what did the killer say?"

"Nothing useful. I only caught a few sentences while he was passing by. 'I never would have expected something like this in Pennycross, let alone in the high school.' Then a woman asked if he thought the kids would be safe, and he said, 'I really think it was a one-time thing, but Dahlgren is right on it.' Then they moved on, or got lost in the crowd, or whatever."

"But you are absolutely sure it was the killer?" I asked again.

"How many times do I have to say it? I'm sure!"

I honestly didn't know if I should be horrified or elated. Obviously, the idea of publicly rubbing elbows with a murderer was enough to make me want to turn hermit, but at the same time, it meant that our assumptions and deductions were correct. The killer had ties to PHS, and he was still around.

Madison and Deborah acted just like I felt, and Deborah decided that the only appropriate reaction was to go over all our security procedures again during the agonizingly slow trip out of the parking lot and the much faster drive to the house.

I appreciated her good intentions, but I was about ready to zip her into the bowling bag by the time we got home. Fortunately for all of us, she didn't come in, just switched cars so she could go back to her place.

The rest of Sid's skeleton was waiting in the armoire, so he pulled himself together and then searched the house—checking the perimeter, he called it, which I assumed he'd learned in a game or a book. He also announced that he'd be keeping watch downstairs every night since he didn't sleep anyway. It made him feel better, so I didn't mind, but I still armed the alarm system.

Madison asked, "Do you really think the killer is going to come after you again, Mom?"

"Not really. Why should he? He knows who I am, but it's obvious I don't know who he is or I'd have told the cops."

"Then why did he try to . . . You know, last night?"

"I've been trying to figure that out. Scare me, maybe? It just seems so stupid in retrospect. If he did hide Irwin's body to make sure nobody made a connection with PHS, then why bring attention back to the school with an attack?"

"Maybe you're making him nervous, and he's losing it."

"That makes as much sense as anything, and if you're right, that's going to make it easier to catch him."

What I didn't say was that it also made it more likely that he'd try more violence—she was worried enough.

41

Over the course of the next week, I learned that being on red alert isn't nearly as exciting as it sounds.

Mostly it involved a lot of texting back and forth between Deborah, Madison, and me so that we could coordinate our schedules to the nth degree to ensure that Madison and I were never alone. Deborah had decreed that having Sid around was good but not sufficient because his rescue powers were limited, especially when only his skull and arm were present.

I knew I shouldn't complain, because Deborah was taking the brunt of it by going to every rehearsal with Madison, and once tech week started on Monday, that was a lot of hours. Still, it was wearing. I had the uncomfortable thought that if the sword of Damocles had been hanging over my head, I'd have pulled the thing down myself, just to get it over with.

At least I had one comfort. Since Sid had declared that

he'd heard the murderer at the big meeting at PHS, that meant Charles was in the clear. My friend would have had no reason to attend that meeting, even if he'd known about it, and if he had been there, I'd have seen him. A man who dresses the way he does tends to stand out in a crowd.

Since I was still feeling guilty for having let Sid convince me that Charles was a suspect, I talked Charles into letting me buy him lunch at Jasper's Diner on Wednesday. It was another wonderful spring day, and Charles is a fascinating companion. Though his area of expertise is the Pax Britannica, his knowledge of English history is broad. That day we were talking about the House of Tudor, but I was having a hard time keeping track of all the family connections.

"Allow me to illustrate." He produced a pen and a Moleskine notebook from his pocket and started to sketch out the family tree.

At first I was just watching what he was writing, but then I noticed what he was drawing with.

"Charles, where did you get that pen?"

"Hm? Oh, the finger bone." He held it out for me to take. "Amusing, isn't it?"

"Hilarious. Where did it come from?"

He looked taken aback by my tone, and I couldn't really blame him.

"It belonged to Patty Craft. You'll remember that I assisted her sister in packing up her apartment, and there were a number of odds and ends she decided weren't worth the expense of shipping to her home, so she offered them to me. I accepted a few as mementos, but I've been meaning to pass this particular pen on to one of our colleagues in biology or forensic anthropology."

"Can I have it?"

"Certainly, if you like."

"Thanks."

He went back to the Tudors, but I had no idea what he told me for the rest of that meal, and I didn't even look at the family tree he'd drawn for me. Instead I kept looking at the pen.

There were three of them just like it in my house, and all of them had come from Tristan's father.

So had this one. The printing on the side said, *Adam McDaniel, Pharmaceutical Sales.*

42

It's a good thing I didn't have any more classes to teach that day because I don't think I'd have done a good job. After lunch, I went back to my mother's office and tried to work, but instead I kept twirling that blasted bone pen around in my hand, trying to figure out what it meant.

No, that wasn't true. I knew what it meant—it meant that Adam McDaniel had known Patty Craft. The question was, did it mean anything else? I was afraid that it did. I made a phone call to gather one more piece of the puzzle, and after that, I was convinced. Then it was just a matter of trying to work out how everything must have happened.

I got home just as Deborah dropped off Madison and Sid, and though I considered asking her to stay to talk, I decided I wanted to speak to Madison and Sid first. If my theory didn't hold water, I'd rather they be the ones to poke holes in it.

Hugs were exchanged, Sid's bones were retrieved from the armoire, and I said, "Have a seat, both of you."

"What's wrong, Mom?"

"There hasn't been another murder, has there?" Sid asked.

"No, and I may have solved this one."

They sat immediately. Even Byron seemed to be giving me his full attention.

"I had lunch with Charles today, and he pulled this out." I held up the pen.

"Hey, that's like the one Tristan's father gave me," Madison said. "Does Charles know Mr. McDaniel?"

"No. He got it when he helped Patty Craft's sister clean out her apartment. Apparently Patty knew Mr. McDaniel."

Judging by his sudden bone rattle, Sid got the point right away, but Madison wasn't making the connection.

"So?" she said.

"Patty died of an overdose—it could have been suicide or it could have been an accident. Or it could have been murder, but the killer would have needed access to drugs. Like a pharmaceutical sales rep would."

I waited for either of them to argue the point, but neither did, so I went on. "Mr. McDaniel also knew Robert Irwin, or at least they'd met. He was part of the PHS search committee that interviewed Irwin."

"What about the Sechrest Foundation?" Madison asked. "What does Mr. McDaniel have to do with that?"

"I haven't met Tristan's brother yet, but you have, Madison. Did he seem particularly intelligent?"

"God, no. He didn't even know what *Hamlet* is about."

"That was the impression you'd given me. But according

to Mr. Chedworth, Adam made ninety-fourth percentile on his SAT." I'd had a hunch Chedworth would remember it if somebody like Adam had done better than expected, and sure enough, he'd been shocked enough that he remembered the score several years later.

"No way he scored that high!" Madison said.

"Mr. Chedworth also said he didn't take the test at PHS. He couldn't remember exactly why, something about going out of town that weekend and it being easier to use another testing location. It's allowed, so nobody questioned it, not even when they saw his score."

"You think he hired somebody from the Sechrest Foundation to take the test for him?" Sid said.

"I think his father did. I went back and found that picture of Robert Irwin from your dossier, Sid." I'd left it on the coffee table, and now I handed it to them. "That's what Irwin looked like around the time Adam got that SAT score."

"He looks like Adam," Madison said.

"I don't know exactly how the Sechrest Foundation runs their scams, but maybe each parent involved gets to meet the person impersonating his or her child, just to make sure it's a close enough match. Even if that never happened, Irwin would have to have known Adam's name—it was on the fake ID he was using. Then, years later, he runs into Mr. McDaniel—Adam McDaniel Sr.—and he remembers Adam Jr."

"Okay, there's a connection," Sid said, "but—"

"Remember what we know about Irwin. He's sleazy and he needs a job. And what do you know—there's a guy on the PHS search committee who he can put pressure on. He makes a point of talking about the SAT in the meeting, even though it isn't relevant. Mr. Chedworth knew right away he didn't want to hire him, and I don't think he'd have been subtle about letting Irwin know. But despite that, Irwin is so sure he's going to get the job that he spends hours looking at apartments. Unless, of course, he's just killing time until he has a chance to go back to PHS and meet privately with McDaniel. The two men argue; McDaniel snaps and kills him. Or maybe he intended to kill him from the start. Either way, Irwin is dead."

"And what about Patty Craft?" Madison asked.

"I think that goes back to Sechrest, too. Frisenda said Craft had done some work for him in addition to taking the tests—maybe she was the one to make arrangements with McDaniel or maybe she collected payment. That had to have been done in person, in cash—nobody would want a paper trail for that. She wasn't sleazy—or at least Charles didn't think she was—but she was sick and she was desperate, and she knew McDaniel had paid somebody to take his son's SAT. I think she might have been blackmailing him—not for money, but for medicine. A pharmaceutical sales rep has access to all kinds of sample drugs, but surely McDaniel's bosses would notice at some point. And Craft was dying anyway. It wouldn't take much to push her right over the edge. It could even have been a mercy killing."

"Yeah, right," Sid said.

"Whatever his motives, the woman was dead and he was safe. But that same week, here comes Irwin, and he's threatening a different kind of blackmail: 'Make sure I get this job or I'll tell people about your son's amazing SAT scores.' It's no wonder McDaniel lost his temper."

Sid said, "Okay, this all works for me, but why would McDaniel go to so much trouble to hide the body? He could have claimed it was an accident or just run off and left the body to be found the next morning."

"I don't know if McDaniel knew that Craft and Irwin had dated, but he knew they were both connected to Sechrest. So he must have been afraid that the police would find that connection if they investigated Irwin's death, and it might lead to him. Why take the chance? He'd killed twice—hiding a body is small potatoes compared to that."

"You don't think Tristan knows about this, do you?" Madison said in a small voice and pulled Byron over to hold on to, as if he were a teddy bear.

"Sweetie, I don't know. I hope not."

"He's a good actor—he could have just been acting like he was interested in me to find out what we were up to. I was texting him that night you were at the parent-teacher meetings—I may be the reason you were almost hurt."

"Madison," Sid said, "am I or am I not the most annoying eavesdropper you have ever met?"

"Um—"

"I am, and I listened in on all your mother's dates when she was growing up, and all Deborah's dates, too. I can tell the difference between when a guy is really interested in a girl and when he's not. Tristan really likes you."

"Really?"

"Sure as sacrum."

She smiled, but then said, "None of that matters now, anyway. The important part is that Mom caught the murderer."

I hated having to say it, but I had to. "No, Madison, I haven't. I know who it is, but I can't catch him because we can't prove any of this. There's no proof of anything. Unless something changes, McDaniel is going to get away with it."

Sid, bless his bones, didn't even hesitate. "Then we're going to change something."

Several hours, a pepperoni pizza, and most of a carton of red velvet cake ice cream later, we knew what we were going to do.

By the time we had our plan worked out, I was exhausted and both Madison and the dog were asleep on the couch, but Sid was jumping up and down in excitement.

"Can I say it? Can I say it?"

"Go ahead. I know you've been resisting the impulse."

He struck a dramatic pose. "The play's the thing wherein we'll catch the conscience of the killer."

43

Getting the pieces into place wouldn't have been possible if Deborah hadn't already established herself as an invaluable member of the tech crew for *Hamlet*. She was able to sneak in what we needed and hide it backstage in the midst of the last rehearsals.

On Thursday, I had to teach a class at PHS that included Tristan without giving anything away, but that was nothing compared to Madison's situation. She had to rehearse with him, and since their characters were nearly inseparable onstage, she was side by side with him all through those last rehearsals.

Finally it was Friday night. Rather than just drop Madison off at her call time, I stayed so I could get into the theater as soon as they opened it to the audience. This was nothing particularly unusual—I like to get the best seat I can wrangle and have often had to save seats for my parents and Deborah, too. But this time I wanted to be off to the side, where I'd be able to see both the stage and McDaniel. To make sure he sat where I wanted him to, Sid had printed up two cards that said, *PTO President* and *Guest*, and in the middle of her other duties, Deborah had left them in second-row seats on the aisle. There's something about school events that makes people oddly obedient. Any number of people saw those cards and grumbled about them, but nobody moved them.

I saw McDaniel arrive and start chatting with people in the crowd. Somebody pointed out his reserved seats, and he looked surprised but not suspicious as he made his way to the plum location. He nodded in my direction as he came down the aisle, but I pretended I hadn't seen him. I'm not the actress in the family, and I was afraid he'd know what I'd figured out about him just by looking at me.

Adam Jr. wasn't with his father at first, so I thought he'd come up with an excuse to keep from attending—something that would please Madison and probably his brother, Tristan, as well. Then, a few minutes before the show was due to start, he came stumbling down the aisle looking for his father. He ran into one woman, and I saw her recoil and say, "He's drunk!" to her companion. Perhaps the boy had decided that since he couldn't avoid watching the play, he could at least deaden the pain with booze. His father muttered at him angrily once he sat down, but all he did was shrug, pull out his phone, and start texting.

Finally the house lights dimmed, and Deborah came rushing in to sit in the seat I'd saved for her. "Everything okay backstage?" I asked, trying to sound casual.

"All set, except that Ophelia ripped her dress again and needed a quick repair job." Then she whispered, "Is he here?"

I nodded.

And the show curtain raised.

Madison had been in theater since she could first toddle across a stage, so I'd long since lost track of how many plays I'd sat through. Admittedly the performances had varied in quality widely, but I'd always enjoyed them before. This time, I honestly didn't know if the production was any good or not. I was too focused on what was coming after the play.

Finally Fortinbras arrived, sadly surveyed the corpse-strewn scene, and gave his lines. Judging by the enthusiasm and volume of the applause as the curtain went down, apparently the cast had done a fine job.

The curtain calls began, starting with the smaller parts—of course I cheered as loudly as I could for Madison as Guildenstern—and working up to the Prince of Denmark himself. When the boy playing Hamlet came onstage, he was holding Sid's skull, and after he bowed he assumed the traditional pose of Hamlet regarding the skull of Yorick. Madison had suggested the bit and had been worried that she'd have to talk people into it, but both Becca and Hamlet had loved the idea. So did the audience. Flashes from cameras and phones lit up the audience, and even Adam Jr. showed enough interest to take a picture.

The official plan was for the cast to then join hands to bow en masse, but before they gathered and as the applause for Hamlet quieted, Sid started speaking.

"Friends, Romans, countrymen, lend me your ears."

In fact, Sid wasn't actually speaking—we'd been afraid he wouldn't be able to project well enough. Instead he was moving his mouth to a recording that Deborah was playing—she'd left her seat in the middle of the second act to sneak backstage and handle the effects we needed. Sid was, however, moving his jaw to the words—lip-synching, without the lips. Hamlet was staring at the skull in his hand in astonishment, and I was just hoping he wouldn't drop it, or worse still, throw it. Madison had promised to catch it if he did, but I wasn't sure if she was close enough.

At first the audience thought it was a joke, and there was laughter. But the voice went on. "Murder hath no tongue, nor do I, but both murder and I doth speak this night. Here in this humble place of entertainments, murder has been committed, foul murder for a foul purpose. You there, you near the door from theater to school, canst thou not see the blood, feel the violence, know what has been done? 'Twas a Thursday when death did come here, and though the body be not present, still the stench of murder lingers 'til murderer admit his sin. Reveal yourself, O killer, for though thy victim be a blackmailer, ne'er did he deserve to be treated so. Confess. Confess. *Confess!*"

A spotlight suddenly lit McDaniel's seat, and there were gasps all around.

But nothing else.

I was watching McDaniel the whole time, waiting for him to break, but it never happened. He jerked when Sid first said "murder" and he stayed stiff the entire time, but that was the only reaction from the man. Adam Jr. looked as if he'd seen a ghost, but his father expressed only bafflement. Then in a display I'd have admired had it been in a good cause, he started laughing.

The rest of the audience hesitated for a second, then most of them joined in. The cast made their belated bow in confusion, and the applause was even louder now that everybody thought they'd pulled off this amazing bit of theater.

In the middle of it all, McDaniel turned toward me and caught my eye, and then the vicious bastard winked at me.

44

With the bowing over, the curtain went down and the audience started moving slowly toward the exit. I just sat in my seat, stunned, staring at nothing. I'd accused the man of murder—in public—and he'd reacted less than if a mosquito had bitten him. There was nothing we could do to him, and he obviously knew it.

Deborah came back after a few minutes. "He didn't crack, did he?"

"You were watching from backstage?"

"Yup. Any other ideas?"

"Stay on red alert for the rest of the school year, then move out of town and transfer Madison to another school."

She thumped me on the skull as if I'd been Sid.

"Hey!"

"Stop talking that way or I'll do it again. So we had a dumb idea."

"It should have worked."

"Yeah, it should have, but it didn't. We'll try something else."

"Like what?"

"I don't know. You and bone boy will come up with something."

"Why are you so sure?"

"It's family dynamics. You're the smart one. I'm the practical one."

"Want to switch places?"

"Hell, no."

"You're smart."

"Of course I am, but you suck at being practical."

By now I was seeing cast members joining their friends and family in the auditorium. Several were accepting congratulatory bouquets.

"Coccyx," I said. "I should have brought Madison some flowers. Where is she anyway? She's got to be as upset as we are."

"As you are. I'm not upset—this thing isn't over. Wait here, and I'll go find her."

Deborah was gone for what seemed like a long time, as other families chatted and the theater emptied out. When she did show up again, she looked worried. "Did Madison come out this way?"

"No, I've been sitting here the whole time."

"Well, she's not backstage." Deborah spotted the show's director on the stage, hugging the actress who'd played Ophelia. "Becca, have you seen Madison?"

"No, ma'am, not since the curtain calls."

"I can't find her."

"Hang on." She opened the curtains enough to stick her head through. "Anybody see Madison back there?" We heard garbled voices, then Becca turned back to us. "Jo said she saw her out in the parking lot."

"By herself?"

She went back through the curtain and repeated my question.

"No, Jo says she was with some guy. And could you ask her to bring back her costume? Jo needs to Febreze them all for tomorrow night's show."

"I'll check outside!" Deborah said and took off out the side exit. I pulled out my phone and entered Madison's number. It went to voice mail. I tried again. The same thing. Then I texted Sid. There was no response.

Deborah charged back in, accompanied by Officer Raymond. "Louis was out directing traffic, so I grabbed him. Have you seen her?"

"No! I tried calling but she didn't answer."

"You're sure she didn't go off with her boyfriend?" Officer Raymond said.

"Louis, if you ask me that one more time, you're going to have to arrest me for assaulting an officer," Deborah said. "Madison would not go off without telling us."

"Let's check backstage again."

This time I went with them. Most of the cast was long gone, but Becca was still basking in the glow of a successful directorial debut while Jo hung up costumes on their labeled hangers.

"Jo saw her outside," I said.

"Excuse me—Jo, is it?" Officer Raymond said. "I understand you saw Madison Thackery leaving."

"I don't know if she was leaving, but I saw her in the parking lot when I went out to my car to get my bottle of Febreze."

"Was she alone?"

"No, she was with somebody. I think it was a guy, but he had on a hoodie and I didn't see his face. He was holding something up over her head, and she was grabbing for it. You know, messing around. Does she have a new boyfriend?"

Officer Raymond looked at me.

I said, "Was it Tristan?"

"I don't think so—this guy looked taller than Tristan. Wait, I know it wasn't him. I saw Tristan a few minutes after that, when he brought me his costume."

While Raymond started asking about the guy's height and the color of the hoodie, I tried Madison's number again. This time, before it went to voice mail I heard a buzzing. Not over the phone, but close to where I was.

"Everybody be quiet!" I snapped. "Where's that noise coming from?" I dialed the number again and tracked the sound to a set of shelves along one wall. "That's Madison's bag!"

I grabbed the purple and black bowling bag Madison used to transport Sid's skull and looked inside. "Here's her phone. Her regular clothes and wallet are in here, too. And—" I'd started to say that Sid's hand and his phone were in there as well, but stopped myself in time. "All her stuff is in here."

Deborah said, "Call it in, Louis. Now."

Raymond stepped a few feet away to use his radio, but I didn't need to hear him to know what he was reporting.

My daughter was missing.

45

Jo and Becca must have realized something was really wrong, because they came over and asked what they could do.

My mind had gone blank, but fortunately Officer Raymond's had not. He asked them for a list of cast members along with home and cell phone numbers. More police arrived while they were gathering the information, and once they had it, Raymond put the other officers to work calling the cast to find out if anybody knew where Madison was or if they'd seen who she'd left with.

"The man you need to be speaking to is Adam McDaniel," I told Raymond.

"Why him?"

"Because he's a murderer."

"Excuse me?"

"What my sister means to say," Deborah said, "is that somebody accused McDaniel of being a murderer at the end of the play tonight." She described what had happened, though of course not mentioning her own supporting role. "So if that guy really had something to do with a murder, you should talk to him first."

"It was our skull that was doing the talking," I put in. "Maybe McDaniel thinks Madison had something to do with it." I knew it sounded crazy, but trying to explain how I knew about the murders would have sounded even crazier. "Please, just send somebody to his house."

"Okay," he said in a patient voice, "we can do that. But in the meantime, I want you to put together a list of Madison's other friends so we can check with them. Okay?" It was make-work, and I knew it was make-work, but it couldn't hurt, so I sat down in the auditorium to pull the names from Madison's and my phones. Once I handed the list over, the police started calling those people.

At some point, Mr. Dahlgren showed up.

"Dr. Thackery, Georgia, I am so very sorry. Is there anything I can do, anything at all?"

I thanked him, but all I wanted was Madison, and she was gone.

Dahlgren took Raymond to check the security tapes, but it was the same lousy system—there hadn't been time to replace it since I was attacked—so the tapes showed a lot of nothing.

After a while, Raymond came to talk to me. "Okay, we've caught up with most of Madison's friends and fellow cast members, but nobody has anything for us. We're putting out an alert, and we need a description."

"Green eyes, strawberry blonde hair," I said. "Dressed in an Elizabethan courtier's costume. I took a picture with my phone when she was onstage." I e-mailed both that one and a recent picture of her in normal clothes. "Did you talk to McDaniel?"

"Yes, we did, but he didn't know anything about your daughter's disappearance."

"Did you search his house?"

"McDaniel gave us complete access. She's not there."

"What about his son?"

"Tristan was there with him."

"Not Tristan. Adam, the jerky one. Madison hates him."

"Mr. McDaniel said Adam was on his way back to his dorm in Springfield. We reached him on his cell phone, and he said he hadn't seen your daughter tonight other than onstage."

"He's lying!" I said in a too-loud voice, and though everybody in the auditorium looked at me with sympathy, I could tell nobody believed me. And why should they? What could I say that wouldn't make me sound more like a distraught mother than I did already?

Raymond pulled Deborah aside, and after a few minutes where he spoke softly and calmly while she got angrier and angrier, she came back and said, "Let's go home, Georgia. We can't do anything here."

I wanted to argue with her, but she was right—we couldn't do anything there, not when nobody believed me. "I want her things."

"Louis," she called, "give me my niece's bag."

"Sure, Deborah, I can do that." He brought it over and said, "We will call you the second we hear anything, okay? Just stay home, get some rest, and if you think of anything else that will help us, you can call me." He started to hand me a business card, but Deborah grabbed it.

"We told you who took her, and you won't believe us.

267

Remember that so-called crank call you got? Wasn't it about a murder here? Right when that guy disappeared? And now McDaniel—who had access and who knew the man—is accused of murder. But you won't do anything."

"We're doing all we can," he said in an even tone, but I could tell it cost him.

"It's not enough," she snapped, and she brushed past him.

I should have felt badly for him—I knew it wasn't his fault—but I brushed by him, too.

Deborah and I had driven separately, but she led me to her truck. "We'll get your minivan later. After we get Madison back." As we drove out, I saw police officers with flashlights searching the school grounds. It felt wrong to leave them there hunting, but I knew Madison wasn't there.

Byron seemed to be able to tell that something was wrong as soon as we came in the door—he kept looking for Madison and making unhappy sounds. I patted him absently then went to check the answering machine. There were no messages waiting.

"I need coffee," Deborah said.

I nodded, and though I didn't really want any, when she put some in front of me a little while later, I drank it. We didn't talk, but I knew what she was thinking. I was thinking it, too. Not only had our ludicrous attempt to catch a murderer failed, but it had backfired so horribly that Madison was gone. Maybe she was already—

I stopped the thought, refused to think it.

Deborah tried to get me to go to bed, but I couldn't. The most I would do was wrap myself up in an afghan and put my feet up while I waited for the phone to ring. Byron got onto the couch with me and laid his head in my lap. I'm not sure which of us was comforting the other, but it helped. A little.

Deborah couldn't settle at all. She made more coffee; she brought me a sandwich I didn't want; she put out food for Byron; she washed my dishes. She turned the TV on and off a dozen times and checked e-mail on her phone every few minutes. Finally she threw herself into the armchair and tapped her foot against the floor over and over again.

After forever, I pleaded, "Deborah, please stop making that noise!"

"Fine," she snapped. "I'm sorry!" She held herself perfectly still. "Is that better?"

"Yes, thank you," I said.

There was still a noise. Not tapping, though. More like scratching, and it was coming from the bowling bag. "Is that Madison's phone again?"

"No," she said, and I could tell she'd heard it, too. "Her phone is there on the coffee table."

"Then what—?" I shoved Byron out of the way so I could get up, pick up the bag, and look inside. "Oh, my sacrum," I breathed.

It was Sid's hand. It was moving.

46

"Deborah! Look at this." I gingerly reached inside, took the hand, and pulled it out, still wriggling. The bones shouldn't have been staying together, either, but they were. "It's Sid's hand."

"What in the hell? That means his skull is here in the house, doesn't it?"

"Apparently not. He's controlling it from wherever he is." I briefly explained the experiments he and Madison had been trying. Meanwhile the hand tightened around my own, not painfully, but as if Sid were there to hold on to me. "He's got to be trying to tell us something."

"I don't suppose he knows sign language."

"Maybe he does, but I don't. Find something he can write with."

She grabbed the pad and pen we use for grocery lists from the kitchen. "Now what?"

"Put them on the table." I pulled at Sid's hand, trying to

tell him that I wanted him to let go, and he relaxed his grip. Then I put it on the table, on top of the pad, and tried to wrap his fingers around the pen. It took a minute, but he got the message. As I held the pad steady for him, he printed letters slowly, as if it were a great strain.

Madison ok with me

"But where are you?" Deborah demanded.

"He can't hear you!" I said. "Only his skull can hear."

"Please don't try to pretend that there are rules for this."

"Of course there are rules. Sid's just changing them." The way he had before when I was in trouble.

in a cabin no ashfield

"North Ashfield," I translated. I waited for an address or something more to identify the location, but there was nothing. "Come on, Sid. We need more."

Finally, he wrote another sentence.

junior has us

Then he stopped. The hand was still hanging together, but so loosely I was almost afraid to touch it for fear of breaking the connection completely.

"I knew it!" Deborah said. "That SOB McDaniel must know exactly where they are. I'm calling Louis right now and—"

"And telling him what? That a disembodied skeletal hand told us that Madison is in North Ashfield? He already thinks we're losing it, Deborah, and you know that McDaniel was doing his best to encourage that. Even if Louis did believe us, he wouldn't be able to arrest anybody on the basis of a mysterious note."

"So what now? We wait for bone boy to tell us more?"

"Oh no. We get in the car and go to North Ashfield. If we have to drive down every street in that town and knock on every door, we will find Madison and Sid."

"Now you're talking."

It took us about half an hour to gather everything we might need: my laptop for looking up maps, cell phones and chargers, and the baseball bat that was the only weapon I owned. We also packed up the rest of Sid's bones in his suitcase, even though none of them were showing any sign of animation. The hand wasn't moving anymore, either, but it was still hanging together, so I put it into the bowling bag on top of a towel.

We thought about bringing Byron along—I didn't know if he'd be able to track Madison, but I was quite sure he'd be able to bite somebody if the need arose—but we weren't sure if stealth would be called for, so finally decided to leave him behind.

I asked if we should retrieve my minivan, but Deborah said, "We're taking my truck. It's better on rough roads. Plus I've got my kit to deal with any locks, and a tire iron for dealing with Adam Jr."

As Deborah drove, I used Sid's cell phone to call the Pennycross police tip line. It was the same woman answering the phone—apparently she never left the station.

I said, "This is about Madison Thackery. She's being held in a cabin in North Ashfield."

I know the woman recognized my voice, but she was professional. "Can you give me any more information?"

"Talk to Adam McDaniel—he'll know where." Then I hung up.

"Did she believe you?" Deborah asked.

"Of course not, but I had to try. Now we know it's up to us."

I didn't look at the speedometer during the drive—the trip seemed to take forever, yet when I later counted up the minutes, I realized it had taken less than half the time it normally did to get to North Ashfield. Of course, traffic at five in the morning is pretty much nonexistent, which helped considerably.

While we drove, I'd called up a map of the town. It's smaller than Pennycross in terms of population, but considerably more spread out, with some surprisingly isolated spots thanks to the Twin Lakes on the east side of the city limits. I knew there were roads clustered around those lakes that weren't showing up on the map, and since Sid had written "cabin" I thought that should be our first target.

Sid had other ideas.

We stopped for gas at a self-serve station on the outskirts of town, and when Deborah turned off the truck to fill the tank, I heard movement from the bowling bag. The hand was moving again. By the time Deborah got back in, I'd given it the pad and pen, and the hand had just finished writing another message:

warm

"How does a skull get warm?" Deborah wanted to know. "Did they put him in a fire?"

Fire could destroy bone, but it would have to get a lot hotter than warm for that to happen. "Maybe he's not finished."

But though we waited a few minutes, that was it. I even checked for street names in town that began with "warm," but there was nothing.

"I'm going to get moving," Deborah said. "He can explain what he meant when we find him and Madison."

"Good plan." I left the hand, pad, and pen in my lap in case Sid sent another message.

She pulled out of the service station and drove east, toward the lakes, but a mile down the road, the hand started writing again.

cold

"Turn around! We're going the wrong way."

Deborah looked at the message. "Son of a—I will never call Sid boneheaded again."

She made a U-turn, and after a mile, we got:

warmer

It took a lot of back and forth because apparently the people who'd designed North Ashfield's streets didn't believe in straight lines, but after over an hour of tracking and backtracking, we were driving on a road through dense woods that was technically two lanes, but which was more like a lane and a half, when we got:

HOT

"There's no cabin here," Deborah protested.

"Turn around."

She maneuvered the truck through a three-point turn, and we went past that area again.

I said, "Is that a driveway?"

"More like a trail," she said.

Had it not been approaching dawn, I don't think I'd have seen it. "Can you get the truck down there?"

"Watch me!"

"No, stop, they might hear us coming."

"You're right, you're right." She pulled over as far off the road as she could get. I shoved my phone in my blue jeans pocket and I patted Sid's hand in an effort to let him know we were on the job, but he grabbed the pen again and scribbled two words:

gun

hurry

"Deborah! Sid says there's a gun."

"Damn it!" Then she drew herself up. "Screw the gun. I'm going in. You stay back here."

"Are you insane?"

"I'm getting Madison out of there, and if one of us has to get shot to do it, it's going to be me." She took off down the track. I was going to go after her, but I had an idea. I took Sid's hand to the back of the truck, where Deborah had stowed Sid's suitcase. Once it was open, I put the hand on top of the lifeless stack of bones and waited.

Nothing happened at first, but then the hand wiggled around, as if feeling where it was. Then almost painfully slowly, the bones started pulling themselves together. It took an eternity longer than it ever had before, but finally a nearly whole skeleton climbed out of the back of Deborah's truck.

And promptly started walking the wrong way.

"Oh no, you don't," I said, and I held Sid's hand so I could lead him down the track. It wasn't easy going—the way was badly rutted from the past winter and overgrown with the first weeds of spring, but we managed it. The skeleton was moving better and better the farther we went, and soon we caught up with Deborah.

My sister is usually close to unflappable—it comes with being the practical one—but she had a tough time holding in her reaction to Skull-less Sid.

She'd stopped behind a trio of trees that had grown close together, and those of us with eyes ducked behind them to get a look at the cabin. It was small, about the size of a one-bedroom starter house, and though the windows were shuttered, I could see light shining out through the cracks. There were three cars parked in the grassy clearing next to it. Two were out in the open, but the dark blue one closest to the house was mostly covered with a tarp, and I had a hunch that we'd found Robert Irwin's missing Honda.

Now that Sid's skeleton was no longer rattling, we could hear raised voices from inside the cabin. Deborah drew herself up, and I could tell she was getting ready to storm in, gun or no gun. I grabbed her sleeve and pulled on the tire iron. When she looked stubborn, I put Sid's hand around the iron. She hesitated, then nodded and released her grip.

Sid straightened his shoulder blades, made for the front door, and started beating it down with the tire iron. He'd never shown anything but human strength before, so I don't know if he somehow surpassed that or if the door was just flimsy, but he broke through after only a dozen blows and stepped inside.

That's when the screaming began. Had it been Madison's voice, Deborah and I would have started running, but it was Adam Jr. who was screaming. There was a gunshot, another, then silence. We launched ourselves and pushed our way in through the splintered remains of the door.

Sid—all of him, skull included—was standing over an unconscious Adam Jr. There was a rifle on the floor next to him. Sid turned in my direction, and just for a second I saw him as the boy must have—a looming monster of bare bones, armed with a heavy bar of steel. Then he raised his fist triumphantly and said, "The Bone Ranger rides again!" And it was just Sid.

"Did you shoot him?" I asked.

"Of course not. I scared him good, though—he's fainted."

"Where's Madison?"

Before he could answer, I heard her calling from behind a closed door. "Mom?"

It wasn't locked, but even if it had been, I wouldn't have needed a tire iron to get through.

Madison and Tristan were on the floor, crouched behind a bed, but in an instant she'd jumped up and was holding on to me. When Deborah poked her head in, Madison grabbed her, too, and the three of us were hugging and crying and saying nothing that made any sense at all. Eventually we calmed down enough to take notice of Tristan, who was staring up at us with an expression made up of equal parts relief and trepidation.

He said, "Adam?"

"He's alive," Deborah said in a tone that said how little she cared.

At that moment we heard an amplified voice from outside the cabin. "This is the police. Put down your weapons and come outside with your hands up."

I looked at Deborah and knew we were thinking the same thing. Sid!

But when we all went back through the main room of the cabin, Sid was nowhere to be seen. The tire iron was on the floor, and Adam's hands had been tied. Since I wasn't hearing screams of terror from outside, I decided Sid must have decamped and found a place to hide, which was a very good idea.

"I repeat, this is the police. Put down your weapons and come out with your hands up."

Deborah, Madison, and I obeyed the weapons part, but Madison kept holding our hands as we went out the door.

47

Our tardy rescuers were a combination of North Ashfield and Pennycross police officers, including Deborah's pal Louis Raymond. Though from his glower, I wasn't sure if he still considered her a pal or not. She looked directly at him, then, as Charles would have said, cut him dead.

Once the police determined that none of us Thackerys were armed, a trio of policewomen came running with blankets and hot chocolate and tried to gently separate us. It didn't happen—Madison kept a firm grip on both of us. I don't know if it was for comfort or to make sure we kept our stories straight, but I was content with either answer.

Adam was treated far less politely, but the police weren't quite sure how to handle Tristan until Officer Raymond took us back into the cabin, sat us down, and asked Madison what had happened.

"I was backstage at the play and saw Adam messing 'round with Sid—I mean, with my skull."

"I beg your pardon?"

"A prop for the show," I said. "The kids call it Sid."

Madison nodded, grateful for the save. "I told Adam to put the skull down, that it was mine, but he ran out the door with it. I chased after him, but when I caught up with him, he kept waving it over his head where I couldn't reach it. So I kicked him."

"Good girl," Deborah said.

"But not smart," Madison said. "He got mad and pushed me down." She looked at her hose, and for the first time I noticed the tear on one knee and enough of a bloody scrape that I started wishing that Sid had done more than scare that zygomatic creep. "Jo is going to be mad at me."

"Don't worry about the costume," Raymond said. "Just tell us what happened next."

"Adam had gotten to his car by the time I got up, and I started beating on the hood."

"That was a pretty strong reaction to him taking a skull."

"I know," she said sheepishly. "I lost my temper, big time, but he made me so mad. Taking something that's mine and pushing me down and all."

Of course I knew why she'd gone to such lengths to get Sid back, and I would have been angry at her if I hadn't known that I would have done the same.

Madison went on. "I kept yelling for him to give me it back. Finally he opened the passenger door and said something like, 'You want it—come get it.' He held out the skull, but when I reached for it, he grabbed me and pulled me inside the car and just drove off with me hanging halfway out of the door.

"I wasn't going to get in the car with him—I know you're

not supposed to go with somebody like that—and I tried to get back out, but he slugged me."

"Where is that—?" Deborah said. She started to stand up, but Madison pulled her down.

"Did he knock you unconscious?" Raymond asked.

"I guess. He hit me pretty hard and I was kind of out of it. By the time I woke all the way up, we were parked here and he dragged me inside."

"Then what?"

"He started drinking. Well, drinking more. I think he'd been drinking before—I could smell it on him. He had, like, a whole case of beer in the basement, and I don't know how much he went through."

"The kid acted drunk at the school," I said.

"He kept fooling around with the skull, too," Madison said, "trying to see how it had talked at the end of the play."

"You mean when it accused his father of murder?" Raymond asked.

"Is that what it said?"

I was so grateful for all the acting Madison had done. Had I not known the truth, I'd have believed she was baffled myself.

"Apparently," he said, looking at Deborah. She ignored him. "What happened next?"

"That's when Tristan showed up."

"Was he in on it, too?"

"No way," she said firmly. "He said he'd heard I was missing and was afraid Adam had done something stupid, so he came to find out for sure. I guess the family comes out here in the summer a lot, and Tristan knows Adam uses it for partying sometimes.

"Tristan was really mad at his brother for grabbing me that way, and kept trying to convince him to let me go because it was only making things worse, but Adam said they couldn't because I knew too much."

"What did you know?"

"I have no idea. It got kind of confusing after a while. My head hurt because of Adam hitting me, and when I asked for an aspirin or something, he said I should drink a beer and I'd feel better." She made a face. "It didn't help my head at all, but Adam kept telling me to drink. He made Tristan drink some, too. After a while he got that rifle out and started messing with it. He said he and Tristan had to defend their dad. Tristan finally got him to let us go into the bedroom." She looked embarrassed. "Tristan said we wanted to make out, but he really meant to try to help me get away. Only he wanted me to promise not to tell anybody what had happened. I kept telling him it would never work. My mother knows me better than that. I'd never have left the theater wearing my costume!"

It wasn't funny, certainly not in light of what had nearly happened, but I couldn't help snickering. Deborah gave me a dirty look to make me stop.

Raymond nodded for Madison to continue.

"Tristan and I were still in the bedroom when we heard some really loud noises."

"That was us," I said. "We broke down the door."

Madison said, "Then I heard a gunshot, maybe two."

"The kid missed," Deborah said, "and passed out. Drunk, from what Madison just said."

"Mom and Aunt Deborah came for me, and a little while later, you guys showed up. That's all I know. No, wait, one other thing. When we heard all the noises and the gunshots,

Tristan threw himself over me. He really didn't want me to get hurt."

"We'll keep that in mind." Then he turned to me. "Can you explain your part in this?"

"We got an anonymous call that Madison was in a cabin in North Ashfield and came looking for her," I lied.

"And you didn't see fit to call the police here or in Pennycross?"

Deborah made a sound of disgust. "After the way you treated us last night when Madison went missing? As if we were a couple of hysterical females? Since you obviously weren't going to believe anything we said, we came and found the place on our own."

"So you broke down the door? That's impressive."

"I thought about picking the lock," Deborah said with a smirk, "but this way was faster."

I suspect he'd have asked for more details, like how we'd actually found the cabin, but another officer called him away. Not being Sid, I couldn't hear everything they said, but I did catch the words "body" and "freezer in the basement."

After all that time, we'd finally found Robert Irwin's body.

The police might have continued to pester us, but when Madison realized there'd been a corpse in the basement the whole time she'd been there, she started shaking and then sobbing, which made me cry and Deborah fume, so they finally let us go home. One of the professionally supportive officers walked us back down the track to where Deborah's truck was parked, and held back the lone reporter who'd realized there was a big story brewing.

I checked the back of the truck and saw that Sid's suitcase was closed, even though I was sure I'd left it open before. I couldn't very well check inside in front of the police officer and the reporter, and there was no room to move it to the front of the truck, so I lightly rapped "Shave and a haircut" on it. After a second, I heard Sid tap back: "Two bits." He'd found his way back.

As we started to pull out, a Pennycross police car arrived, and an officer escorted Adam McDaniel Sr. out of the back-seat. This time it was I who caught his eye, and I deliberately winked back at him.

48

When we got home and Madison had been thoroughly greeted by Byron, she admitted that she was starving. Deborah and I nearly came to blows over who was going to feed her. I finally let my sister take over at the stove, but only because she's better at omelets than I am. Besides, I couldn't stand for Madison to be out of my sight for long enough to cook, and of course I had to treat Sid like the hero he was.

Though Deborah was trying to act as if she were taking it all in stride, she showed she was more upset than she wanted to admit when she set the table for four people.

Sid grinned and took his place at the table, and when Deborah started to apologize, he said, "That's okay. I'll take some orange juice. And a mop."

The fact that we all laughed as if it were the funniest thing we'd ever heard showed just how fried we all were.

After that, I insisted we set the alarm, turn off all the

phones, and go to bed. Madison and Byron shared my bed with me, and Deborah took our parents'. As for Sid, I expected him to go up to his attic to catch up on the breaking story we'd just lived through, but I kept hearing him clattering around the house, checking on us and humming happily.

I wished that could have been the end of it, but of course it wasn't. There were more talks with the police, and calls and visits from local reporters. I even tossed my old boyfriend a bone, so to speak, and gave him an exclusive interview. Plus I had to call my parents and tell them the whole story before they learned about it some other way.

Under the circumstances, the second performance of *Hamlet* was postponed. Guildenstern was actually willing to go through with it, but Rosencrantz's father and brother were under arrest. Plus the auditorium was finally being processed as a crime scene.

Fortunately, PHS's spring break started on Monday, which gave Mr. Dahlgren a chance to put a plan in place to soothe parents and students alike and meant I had time to find a therapist to help Madison get past her ordeal. It was so close to the end of the semester that I couldn't take the whole week off, but between me, Sid, and Deborah, we made sure Madison was never left alone.

By the following Monday, Madison said she was ready to go back to school and, after consulting with her therapist, I allowed it and went back to work myself, though only at McQuaid. Mr. Dahlgren had called during the break to let me know that Mr. Chedworth had recovered more quickly than expected and would be returning for the rest of the school year. Chedworth himself called later on to apologize for any financial losses, but though I'd miss Ms. Rad and

Lance, I was just as glad to get my time back. Sid decided he was perfectly happy staying home from PHS, too.

That Wednesday, Deborah brought over a Chinese take-out feast so we could catch up while we ate. Sid tried his drink and a mop joke again, but it wasn't as funny the second time.

"So I was talking to Louis today," Deborah started to say as we handed around the sweet-and-sour pork.

"I thought he was mad at you," Madison said.

"He's getting over it. He knows the team won't win without me."

"Yeah, it's all about the bowling," I said drily. "What's the word on the investigation?"

She said, "Well, since they found Irwin's body in McDaniel's freezer, the guy can't pretend he didn't know it was there, but it looks like his lawyer is planning to claim either self-defense or accident. He supposedly only hid the body because he panicked."

"Will he be able to get away with that?" I asked.

"It depends on how good that lawyer is."

"What about Patty Craft?"

"They're not even going to be able to charge him with that. Louis says they're all sure he had something to do with her death, and it's clear that he'd been giving her drug samples for a while, but there's no proof he killed her. It could still be an accident or suicide—they can't even get enough of a case to charge him with mercy killing."

"Coccyx!" I said. "What about his charming son?"

Deborah snickered. "First off, the guys at the station have been having a field day with all of Junior's stories of being attacked by a walking skeleton. They're blaming it on the beer, of course, combined with seeing Sid's big speech at the end of *Hamlet*. Louis still suspects me of having something to do with that, by the way, but he can't pin anything on me."

"But he does have evidence to use against Adam, right?"

"Plenty. Kidnapping charges to start with. He tried to claim Madison went with him willingly, but his own brother is telling what really happened. He's also being charged with helping to hide Irwin's body. Unfortunately, Louis doesn't think they can charge him for the attack on you. Which seems to have been his own idea, by the way. He says he was just trying to scare you off, but Louis isn't sure he believes him. As for Adam Sr., he was smart enough not to do anything that stupid even though he knew you were asking questions."

"How did they find out about that, anyway?" I asked. "I know I'm not the most subtle sleuth in the world, but I was nowhere close to figuring out that the McDaniels were involved."

"It turns out Adam Sr. was working with the Sechrest Foundation, and had been for years. After he hired Irwin to take Adam Jr.'s SAT, he started helping Frisenda find more parents willing to pay for help cheating. For a commission, of course."

"Hence his devotion to the PTO," I said. "That means it wasn't just his son's reputation he was worried about—it was his own. I should have known."

"Anyway, Frisenda told him all about you."

"That slimy tibia! Now I'm doubly glad I sicced Charles on him."

"How's that?" Deborah asked.

"When I told Charles what the foundation is really about, he said it was a pox upon our community and was not to be borne. It turns out he has friends at several of the big standardized testing companies, and they were very interested in hearing about the cheating. Plus he spread the word through the adjunct network—even put Sara Weiss on the job. Between them, they took it viral."

"The Sechrest Web site disappeared today," Sid added.

"What about Tristan?" Madison asked.

"Thanks to you, he's not being charged with anything," Deborah said. "He probably did know about Irwin, but only long after the fact, and he seems to have believed his father's story that the man's death was accidental. And he really was trying to save you from his brother."

"He's left PHS," Madison said. "He's going to live with his mother in Boston now. He texted me a few times, and I thanked him for what he did for me, but . . ." She shrugged. "I don't think I could ever trust him after this."

I was glad of that. No matter how nice Tristan was, the last thing I wanted was to be connected to the McDaniel family in any way, shape, or form.

"So that's it," I said. "Back to normal."

"Yeah, like this household is ever normal," Deborah said. "And speaking of Sid—"

"Hey!" Sid said. "I resemble that implication!"

She said, "I never did hear exactly what you did to Adam to make him faint like that."

Madison and I had heard the story—several times, in fact—but he enjoyed telling it so much that we could hardly disappoint him.

"It was like this," he said. "Once I beat down the door, I stepped in and he started screaming like a little girl."

"Ahem," Madison said.

"Okay, like a little boy. He had a rifle in his hand, but I

walked right over to him and reached for it. He shot at me twice. Pow. Pow. He didn't even knick me. So I grabbed the rifle and with my other hand reached over and took my skull back. Then I popped it back on my spine and started to give my speech from before. Only he kept screaming and then fainted before I could finish. Then you guys came in."

"Wait, where was your skull?" Deborah asked.

I looked at Sid curiously. I hadn't thought to ask him that before.

"Um, Adam was holding it," he said.

"How was he holding your skull and the rifle?"

"Yeah, Sid," Madison said. "That doesn't make sense."

"Well, the skull was holding him. Sort of."

We waited for more.

"Okay, he had my skull in his hand when I started breaking down the door, so I . . . I bit him. I was still holding on to his arm when the rest of me broke into the cabin."

That turned out to be even funnier than his joke about the drink and the mop.

49

As life continued to settle down, I was just satisfied that the members of my little family seemed to be happy with one another, and though I knew our unusual living arrangements were bound to cause more problems in the future, I had reason to feel that we were going to be able to work them out.

On Saturday, Madison went to work with Deborah as usual, leaving me to perform my usual assortment of boring errands and household tasks. Sid came down late in the afternoon to help me fold sheets, which gave me a chance to bring up a subject I'd been pondering for several days. Though he was showing no signs of boredom or restlessness yet, I knew it was only a matter of time before he did, and I thought I might have a solution.

"Sid, I've been thinking about those times you graded papers for me."

"Then you're going to let me keep doing it?" he said eagerly.

"I'm sorry, but no."

"Even though you said yourself that I did a good job?"

"No, I said that you did a great job, and you did. But I can't let you do my work. It's too much like Patty Craft and Robert Irwin taking the SAT for other people."

"Oh. I hadn't thought about that. Okay, I see your point. No more grading."

"Besides, you're going to be busy."

"Well, there is the Altador Cup challenge coming up on Neopets.com, but it won't take up that much of my time."

"I'm not talking about gaming. I'm talking about you going back to college."

"Um, Georgia, I think teachers would be a little suspicious of a skeleton in class, or even a bowling bag on top of a desk."

"I've got two words for you: distance learning."

"Kind of hard to see the blackboard if you get too distant."

I thumped his skull. "I'm talking about taking classes online. Schools all over the country have added distance learning courses, including McQuaid. You could even get a degree online."

"Excuse me?"

"You could go back to computer science, if you want to, or if you major in English, I'd feel completely justified in letting you assist me. But if you want to study something else, that's fine, too."

"You mean it?" He started to grin, then stopped. "Wait, can we afford tuition?"

"The standard McQuaid adjunct deal includes continuing

ed credits, and I bet my parents' deal is even better, so that'll cover part of it. We'll have to fudge your name and stuff but—"

I didn't bother to go into details right then because Sid was yelling, "I'm going back to school!" He started bouncing up and down, then dancing, then breaking into a move I was dreadfully afraid was twerking. I gave up on conversation and joined in, though I did maintain enough dignity to skip the twerking.

Madison picked that moment to come home and saw the two of us dancing like complete idiots, and without hesitation or asking for an explanation, she started dancing, too. Even Byron joined in by running around and in between us.

That was how I knew we'd be fine. As long as we could dance together, everything else could be managed.

First in the Family Skeleton Mysteries from

Leigh Perry

A Skeleton
in the Family

Moving back into her parents' house with her teenage daughter was not Georgia Thackery's "Plan A." Neither is dealing with Sid, the Thackery family's skeleton. Sid has lived in the house for as long as Georgia can remember, but now he's determined to find out how he died—with Georgia's help of course.

PRAISE FOR THE SERIES

"You'll love the adventures of this unexpected mystery-solving duo."

—Charlaine Harris, #1 *New York Times* bestselling author

"[A] charming debut . . . Just plain fun!"

—Sofie Kelly, *New York Times* bestselling author

leighperryauthor.com
facebook.com/TheCrimeSceneBooks
penguin.com